ROYALLY DECEIVED

J.D. CAROTHERS

Editing by Sarah Calfee from Three Little Words Romance Editing

Content editing by Royal Reads Services

Cover design by Mayhem Cover Creations

This is a work of fiction. Names, characters, businesses, locales, events, and incidents are either the products of the author's imagination or used in a fictitious manner. Any resemblance to actual persons, living or dead, or actual events or places is purely coincidental.

ISBN: 978-1-957997-05-6

To Jeff (my husband and my prince),
Audrey M., and Suzi V.
for being wonderfully supportive,
encouraging, helpful, and patient
during this journey.

.

.

Prince Xander has one job to do: become king. Unfortunately, that means the confirmed bachelor must find a bride.

Engaging the help of an elite matchmaking service guarantees finding a suitable wife. What he didn't expect was to be friend-zoned by one of the ladies ... especially when she's the first woman to spark his soul.

When Ariana loses her job in a NYC PR firm, she heads to London following her dream of becoming a romance writer. A friend's matchmaking service is the perfect starting spot for research into royal love lives. Swearing off men was supposed to be easy, until Prince Xander asks for help.

Monarchy, matchmaking, and murder entangle Xander and Ariana in a dangerous plot. Will it turn their friendship into forever love or will fate keep them apart?

This is Book 2 in the series, but it can be read as a standalone. HEA guaranteed.

For more information, visit
jdcarothers.com

AUTHOR'S NOTE

Royally Deceived is a standalone romance novel with suspense, murder, and a happily ever after for the main characters. It is book 2 in the *Murder and Romance are on the Menu* series. The first two books in the series share the stories of two brothers, Xander and Evan. The first book, *Thrill Ride*, tells Evan's story. This book, *Royally Deceived*, is Xander's story. It begins with a parallel timeline to Evan's story in *Thrill Ride* and continues beyond the end of *Thrill Ride*. However, the books can be read in either order.

CHAPTER ONE

XANDER

The next time I see my brother, I'm going to bloody well kill him. My head is throbbing from the Boulevardier cocktails he kept shoving in my hand last night. By now, the wanker should know getting me pissed isn't going to change the fact my life is ruined.

Finally, daring to crack my eyelids apart, I cringe at the clock's glowing display—3:00 a.m. Groaning, I stagger into the loo, splash icy water on my face, and down a couple of ibuprofen. On autopilot, I return to bed, carefully crawl beneath the comforter, and attempt to bury my head under the pillow without jostling too much. I'm too old for this shite, even if my life is a cocked-up mess. Fortunately, these thoughts fade as sleep happily takes over.

Too soon my ever-prompt assistant Edmund begins pounding on the door. Okay, maybe he didn't really pound, but in my state, a tap would've been too loud. He's far too cheerful as he waltzes into my room. "It's 8:00 a.m. Rise and shine, Your Highness."

"Go away, Edmund. Come back in an hour or two."

He yanks the curtains open, making me wince as bright light streams in.

"Unfortunately, I can't do that, sir. Your diary is full, and you need to prepare for the day. Time to get up. Breakfast will arrive in twenty minutes."

"Give me a few minutes to pull myself together. And find the ibuprofen!"

Making my way into the shower, eyes half-closed, I lean against the wall, letting the water trail down my body for several long minutes to wash away the remnants of last night. If only the real cause of this headache could swirl down the drain too ...

Turning off the tap, I sigh. Having lost my internal battle with the obligations of my position, I once again give in to the life I can't escape.

I'm toweling off my hair when I hear my phone ringing in the other room. "Here we go," I gripe. I reach the phone on the fourth ring and answer it. A refined voice says, "Hello, this is Meredith Marshall, the matchmaker from M-Cubed."

I vaguely remember leaving her a message last night about being another prince needing her help. It probably didn't make much sense given I was well on my way to being pissed at the time. I'm surprised she's ringing back so quickly. "Thanks for calling, Ms. Marshall."

"Your Royal Highness, it's a pleasure to speak with you. Please call me Meredith. How may I be of service?"

Each throb of my head suddenly feels like another tick on the countdown clock to marriage.

It's real now.

I clear my throat and answer. "I can't believe I'm saying this, but I need your help to find a wife."

She doesn't hesitate. "I'd be delighted to help you. We have a discreet process that leads to successful matches."

To her credit, she knows how to make my awkward request seem almost normal.

"I'm counting on it. Can you find me someone within the next month or two?"

"Um. That's a rather short time frame. If I may ask, why the hurry?"

"I have to be married before my father's sixty-fifth birthday, which is less than four months away."

"Why the tight deadline? Is this a present for him?"

"I hadn't thought of it like that, but in a way, it is. Father has decided to pass the throne to me on his birthday, which requires me to be married by then. I'm duty-bound by the laws of Catalinius to find a wife."

"I understand now. Lady Harper Sinclair is rumored to be of interest to you. Should I include her on the list of potential matches?"

I shudder at the thought. "Definitely not. The tabloids are wrong."

"They usually are, but I needed to confirm. May I ask you a few questions about what type of women *do* interest you?"

"Of course. Anything that helps your process will ultimately help me."

"What are the three most important qualities your future wife should possess?"

I exhale slowly, explaining, "That's a tricky question to answer. Our laws are rather unusual. If the king ruled until his death, I would be able to take the throne regardless of whether I was married. Of course, the king routinely reminds me of my duty to provide an heir, but my siblings could handle that. To be honest, I'm not sure I'd marry at all but for my father's desire to place me on the throne now."

"But you must have some idea of qualities you desire in a wife, correct?"

"I'm not looking for a love match. All I need is a future queen. Ideally, she will be intelligent, reasonably attractive, and willing to work independently on projects that'll benefit my country." Betrayal destroyed my hope for true love long ago.

"That's helpful, but hopefully, I can exceed those expectations. I'll need three weeks to select candidates. Will you be able to meet them in a secluded setting in London, or do I need to bring them to a secure location in Catalinius?"

"London is best. I'll be there for a conference and some fundraisers. You can talk with my personal assistant, Edmund, to hammer out the details."

Ending the call, I can't help but wonder if I've solved my problem or merely made an elite matchmaking service significantly richer.

CHAPTER TWO

ARIANA

I'm already on my third—or is it fourth—cup of coffee, and it's only 11:30 a.m. But caffeine is all that's keeping me going after only three hours of sleep for the third night in a row.

Taking another gulp of the magic wake-up potion, I inwardly laugh at my naïve younger self. Moving from Los Angeles to New York for this job six years ago, I was a wide-eyed, enthusiastic 24-year-old. The hours were long, but it was the only way to get the experience. Fortunately, the clients were interesting, and the company awarded regular promotions and raises.

But I thought as I climbed even higher on the corporate ladder at Platinum International PR, I'd have better control over my job and time. With a larger support staff to assist with tasks, I would have plenty of time to focus on the big picture issues.

Boy, was I wrong.

The promotion to Director of Charitable Events last year came with a substantial salary increase but brought with it even longer hours, less time for a social life, and reporting directly to the company's founder, Shelly.

Speak of the devil.

"Good morning, Shelly. Do you have time for me to brief you on the new client I spoke with this morning?"

"Not now. I'm going to be late for my business lunch at The Lamb's Club, so you need to finalize the arrangements for the London fundraiser by the end of the day. Gotta go." She tosses a paper on my desk, and without missing a beat, her heels rapidly click across the marble floor as she rushes to the elevator.

Suspecting it's going to be a long afternoon, I pull my hair into a ponytail and lean closer to see how difficult it will be to finish Shelly's list.

She wants me to deal with the last-minute changes to the menu and room setup for the London fundraiser. The charity's founder, Alex Leonardo, needs info on when and where to meet us before it starts. Hotel reservations must be confirmed. The press release needs proofing. The list goes on and on, and it's already almost noon on Friday.

Damn her, this is the list she insisted on handling herself, but Shelly always spreads herself way too thin. I could have been halfway through these tasks yesterday. Now, the new client's proposal will have to wait until next week. And even pushing that off, how am I going to finish everything this afternoon?

To make matters worse, it's five hours later in London, and our office phone system has been down for the past two hours. IT can't tell me when it will be up again, and my company mobile phone was crushed by a cab when I dropped it last night. Shit. Shelly is never going to reimburse me for the international calls on my personal phone, but what other choice do I have now?

Better dig in. Nothing says it's wrong to start with the most enjoyable task—contacting Alex. It's too bad he prefers texts due to the time difference. Hearing his husky British accent would be preferable to me. It's a little embarrassing since he's a client, but his deep voice and my mind's image of him have invaded my dreams more than once, and he would be the perfect fuel to banish the nightmares about my ex. Thoughts of him send warmth to the best places.

Sighing, I grab my phone and type.

> Me: Alex, Shelly wanted me to let you know everything is set for the fundraiser in London. The plan is to meet in the lobby 30 minutes before it starts.

> Alex: Who is this?

> Me: Sorry, I'm texting from my personal phone. This is Maddie from Platinum International.

> Alex: Got it. Will meet in the lobby. How's your 10K training going?

> Me: Not bad. Pulled a thigh muscle running downhill. Taking it easy for a few days.

I'm shocked he remembered. No one else even noticed my limp this week, much less asked how my training is going.

> Alex: Massage was crucial to my quick recovery when I did something similar last year. Ask your boyfriend to help.

> Me: We broke up earlier this week. Turns out Brian's a jerk.

> Alex: Too bad. You need someone with strong hands to get up in there and really work your thigh muscles.

Too bad the windows don't open in high-rise buildings. It's getting extremely warm in here. How can he turn me on this much when I don't even know what he looks like?

> Me: That sounds heavenly. Are you offering your services?

Crap. I need a better filter today. I shouldn't have hit send, but I instinctively thought he was flirting. Shit. How could I forget he's the client! What is wrong with me? He was probably just being clinical as one runner to another. Will he think I'm trying to flirt with him? Am I? Maybe? I *am* single now but that was too much. Shit!

Me: Just kidding. If it doesn't get better, I'll check into physical therapy.

Alex: If I can't be your physio, let me take you drinking when you get to London? It sounds like you need to get smashed.

Me: LOL. It would be unprofessional to get drunk with a client.

Alex: I won't tell. That's what friends are for. After working together on the fundraiser for almost a year, it's the least I can do.

Me: I'll be ok but wouldn't mind grabbing one drink. By the way, how's your little sister? You said she was in an unhealthy relationship.

Alex: She's ok now. Fortunately, she finally woke up and dumped the guy. She should've listened to her big brother's advice sooner.

Me: Overprotective family can be a pain. Believe me, I know. Give her some space.

Alex: I'm trying but it's not easy.

Me: Why not? Are you a pain to everyone?

Alex: LOL. You'll have to decide for yourself when we meet at the fundraiser.

Me: See you in London.

Alex: Looking forward to meeting you in person.

Me too. More than you know. He's raising money for clean oceans, he's flirty, he's always flying somewhere interesting, and his voice is hot as hell. Since I've never seen his photo, he's a little mysterious too. Of course, in my mind he's gorgeous.

Back to the list ...

At 6:00 p.m., exhaustion replaces any remaining adrenaline or caffeine in my body. But I finished all the tasks. Whew.

As I'm grabbing my purse to leave, Shelly interrupts my departure. "Is everything set for London?"

"Yes. Every item on your list is done."

"Excellent. Thank you. I knew you could handle it, but I have some bad news." She frowns.

"Oh no. Are you okay?"

"I have to let you go. Security will give you time to pack up."

"You've got to be kidding!"

"Unfortunately, I'm not. Today is your last day."

This can't be happening. How can she do this to me after all I've done for her? Why is she destroying my career? Where will I find another job? I have bills to pay.

I have so many questions, but in my shock, I only manage to choke out one word. "Why?"

Placing my palms on the desk to steady myself, my eyes are laser focused on Shelly, willing her to provide an explanation that will somehow make sense of this nightmare.

"We're overstaffed, the economy is lagging, and we need to make cuts in upper staff positions."

She doesn't even have the decency to look me in the eye as she spouts the lies.

And they are lies.

"That doesn't make any sense. We're busier than ever. Did I do something wrong?"

"I've given my explanation. The decision is final. But feel free to use me as a reference." She walks out without another word.

Unbelievably, Shelly ended our six-year working relationship in mere minutes. Then something else hits me.

The bitch waited to fire me until she was certain her damned list was done. She had this planned all day. How dare she?

If my life was a cartoon, my face would be bright red, and steam would be pouring out from my ears right now.

My swelling anger is overshadowing the hurt and disbelief of a few minutes ago as further realization sets in. Shelly fired me, lied to me about the reason, and has the audacity to have security here. He must believe I'm some … I don't know what.

The uniformed guard silently places a lonely cardboard box on my desk.

For a moment, I stare out the window, trying to process what happened. I've busted my butt for Shelly and this company. Work has been my first priority for the last six years at the expense of almost everything else. Apparently, loyalty and hard work are meaningless to her. That should have been clear when Shelly barely gave me time to grieve after my grandmother passed away earlier this year.

With that eye-opening thought, I numbly pack the few personal items from my desk. It doesn't take long despite my years at this company.

Leaving my ID badge on the desk, I take a last, hard look at it. Below my photo, it reads

Ariana Madison
"Maddie"
Montgomery

To this day, it annoys me that I've let the nickname Maddie stick this far into adulthood. I should have let it go and started using my first name Ariana when I moved to New York. Oh well, that's the least of my problems today.

My eyes scan the office one final time before the guard hustles me out.

Five minutes later, on the curb outside the skyscraper, tears start streaming down my face, landing like sad raindrops on the box I'm still clutching.

♛

At my apartment, I change into pajamas and crawl into my bed with a comforting pint of full-fat, chocolate ice cream, a box of tissues, and the TV playing a rom-com.

I never would've thought so many disappointments could fit into a single week. Dumped my cheating boyfriend. Got fired. Cancelled my trip to London for the fundraiser. Lost the opportunity to meet sexy-sounding Alex in person. Ugh. I breathe in deeply, letting the air out slowly.

During the third movie in my mini marathon, my eyelids flutter closed, and my thoughts take a different turn. Nana Ariana, the only grandmother I ever knew, would tell me to spread my wings and seek adventure—so what if you skin a few knees along the way. But my parents would tell me not to take risks. They'd do anything to shield me from harm. Sometimes, I wonder if that's why they still refer to me by my childhood nickname. Originally, they called me Maddie simply to honor my other namesake, grandmother Madison, but now it's their way of holding onto me. They want me to remain under their protective umbrella.

Mom and Dad would rather smother me with love and protect their only child than watch me experience hurt. Their hearts are in the right place, but this is my life, and I can't let guilt over their worrying decide my future.

But the child in me hopes I can follow Nana's advice without causing my parents too much worry. My move to New York already freaked them out, but they eventually adjusted.

They'll adjust again. Won't they?

CHAPTER THREE

XANDER

etween budget meetings at the palace, there's a text from my brother asking if I'm still among the living. Rather than text back, I escape to the library and ring him. "Evan, I'm not sure whether to beat the living daylights out of you or be grateful for the drinks yesterday. I'm completely knackered today."

Laughing, he says, "A simple thanks will do. The way you hurled yourself through my front door without even knocking, you needed a few stiff drinks before you did something you'd regret. You'd have done the same for me."

"I know. I still can't fathom that *His Majesty* gave me an ultimatum yesterday. Can you believe he told me to find someone immediately or he will pick a wife for me? It's bloody wrong."

"It's not like Father sprang the news on you for the first time yesterday. You've known for almost a year now."

"I know, but his ultimatum was more than I could handle yesterday. I've always been willing to do my duty, but why must I be married to be King of Catalinius? It's an antiquated, archaic rule."

"I agree. The rule should change, but we don't have that power. You shouldn't have waited this long to pick someone. I tried to remind you to get your shite together, but you wanted none of my advice last time I brought it up."

Raising my voice slightly, I say, "Father never mentioned retiring until early last year. I thought it was a kneejerk reaction to his health scare. I assumed he'd change his mind when he realized he wasn't dying."

"I'm not the villain here. I get it. You've been in denial. And I'll admit, at first, I didn't believe he would actually retire. But when he and Mum started planning a month-long vacation to the South Pacific for this fall, I assumed that meant he is still planning to take advantage of former King Lorenzo's Royal Retirement Decree, didn't you?"

I collapse in a nearby chair. "You're right. I've been so busy with my charities and other duties that I didn't pay enough attention. Besides, I didn't want it to be true. Damn that decree."

"If you'd been forced to take the throne as a teenager you would have come up with a way to step aside too."

"I know. I can recite the story by heart. After reigning for many years, King Lorenzo wanted the freedom he'd been deprived of as a young prince. So, he decided to allow monarchs to retire, but only if the crown prince or princess was at a stable and settled point in his or her life."

When I come up for air, Evan picks up the story. "And King Lorenzo, clever as he was, made it almost impossible for Father to change the conditions under which monarchs are allowed to retire. He'd have to abdicate to change the rules, putting a substantial blemish on his reputation and legacy. He would never do that."

"Correct, dear brother. Therefore, in Catalinius, the reigning monarch is allowed to retire at age 65, but only if the crown prince or princess is married. If that condition isn't met by the reigning monarch's sixty-fifth birthday, then the king or queen must remain on the throne until death. Blah. Blah. Blah."

"Our monarchy's rules are a tad unusual, but you're stuck."

"When I near Father's age, I may praise that decree but not now. Bloody hell, I'm not ready for marriage."

"You're thirty-six. A bunch of our friends are already married. You're not exactly a young lad."

I can practically see the smirk on his face. "Careful, Evan. You're only two years younger than me, and I don't see *you* heading to the altar any time soon."

His voice sullen, Evan says, "I'm in a different situation. As the spare, no one cares what I do. That's one reason I'm leaving tomorrow for a few weeks in Las Vegas."

What's up with the depressed tone? He has the perfect life. A title. No pressure. Plenty of money. Women with no strings. Trips to Las Vegas on a whim.

I'm still shaking my head when Evan continues, "You have loads of time before his birthday. It mystifies me, but the tabloids call you the *deliciously handsome prince*. Women will be lining up to marry you and become the next queen. It's simple—choose one of them."

"Very funny. Just what I need, a queen wannabe." I rub my palm over my eyes.

"By the way, is Father insisting you marry a royal?"

"That's his preference. He wants my future wife to know what she's getting into. Did I tell you that he suggested I consider Lady Harper? Ugh." Shivering at the thought, I ask, "Can you believe it? The mere idea of marrying her leaves a bad taste in my mouth."

"No way! Can you imagine being stuck in her love affair with the paps? They eat up her publicity stunts."

"Agreed. Father ignores the tabloids though. And Harper is careful to appear prim and proper when she's around our parents. Father referred to her as sweet. If only he knew. Harper is a catastrophe waiting to happen."

"I know. We've all heard her sharp tongue when our parents are out of earshot," Evan says.

"I've got it! The best solution is for us to trade places. I'll abdicate, then you marry someone, and you get to be king," I say, waiting for Evan's explosion.

"You can forget that idea! Besides, you've always wanted to be king. Get busy and find a wife." Evan huffs.

"I'm just winding you up. You'll be happy to know I already talked with the matchmaker Prince Karl used. Thanks for the suggestion last night. She's setting up some introductions while I'm in London for the Worldwide Economic Conference. I'm not sure how well it's going to work. But right now, I don't have another option."

"At least it's a step in the right direction. I'll return before Father's birthday but let me know how the search is going."

"You aren't going to the US on official business, are you?"

"No. I'm taking a short break. You remember Sean, right?"

"Your friend from college. Doesn't he own the Grand Athena in Las Vegas now?"

"That's right. I'm going to visit him for a few weeks. *Your* path is set, but my role in the monarchy going forward isn't. I need time away from here to clear my head and sort things out."

Why does he sound so confused? He can do anything he wants. It's strange that we both believe the other one has it easier, but we don't want to trade places.

"You'll work through it. As long as you serve the monarchy, whatever you do will be fine with everyone."

Evan mumbles something—Did he say, "That's the problem"? But before I can ask him to repeat it, he says, "Hang in there. Sorry I'm missing Alex's fundraiser."

"You mean *my* fundraiser."

"Just keeping up appearances. You sponsored it as Alex instead of Xander, didn't you? By the way, what did you use for a surname this time?"

"One of my middle names. I went with Alex Leonardo. I don't dare let *His Majesty* find out I'm sponsoring a fundraiser for Clean Oceans when he's supporting offshore drilling. He would put a stop to my participation in the charity event in a heartbeat."

"No kidding. Give me a call to let me know how everything goes in London."

"Will do. Have fun in Vegas but stay out of trouble."

I hear him snicker before the line goes dead. That doesn't bode well. Hopefully, the PR team won't have to clean up after his trip like they have on so many of his prior excursions. I'm glad that's their problem, not mine.

But I'll be the one calling the PR team if it leaks that I've hired a matchmaker. Too bad my Alex alias wouldn't work for that.

CHAPTER FOUR

ARIANA

After crying, sulking, fuming, and doing some soul searching for a few days, my plan crystallized. Rereading Nana Ariana's last letter confirms my decision. I booked my flight and lodging. Now it's time to pack, but where is my second suitcase?

As I'm crouching to look under my bed, the phone rings. Answering, I hear a meek voice.

"This is Lisa. Do you remember me from Platinum International?"

"Of course. Your graphic designs are phenomenal."

"Thanks. I heard what happened to you. Are you okay?"

"I've been better but I'm working on a plan." This is awkward. We don't know each other very well. Why is she calling?

"That's good. Um. I'm not sure I should've called. We're all on edge, wondering if we'll be next."

"I certainly didn't see it coming, so I have no idea what Shelly has planned."

"Um. You were always wonderful to work with and what happened to you wasn't right. You deserve to know the real reason Shelly fired you."

"Thanks, but I doubt she'll ever tell me."

"Well … That's why I'm calling. I wanted to warn you not to use

Shelly as a reference. She gets upset anytime someone asks for you. I also overheard her say that you were becoming too popular with the clients, and she didn't want competition. She sounded jealous."

"That's ridiculous. I wasn't competing with her. I was helping build her business and making sure the clients were satisfied with our work."

"That's why I thought you should know. She sounded irrational. Now a bunch of people aren't sure what to do, but I've already started looking for other opportunities. Shoot. My break's almost over. I have to run. Good luck with your plan."

"I hope things work out for you too, and thanks for letting me know what you heard. I appreciate the warning."

Was I fired for doing my job too well? That's messed up. Fortunately, I'm not looking for a reference right now.

I'll have to process this later. My clothes won't magically put themselves in my bags.

Buzz. Buzz. Buzz. I'm never going to get packed. Grabbing my phone, it displays "Mom." Shit. I'd hoped to put this call off a little longer.

"Hi, Mom."

"I've got you on speaker. Dad's here too. We wanted to make sure you got the email info on how to contact us while we're on vacation."

"Hi, Dad. Yes, I got your email. You leave in a couple of days, right?"

"We do. We'd have preferred to use the money for something practical, but Nana's lawyer said we couldn't."

"You'll have a wonderful time. Nana left each of us money for something we wouldn't do otherwise. Enjoy your trip guilt free."

"She was always the adventurer in the family. You have to admire her spunk," Dad says.

"Speaking of her gifts, I'm taking some time away from work and using Nana's gift for an extended trip to London."

"Is that wise? Why now when you're doing well in your job?"

"Consider it my mini sabbatical to work on the novel I've always wanted to write. It's the perfect time in my career to take advantage of a break, and it'll give me a chance to honor Nana's wish."

"But you don't know anyone in London. Who'll check in on you with us stuck on a ship?" she asks.

"Mom, I've always traveled for work. I'll be fine. Quit worrying. It's no different than me living in New York. I have to do this for myself *and* for Nana. Please be happy for me."

"Honey, we love you. We don't want anything bad to happen to you," Dad says.

"I know. I promise to be careful."

"If you're set on doing this, you should reach out to Meredith. She's in London. Do you remember her?" Mom asks.

"Of course. I was hoping to see her while I'm there. Can you send me her contact info?"

"I will. When are you leaving?"

"This week. I'll email my itinerary."

"Don't forget your pepper spray," Dad says.

He's got to be kidding. Does he really believe the airline would allow that? I'll deflect.

"I have some in my purse now. And, I almost forgot to tell you, I'm drafting my novel using my first name. So, if you send me anything, be sure to address it to Ariana instead of Maddie." I'm not sure why they would send me anything, but I'm hoping this is a benign way to bring up the name change.

"I've heard it's common to write books under another name, but why use it for travel?" Mom asks.

"It is the first name on my passport, and it's an immersion thing. Besides, I want to embrace Nana's love of life as I write. It's not a big deal."

"Makes sense. You'll always be our little Maddie, but you remind me of Nana Ariana," Dad says.

Thank you, Dad. Whew!

"She was determined to carve her own path through the world. But we worry about you. We wish there was someone special in your life," Mom says.

"Let's not go there today. If the right person comes along, I'll know. But I need to run now. I'm not through packing. Have a great cruise. I'm sure ships have Wi-Fi. Email me photos."

"We love you. Please stay safe."

"Love you too."

Nana wasn't overly wealthy, but she was more than comfortable. When she died earlier this year, her lawyer said she left moderate, but specific gifts to each of her children and grandchildren. She'd known she was running out of time, so she wrote letters to each of us.

Mine brings tears to my eyes.

Ariana Madison,

You're my namesake and, whether you know it (or appreciate it), are more like me than any of my other grandchildren. I've watched with admiration as you have used your strong will to become independent even when your parents, as wonderful as they are, tried to cocoon you.

You deserve the world, so I'm sharing a gift to help you capture it. But first, indulge me. I have a little advice to share.

Never put yourself in the position to be dependent on a spouse. Stand on your own. You are no one's shadow. Only marry if you find someone who will be your partner. You may each bring different things to the relationship, but it will only work if you are a balanced team. Oh, and it will never work without passion and great sex! I can see your shock, but it needed to be said. So, if you find a true partner who fills you with passion, great. If not, marriage isn't worth it.

Now for your gift. You have always wanted to travel for pleasure and author a book set in Europe. I'm leaving you money to cover the cost of travel, moderate living expenses, and a few extras. It should be enough to last a few months. And no, you can't use it for anything else.

Don't let your work get in the way of your dreams. At the first opportunity, book a flight and go! See where the adventure takes you. You may be surprised.

Take the chance. At heart, you're Ariana, like me. Embrace it.

With all my love,

Nana

CHAPTER FIVE

XANDER

Seated at the desk on the royal jet, my stomach uncharacteristically churns as we speed toward London. My thoughts bounce between two problems: the palace's unwelcome edits to my speech for the Worldwide Economic Conference, and what I'm going to do if this matchmaking process doesn't work.

Once again, the palace's speech writers insist on deleting my comments on the tension between the economic benefits and the environmental harm from offshore oil and gas drilling. Father and I disagree on this issue. As the king his opinion prevails, and understandably, we must appear united to the public. But why is he opposed to mentioning the tradeoffs? It's important we encourage discussion of the risks, and I thought my proposed compromise on the subject would be acceptable, but I was wrong. The palace struck that entire part of my speech.

The king may control my presentation, but I won't let him have the final say on the woman I marry. It's bad enough I'm expected to tie the knot by an arbitrary date, but I'll be damned if he forces Harper on me.

Edmund coughs loudly. Looking up, I meet his raised eyebrows. "Edmund, what was your question?"

"Your Highness, I was wondering whether you plan to dine in your room tonight or prefer a reservation at one of your favorite restaurants or London clubs. I also need to let your security detail know."

"Edmund, you know I prefer for you to call me Xander. No need for such formality when we aren't in public." I shake my head at his insistence on using my title and standing at attention in my presence, but he was trained by his father, the king's personal assistant. "There's no need for a reservation. I'd prefer an anonymous visit to a nearby pub for a drink and bite to eat."

"From a security standpoint that is difficult, sir."

"I highly doubt anyone will recognize me in casual clothes in a London pub. I'm a prince from a country most people have never heard of. And this may be my last chance to do something normal, so tell them to make it work."

Edmund dutifully responds, "Whatever you say, sir."

I smile. His insistence on formalities has its advantages. He knows when to follow my orders.

"Thank you, Edmund. Anything else we need to discuss?"

Consulting his tablet, Edmund says, "I also need to go over your schedule for tomorrow before we land. The press will interview you at the conference tomorrow morning, and you're giving your presentation tomorrow afternoon. Also, the palace emailed talking points for the interview."

I nod. What Edmund means is the palace sent me a list of topics to avoid, skate around, or answer with a "no comment." Even my father receives such lists before his meetings and public talks. But he has the choice whether to follow the advice. For me, my hands are tied. While my upbringing has taught me to tolerate restrictions, I don't have to like them.

As Edmund walks away to buckle up for landing, my thoughts return to the issue of marriage. What if I convince a female friend to marry me as a business arrangement? Would that work? We could agree to stay married for a year or two and then divorce amicably. That would be the simplest solution. No one else would need to know, except the attorneys.

Of course, it would kill Mum if she ever found out, and everyone knows it's hard to keep a secret in the palace with the attentive staff ever present. She'd be horribly disappointed to learn I'd recited vows in the cathedral having already agreed to break them. A contract has problems too. When we divorced, it would become known, which might call into question my right to the throne.

Closing my eyes, I silently hope Evan's idea to use Karl's matchmaker works.

The landing gear skidding along the runway turns my attention to the outside world. I'm welcomed to a foggy, drizzly London evening that matches my somewhat dreary mood.

The plane has barely taxied to a halt when Edmund hustles me down the stairs and into the open door of the waiting limo. Robert and Darren, my two-man security detail, climb in last, and we're quickly on our way to our hotel in Mayfair.

While we wait for Edmund to secure the keycards for our rooms, Robert and Darren are in their hyper-attentive mode, scanning the lobby for threats.

"You two need to change into casual attire for our pub night. We don't want to draw attention," I say. They start to object, but I wave them off. "My plans for tonight are not up for debate. Understood?"

They nod, and we follow Edmund, keycards in his hand, to my suite.

While Robert and Darren do their standard security sweep, I lean against the hallway wall and pull out my phone to text Maddie.

> Me: Forgot to ask when you arrive in London. Let's schedule drinks.

> Maddie: Change of plans. Missing the fundraiser.

> Me: Why? You've worked so incredibly hard on it. I've been looking forward to finally meeting you in person.

> Maddie: Me too. But I am no longer working on the fundraiser.

> Alex: You've done a fantastic job. I can't be the only client who relies on you. I should've known you'd be promoted.

> Maddie: Not exactly. Not with Platinum International now.

> Alex: Oh, I see. You got a better offer. Congrats. Would love to work with you again.

A high-pitched scream comes from the suite. Reception must've given us the keycard for someone else's room.

> Alex: Have to go. Send me your new contact info. Will let you know how the fundraiser goes.

> Maddie: Thx.

Peering into the room, I call out, "Robert, is everything okay? Who did you walk in on this time?"

"That's not the issue, Your Highness. Please stay where you are. We have the situation under control. I'll be out shortly."

A muffled conversation ensues inside.

Robert reappears, nervously twisting the signet ring on his left pinky and avoiding eye contact. "I don't know if you'll want to see what's in the master bedroom."

"What's going on, Robert? Who's in there? Did you surprise a maid?"

"No," he whispers, "Your Highness. Um. It's Lady Harper. She's waiting for you and refuses to leave. We confiscated her phone, which was on a small tripod recording."

"You must be joking!" Pushing past Robert to deal with this myself, I quickly stride toward the master bedroom, and halt at the door. Lady Harper lies seductively across my bed wearing only three strategically placed red bows. "What the fuck?"

She plasters a big grin on her face and says, "Come unwrap your present," as her hand traces a path down her exposed body.

"Bloody hell, Harper! What were you thinking?" Grabbing a

white velour robe from a nearby chair and tossing it to her, my patience wears thin. "Cover yourself up. What would your parents say?"

"Since we're getting married in a few weeks, why would they care?" She grins.

My fists are clenching and unclenching as I say through gritted teeth, "We're certainly not getting married in a few weeks or ever for that matter. What gave you that ridiculous notion?"

"Your father, of course. At the gala last weekend, he gave the impression he'd be thrilled if we were married before his birthday. So here I am. We can celebrate our engagement all night long." She giggles.

No way in ever-loving hell is that going to happen. Exhaling a deep breath, my prince mask returns. "Your offer to marry me is exceedingly kind, but I respectfully decline. Put your clothes on and please leave. Now."

Cheeks puffed and tears welling at the corners of her hazel eyes, Harper cries out, "How dare you treat me this way? We've been destined to marry our entire lives." She flicks her long dark brown hair and shimmies her ample chest, dislodging one of the bows. "I'll be the perfect queen."

If I didn't know better, I'd swear this is an elaborate prank. But knowing Harper, she mistakenly assumes putting herself on display will win me over. While I enjoy the company of beautiful women, this one is too desperate for the wrong kind of attention.

"Harper, we've never even dated. We have nothing in common except we're both royals. You love the paps and media attention. I loathe them. You've never been interested in working on our country's economic projects or my environmental charities. My wife needs to have something in common with me, and you should want something in common with your future husband too. Now, please get dressed and leave. Don't make me ask again."

Her tears disappear as quickly as they started, confirming my doubt as to their genuineness. "Why are you humiliating me? You'll see. I'm the only one for you."

"Goodbye, Harper." Me humiliating *her*? She's got to be kidding when she's the one sporting nothing but three red bows.

Shoulders sagging, she starts dressing. I step into the living room, giving her more privacy than she appears to desire.

While Darren remains by the door to ensure she leaves quietly, I ask Robert to check her phone for photos. Sure enough, she took several with her clothes draped across a chair and her bare legs lounging on my bed. Robert informs me she already posted them on social media with the caption:

Spending the evening with my prince.
You know the one.
Exciting announcement soon.

"Robert, please inform Edmund about this incident and escort Harper out of here."

"Yes, sir. I'll take care of it."

"Thank you. Keep her away from me. If she's willing to do this, no telling what she'll try next. Her last comment worries me that this isn't the end of her campaign to marry me."

"Understood, your Highness. This won't happen again," he says.

"Be ready to leave for the pub in an hour."

"Are you sure you still want to go out tonight?"

"Yes, now more than ever. I won't let Harper's antics ruin my plans to relax this evening."

Robert knows to find a discreet exit, put Harper in a car, and make sure no one sees her leaving. The good news is Father will hear about her stunt. Maybe he'll finally back off the notion she's the right match for me.

While Robert takes care of my uninvited guest, housekeeping removes all traces of her from my bed. That gives me time to leave a short voice mail for Meredith, letting her know I've arrived in London.

Finally, stripping out of my suit, I step under the waterfall jets in the oversized shower, attempting to rinse away thoughts of Harper's outlandish stunt, my desperately short period for finding a wife, and the realization I've hired a matchmaker. Who'd believe the weird reality of my life?

Quickly toweling off and pulling on charcoal jeans and a sweater, it's time to pretend I'm nothing more than an everyday English bloke heading to a pub for a drink.

CHAPTER SIX

XANDER

E xiting the hotel, my vision immediately fills with stars as the paps' flashing cameras click like firecrackers while they pepper me with commands and questions. "Look over here." "When are you announcing your engagement to Harper Sinclair?" "Is King Louis retiring?" "When is the wedding?" "When will you take over as king?" "Smile." "Where's your fiancée, Lady Harper?"

And on and on.

With Roger's and Darren's bodybuilder physiques holding the intruders at bay, we carve a path to the waiting car and slip safely inside without me uttering a word in response. Roger joins me in the back, and Darren takes the front passenger seat, urging the driver to make a speedy escape.

"Thanks. Excellent job."

Roger replies, "We have the situation under control. We'll take a circuitous route to the pub and lose them. Unfortunately, they know how you're dressed now. But hopefully, the pub will be crowded, and no one will notice you."

At least they don't know where we're headed.

No doubt the tabloids saw Harper's photos on social media and recognized the hotel with enough time to congregate, hoping we'd emerge together. Or even worse, Harper leaked the story herself.

Of course, feeding the press royal-approved comments comes with my title, but I have no desire to deal with the Harper issue again tonight.

Staring out the tinted window, memories pour in. Photographers and tabloids have hounded my brother, sister, and me since we each turned eighteen. Unfortunately, at that age, we became fair game. My baby sister, Brianna, suffers the most due to society's double standard. A photo of a woman leaving a hotel room after a night with Evan or me is annoying but no big deal for us. We're tagged the wild princes, and people expect, and sometimes even envy, such behavior. On the other hand, the one time that Brianna was caught leaving a guy's place at an early hour of the morning, the tabloids labeled her the Promiscuous Princess and other unflattering names.

My cheeks heat, remembering the unfair articles. But it's not only our personal lives being displayed for all to judge that irks me. The gossip rags print lies and make stories up out of thin air.

It baffles me as to why Lady Harper loves the attention. I sure as bloody hell don't. Unless the press is talking about issues affecting our country, charitable events, or other worthwhile topics, leave me out. My personal life and liaisons should be private. Of course, it doesn't work that way.

We finally arrive at the pub. The dark green sign adorned with gold letters proclaims The Skinny Frog. Sounds perfect. We don't encounter any cameras as we make our way through the throngs of people hoisting pints to close out their day. So far, so good. Luckily, Darren finds us a small table near the back, and Roger goes in search of food and drink. During the drive, I made it clear that he and Darren are ordering food and alcoholic beverages and sitting with me as friends would. No argument.

Knowing me well, Roger returns with a small pitcher of Pimm's for me and pints of lager for him and Darren. They could leave off the fruit garnish that always accompanies a Pimm's, but the drink packs a punch that is very much appreciated right now. Raising my glass to the men, I say, "Cheers. May the rest of our visit to London be much calmer than today!"

Taking a healthy swig, I savor the hint of tang and fizz trickling down my throat. Relief washes over me, and the untitled Alex takes over for the evening.

Roger and Darren continue to scan the pub for possible threats as we chat about football and other generic topics appropriate for pub night. Neither of them has made it past an inch or two of his lager while I've already refilled my glass.

When our fish and chips appear, I raise an eyebrow as the server says the fish is rolled in panko breadcrumbs and bake fried instead of deep fried. The chatty woman explains The *Chubby* Frog changed to The *Skinny* Frog after the pub's proprietor suffered a heart attack last year and decided to make the food a tad healthier.

The meal isn't what's expected in an English pub, but it's quite tasty.

My thoughts are interrupted when my phone vibrates. It's matchmaker Meredith. She can wait until tomorrow. Tonight is for relaxing and enjoying my Alex alter ego, so I refill my Pimm's again as I admire the cute brunette in tight black leggings at the bar. I don't do relationships, not since a disastrous one in college, but I'm always up for a no-strings night. Maybe she'd be interested in meeting up later. Introducing myself as Alex would make it less complicated too.

I shake my head when it hits me that marriage will mess with my lifestyle. Given this is going to be a marriage of convenience rather than love, hopefully, there will be room for negotiation.

CHAPTER SEVEN

ARIANA

My years in New York City have taught me well—always allow extra time. But with London's uneven pavement, hordes of tourists randomly stopping to take photos, and the city's confusing layout, an extra half hour wasn't quite enough.

Based on my app's directions, the restaurant should be close by though.

There it is.

Five minutes late is not ideal, but acceptable in most situations.

A few more steps, and I'm grasping the handle on the elegant door and double-checking my navy day dress. At the mention of Ms. Marshall's name, the hostess nods for me to follow.

Mom's friend is already seated by the window at a table topped with white linen and a small vase of fresh rosebuds.

"Ms. Marshall, my apologies for keeping you waiting. I'm still learning my way around London."

She reaches across the table to pat my hand. "Don't give it another thought. Welcome, Maddie. It's wonderful to see you again. And please—you're an adult now—call me Meredith."

"It's good to see you too." I beam, remembering the thrill of dressing up and going to plays with Mom and Meredith as a young teen.

"When did you arrive?" she asks as she straightens the napkin in her lap.

"Let's see ... four days ago. It's been almost long enough to adjust to the time difference from New York. By the way, Mom sends her best. I know she misses seeing you."

"I miss her too; we had such good times together. I'll give her a call when she gets back from the fabulous cruise that she told me about. But you are here now, so tell me how you're doing. We haven't seen each other in at least ten years."

"I'm doing well. You're right, it's been about eleven years, perhaps a little longer. I remember you moved here around the time I left for college," I cheerfully respond, perusing the lunch selections.

"Time flies, doesn't it? Let's order and then you can tell me about your plans for your stay in London." Placing her menu back on the table, she discreetly catches the attention of the nearby server as she asks me, "Will you join me in a glass of champagne? We should cele-brate this unexpected opportunity to chat."

"That sounds wonderful."

After we order she says, "Now, tell me what brings you here."

"As I mentioned in my email, I'm taking a short break from work to write a novel."

"How exciting. That's quite a departure from your regular job."

"It is. Businesswoman to novelist is a little scary, but I'm super excited to take the leap."

"What motivated you to make the change now?"

I shrug while overly smiling and beginning my well-rehearsed explanation. "I decided to grab the opportunity to take a short sabbat-ical when it was offered. I've always dreamed of writing a novel but didn't have time because my job was too demanding. Now with the luxury of a bit of savings and a small inheritance from Nana, this summer will be spent exploring my secret passion."

Confusion crosses Meredith's face, causing my chest to tighten. She's going to question my story. Crossing my fingers, I hope she doesn't ask *too* many details about my supposed sabbatical. She doesn't need to find out Shelly fired me and run to share that with Mom.

The waiting is killing me as Meredith concentrates on straightening the silverware, her brow slightly furrowed. She speaks slowly when she finally breaks the silence. "How interesting. I didn't know that marketing companies offer sabbaticals. You're lucky to work for such a ... progressive employer."

Choosing to ignore the note of questioning in her voice, I say, "Platinum International is at the forefront of our field." That's a truthful response even if I omitted the fact I don't work there anymore. "I'm excited to take a break and finally start my novel."

A smile returning to Meredith's face, she says, "A toast, then. To new beginnings." After we clink glasses, she says, "Changes can be exciting. What's your book about?"

That's a relief. She's not going to press the issue, but now for the next hurdle.

A final sip of bubbly does practically nothing for my dry mouth. Setting the glass carefully on the table and twirling the stem between my fingers, my planned words replay in my head one last time. Going for it, I begin. "Believe it or not, the stories Mom has shared about your life in London and your fascinating business are inspiring a part of my writing."

"Does that mean your novel is set here?"

"Yes, that's what motivated me to spend time here. Portraying the setting properly is critical. Also, I'm hoping you'll share with me what a matchmaker to the rich and famous does," blurting out the last part quickly.

There! The big ask is done, but will she help me?

"London has a special vibe. It would be hard to capture its essence without immersing yourself, so you're smart to spend time here. But why do you want to learn about matchmaking?"

"I envision the female character as a high-powered executive who's too busy running her accounting firm to meet the right person. But she's lonely without a partner to share her life with, and she wants a family before it's too late. That's why I need your help. Wouldn't using a matchmaker be the perfect solution for my character?"

Hearing myself say this out loud for the first time, the parallel with my own life is disturbing. I'm not worried about starting a family. But Nana warned me, life can be lonely without a true partner, and work has limited my opportunities to meet one. Work is one of the reasons I've ended up with less than desirable boyfriends. Am I subconsciously writing a character that's at least partially autobiographical? Probably. I've read that's what authors often do, intentionally or not. Still, the thought of putting myself out there again is too painful right now.

"Executives often use my services in similar situations, so it would be a believable option."

With a thoughtful look at me and fingernails gently tapping the tabletop, she hesitates to speak. As the server arrives with our entrees, Meredith says, "Let me think about it while we eat. I've heard fantastic reviews about the new chef's chicken with cherry balsamic glaze, and I must say, it looks divine."

I take a bite of my food. "Let me know if you want to try my lemon poached fish. It's absolutely perfect."

We casually chat for the next half hour about our love of food and different places to eat in the city. She even recommends a play she recently saw. As the meal passes, I wonder if she's going to ignore my request to learn about her work, but once our plates are cleared, Meredith focuses directly on me. Her lips form a thin line, and her eyes narrow to a piercing stare. This cannot bode well for my project.

"You asked about my matchmaking career. My ultra-high-end clientele insist on the most discreet approaches to finding matches. Therefore, it's imperative that no one views your novel as a breach of my confidentiality obligations."

I lean forward, making full eye contact. "I don't want to cause you problems. My goal is to understand the basics of the process, nothing client specific."

Meredith stares back. Then she turns to gaze out the window. When I'm sure she's going to turn down my request, she faces me again and smiles. "I have an idea. I'm hosting a reception the weekend after next to introduce a wealthy gentleman to potential matches. Ideally, we'd have one or two additional candidates. If you're willing to sign a confidentiality agreement, you can participate as one of the candidates. Then you can experience the process firsthand. What do you say?"

And just like that, poof, there goes my hope of this working. My shoulders sag, and I deflate, frowning. "But I'm not looking for a match, and it would be wrong to mislead him."

"You're single, intelligent, independent, and attractive, which makes you a suitable candidate for this client. You wouldn't be misleading him."

Hands splayed, I counter, "But I can't lie and pretend to be interested when I'm concentrating on my novel now. I don't need a boyfriend now, much less a husband."

"I'd never ask you to lie or pretend. Answer his questions truthfully, be honest about yourself, and who knows, you two may hit it off. What do you have to lose? You'll meet some interesting people, enjoy a lovely reception, and learn about the matchmaking process, all in one evening. Didn't you ask me to help you? I'm offering exactly what you requested."

She makes some good points.

If Meredith's okay with me being honest about why I'm participating, then it could work. It seems deceitful to pose as a candidate when my recent breakup destroyed my trust in men. I've sworn off relationships, at least for now. But she's offering the help I need for my book, and writers often go undercover to research stories, don't they? That's all I'd be doing.

I let out the breath I've been holding and say, "When you put it that way, how can I say no? As long as you're sure I'm not taking someone else's spot."

"You're not. It's settled."

Maybe this can work after all. "I have one other request. I've decided to use my first name for my novel. So, I want to go by Ariana."

"That's surprising. I remember your name was quite the debate when you were born. Your parents wanted to name you after both of your grandmothers, Ariana and Madison. You wouldn't believe how much your mother fretted over whether your name should be Ariana Madison or Madison Ariana.

"You've probably heard the story a million times. At family gatherings, they didn't want the confusion of two Arianas—you and your very much alive Nana Ariana, so they decided to call you Madison, after your deceased grandmother. But they were torn because they thought Ariana Madison had a nicer ring to it."

"I know. Ultimately, they decided to go with that name but refer to me as Madison, or Maddie for short. That was fine as I was growing up, and it felt special to have a connection to grandmother Madison since I never knew her. But now's the time for some change in my life. While this book-writing detour is scary, it's also my chance to show the world who I can be. Leaving behind my childhood nickname is a key step in that process for me. And with Nana Ariana sadly also gone now, I'll have the chance to honor her too."

"I can tell that this is important to you."

"It is. Mom has always called me her 'little Maddie.' But I'm thirty years old, and I've felt a connection to Nana Ariana's outgoing, independent nature for a long time. I haven't wanted to hurt Mom's feelings. Writing my book has finally given me the perfect excuse to make the change without any guilt, so I'm cutting that last tether to childhood."

"Ariana it is then. I'll send you the invitation for Saturday. It'll be cocktail attire, and you can find plenty of shops on Bond Street if you didn't bring the right dress. Let me know if you need a recommendation for a salon. I know a fantastic place for hair and makeup that will fit you in."

"Yes, please. I'll look for a dress."

Meredith's phone chimes. "Unfortunately, that's the reminder for my afternoon meeting. Forgive me, but I need to go now."

I pull out my credit card, but Meredith places her hand over mine, saying, "This is my treat. No argument. I can't tell you how happy I am to see you again."

Meredith quickly taps her credit card on the staff member's portable payment device, gives me a hug goodbye, and rushes toward the exit, saying over her shoulder, "See you at the reception."

My plan was to frequent pubs, take walking tours, and casually explore the city rather than attend high-end social events. Fortunately, I have some savings, a little extra from Nana, and haven't maxed out my credit card yet. That's still not enough for a visit to Bond Street, but there must be moderate options elsewhere. The cost of this trip is rising quickly. Hopefully, it's worth it.

A matchmaking reception. What have I gotten myself into?

CHAPTER EIGHT

XANDER

I'm going to lose my mind if I have to answer another effing question about when I'm marrying Harper. Damn it. Annoying tabloid reporters predicting my upcoming wedding and the king's retirement are following me everywhere.

It's the Worldwide Economic Conference, not the Royal Gossip Symposium. Don't the reporters care about the economic and environmental issues we're here to discuss? But every interview has been overshadowed with tabloid-style questions about my relationship status and speculation about Lady Harper becoming the next queen. It's those blasted photos she posted.

Don't get me wrong, I've "no commented" my way through the questions, mustering my best blank expression. But after watching me repeatedly rake my fingers through my hair, Edmund finally handed me some coins for my pocket and suggested fidgeting with them instead. He gently reminded me that an anxious prince with tousled, oily hair is not a great look for the cameras.

Clearly, this marriage situation is getting to me. I'm usually the calm, cool, distinguished prince, or the playboy prince—not the frustrated, impatient one. My priority needs to be my speech at the conference this afternoon to avoid embarrassing myself and the crown. But first, there's another set of questions to face.

After the last interview, we walk swiftly out the exterior doors with the security team keeping pace.

As our driver holds the door open, I slip into the back seat, saying "Edmund, I need an hour to review my speech."

"Yes, sir. I'll have lunch served after you finish your work, if that's acceptable."

"Perfect. Thank you."

In my suite, I shrug out of my suit jacket, take the folder from Edmund, and settle in the Louis XV chair at the polished cherry dining table. It's quite lovely but not my style. After growing up in a palace filled to the brim with antiques, my preference is for contemporary furnishing with cleaner lines. Mum at least let me redecorate my apartment to suit my tastes.

Reading through the speech, our country's position is hard to swallow. Without question, the king and I agree on the monarchy's duty to ensure that the economy of Catalinius remains stable and continues to grow. Where we disagree is on the sacrifices that are necessary to fulfill that duty. In my opinion, we must take a stronger stand on environmental issues to ensure long-term success, even if that slows growth in the short term. But the king worries my approach will not only slow growth but also destabilize the economy.

The outside analysts that my staff engaged are certain my approach is viable and, more importantly, necessary for the long-term health of our nation. But the king repeatedly ignores the fact-based research and instead relies on his advisers who have a vested interest in keeping the status quo. It makes me want to pull my hair out. If we're not careful, we risk ruining our country's natural resources in exchange for temporary economic stability.

It horrifies me to know we're compromising clean water in our oceans and the supply of safe fish that our people rely on. But my efforts at convincing the king have been futile. He's blind to the fact his longtime advisors have placed their own interests above those of our country. My—perhaps should I say *Alex's*—fundraiser for Clean Oceans is aimed at combatting the harm, but it's not enough.

Resting my head in my hands, my thoughts run through every possible option I can think of. Then it hits me. "Aha!"

"What is it, sir?" Edmund inquires as he approaches the dining table.

"I didn't mean to say that out loud, but I know what needs to be done." Writing as quickly as my pen will move, I make final notes on my speech.

After writing the last comment in the margin, I close the folder and sigh.

It's done.

Now I'm famished, and as usual, Edmund has things timed to the minute. I'm never sure how he does it, but I don't complain when a server emerges from the suite's small kitchen and places a wide shallow bowl in front of me. He explains it's seabass atop sautéed mushrooms, carrots, and bok choy in a soy- and ginger-infused broth. My first taste reveals that the moist, firm flakes of the seabass have absorbed enough broth to elevate the delicate flavor of the fish to a new level. And biting into a forkful of vegetables, the mushrooms are soft but firm, and the carrots and bok choy are slightly crunchy. Perfection. Outstanding food may not be my number one pleasure, but it's easily two or three.

And this was exactly what I needed—a reviving meal and quiet time away from the personal questions about my marriage plans, or lack thereof. Now, gathering my speech materials for the ride back to the conference, my focus must return to the business at hand.

It's time to put my plan into motion.

CHAPTER NINE

XANDER

Backstage at the convention center, I'm watching the presenter, who happens to be a friend from my college days. When he finishes, we shake hands, and I lean in to whisper a request. His eyebrows raise slightly, but he acknowledges my confirming nod.

Grasping the podium, it's time to give my speech. "Catalinius has been asked to share information about the economic impact of its offshore oil and gas drilling in the hope other countries can benefit from our experience."

My prepared talk covers the current state of our drilling and future opportunities for extracting not only oil and gas but other minerals from the deep sea, seabed, and the sea's subsoil. It addresses efforts to add safeguards to the exploration and drilling process but omits the fact those discussions are presently at a stalemate. And it's no surprise to the audience that there are many economic benefits from making use of the underwater resources.

But my conclusion deviates from the original speech. Instead of thanking everyone and walking away, I say, "I have time for a few questions," I announce, staring at my college friend in the front row and willing him to speak.

He looks around and finally stands, asking, "Has Catalinius experienced any problems with protesters upset about the negative environmental impact of offshore drilling?"

Perfect. The door is open. "That's an excellent question. Any country considering offshore drilling must be prepared to weigh the economic benefits against the environmental issues that protesters will surely raise. Leaders must make informed decisions in the face of sometimes difficult choices."

More questions follow. They took the bait, giving me the chance to address my concerns after all.

"Is Catalinius concerned about the protesters?"

"We consider all information seriously and analyze the issues."

"Will the king be making any changes in policies based on these protests?"

"Not at the present time."

"Does offshore drilling cause harm to the environment?"

"A number of reports show it can cause harm unless precautions are taken. Other reports dismiss those claims."

"Do you share the king's support of the oil and gas drilling near your shores?"

"My opinions are irrelevant. King Louis is our country's leader, and I fully support my king."

"Does your answer indicate you'll make significant changes when you become king?"

"I cannot predict the future, nor will I speculate."

"Which is more important: economic growth or environmental concerns?"

"Both are critical considerations."

"Isn't King Louis retiring later this year? Do you have plans for policies you'll put in place when you ascend to the throne?"

"The palace has no comment on the king's plans. Thank you for your attention. These are important economic and environmental issues."

Leaving the podium, my lips turn upward in a smug smile as I approach Edmund backstage. "That went well, don't you agree?"

Edmund nods in support but mumbles, "It's not my opinion that matters."

At least my plan worked, and the audience was given the hint that drilling is not completely without risks. Hopefully, that will be enough to encourage the other countries to research it further. Maybe they'll even consider the pros and cons of alternatives, such as offshore wind farms.

My role complete here, Robert escorts me to the town car with Darren and Edmund following. I'm ducking into the backseat when Robert yells, "SCRAMBLE!"

I'm instantly pushed backward into the padded leather, and Robert's 260 pounds land on top of me, making it almost impossible to breathe. There's a loud metallic screech, and the vehicle lurches sideways. The engine roars and wind whooshes in as we're moving. I squirm to look past Robert and get a clear view of us zipping past buildings.

Damn! The passenger door is missing!

"Get off me," I gasp at Robert.

He rolls off, placing himself between me and the gaping hole.

My heart is racing, and I'm working to catch my breath after he knocked it out of me. But I manage to ask, "What the bloody hell happened?"

"Some arsehole motorcyclist came out of nowhere, heading directly toward you."

"Was the crack I heard a gunshot?"

"Not gunfire. The motorcycle hit the side of the car."

"Where are Edmund and Darren? Are they okay?"

"Checking, Your Highness," Robert says tapping quickly on his phone. "They're fine and in a taxi on their way to the hotel."

"Are we being followed?" I ask.

Our driver answers, "No sir, but please make sure you both buckle up. There's no good place to stop, and I don't want to lose either of you."

"Did anyone get the license plate on the motorcycle?" I ask.

"I'll check with Darren," Robert says, snapping his seatbelt and glancing to see if mine is secure.

"That won't help," the driver says. "The license number was obscured with dirt, but it was a late model Triumph Tiger Sport 660 with royal blue trim. The driver was wearing a leather jacket with an unusual purple and white decal. It looked like a type of cat, maybe a leopard or jaguar."

"Outstanding. You're extremely observant," I say.

"Thank you, sir. I'm retired from the special forces. It's always been my job to remember the details."

As a precaution, security runs me through various drills on a regular basis, even though the likelihood of facing true threats is usually low. It's sinking in that this time it was real. We narrowly escaped real harm. Fortunately, when Robert signaled the danger, instinct kicked in and the training paid off, so we're fine, physically. The harder part to deal with is that this wasn't a drill, and someone may want to harm me. To say it's unsettling is an understatement.

"Was it intentional? Was I targeted?"

"Not sure, but it likely was an accident. His throttle was probably stuck open, and he didn't know what to do. We've reported it to the authorities, but I wouldn't be surprised if he crashed somewhere nearby unless he was able to free it."

If that's the case, hopefully he wasn't hurt. But why was he coming through the driveway of the conference center in the first place?

CHAPTER TEN

XANDER

"Your Highness, you need to read the headlines before the palace calls," Edmund says.

I rub my eyes. "Is it already morning?"

"Yes, and the matter is rather urgent."

"I don't remember a call with the palace on today's schedule." My muscles complain as I stretch and stiffly push myself into a sitting position. It's no wonder I'm sore and bruised after Robert shoved me into the car yesterday.

"You can be certain they'll call, sir," He tosses several newspapers on my bed and offers an iPad in his outstretched hand.

"Read them to me. My eyes aren't focusing yet."

"As you wish, sir. The top headlines are 'Prince Alexander signals changes in offshore drilling under his reign,' 'Prince Xander downplays policy disagreements with King Louis,' and 'Prince Alexander will kill offshore drilling.'" Edmund scrolls down on the touchscreen. "Other headlines include, 'Will King Alexander cancel offshore drilling projects near Catalinius?,' 'Prince Xander values the environment over the economy,' and 'Beware: changes to offshore drilling are coming when Prince Alexander takes the throne.' Should I continue?"

"No, that's enough." Shaking my head, I mutter, "I didn't say those things. You heard me expressly voice my support for the king." Swallowing hard, I pinch my lips shut. I may have skirted the edge by planting the initial question with my friend to remind everyone there are tradeoffs and alternatives to consider, but I was careful not to cross any lines. I certainly didn't contradict the king or propose banning offshore drilling.

"Sir, many of the articles rely on reading between the lines, as they say."

"I merely answered direct questions. Father wouldn't expect me to outright lie, would he?"

"Sir, I suspect the palace will be disappointed that you chose to address those questions at all. What should I say when they call?"

"Ugh." Squeezing my eyes closed and rubbing my temples gives me time to decide the best course of action. "Let's not wait for the palace to call. I'd rather be proactive. Call our public relations team and let them know everything was taken out of context. They can issue appropriate statements."

"Very well, sir."

I roll onto my stomach, stretching my back. King Louis is my father, but he's also my king. My intention wasn't to disrespect him. My plan was to stop well short of that. Unfortunately, those headlines imply my remarks crossed the line.

Of course, questions weren't on the agenda in the first place, but other countries need the opportunity to avoid the mistakes we've made. Don't we have a moral obligation to them? Still, I may have gone too far given the palace's directives to avoid these issues.

Regardless, with these headlines, dealing with Father will require some damage control. Hopefully, he'll wait until I return home to deliver the inevitable, stinging rebuke. With the conference over, I can lie low for a few days. I'm attending a couple of fundraisers, but the focus will be on the charities rather than me. As only one of many royals, I should be able to avoid more bad press.

And then there's the matchmaking reception which will keep me here a little longer. I'm figuratively crossing my fingers that it works. Meredith is my best chance to find a bride in time, and bringing home a suitable fiancée will redirect the king's attention to a pleasant topic.

CHAPTER ELEVEN

ARIANA

My stomach drops when I see an article in the morning news about the Clean Oceans Fundraiser—my final project at Platinum International before Shelly fired me. Her excuse about reducing staffing costs didn't make sense that day. And Lisa's call, along with the online ads that popped up for a similar open position at the company, confirmed my suspicion that Shelly lied about her reason for firing me.

Not long before she let me go, Shelly acted a little miffed a couple of times when clients called me directly instead of going through her. But it didn't seem important to me. I never encouraged them to bypass her. But returning their calls quickly made me the go-to person when they needed immediate responses.

And Shelly always spread herself far too thin to have time for the personal touches. I enjoyed listening to our clients' latest life dilemmas, children's accomplishments, and plans for the weekend. Shelly didn't have time for that "nonsense," as she called it. But Platinum International was her company, and apparently, she didn't intend to share the spotlight with a subordinate even if it was good for business. She could have at least waited until after the fundraiser to fire me, but her timing saved the cost of my trip and ensured she was the center of attention.

Looking back, it should have been clear to me. She prefers "yes" people and doormats. Thankfully, that's not me. So, here I am in London writing my novel instead.

It still hurts to have missed the Clean Ocean fundraiser last night after working so hard on the publicity, invitations, decor, menu, and auction items. But when she fired me, my name disappeared from the invitation list. It occurred to me that Alex would probably invite me if I asked, but that would mean explaining my situation to him and, worse, seeing Shelly. No thanks.

The event must have been spectacular though. Closing my eyes, an image of the plush London ballroom appears. Sparkling silver and burgundy décor accent the room I'd seen in photos. White roses, lilies, and greenery flow from tall silver urns onto the candlelit tables. Music plays softly in the background. And I can almost taste the filet mignon and lobster with truffle butter melting in my mouth. Mmm.

In my imagination, I'm at the fundraiser, mingling with the guests in my crystal-encrusted stilettos that are perfect with my long, silver lamé dress accented with burgundy chiffon rosettes. It's like a fairytale.

It's too bad my only chance to put a face with Alex's inviting masculine voice evaporated. There's something about a deep British accent that makes me want to mix business with pleasure.

A buzzing noise interrupts my thoughts. It's an incoming text from Alex himself!

> Alex: Fundraiser was a huge success. Missed meeting you in person.

> Me: Wish I could've been there. Can't find any photos. Press?

> Alex: No. Didn't want a media circus.

> Me: A lost opportunity to advertise the charity.

Alex: Wanted the attendees to focus on donating, not getting their photo into the news. Raised more that way.

Me: Glad the strategy worked. How did the ballroom look?

Alex: Spectacular. It far exceeded your description. The charity took some photos. Check the website tomorrow.

Me: Good to hear. Had the perfect strapless dress to match the theme.

Alex: I want to see a photo of that.

Me: Too late. Returned it.

Alex: Too bad. Are you back to running yet or is your thigh still in need of massage?

Me: Are you flirting?

Alex: Who me? How's the new job?

Me: Traveling for a project.

Alex: Off to a fast start. I'll buy you a drink next time I'm in NYC. You can tell me about it.

Me: Would love that. Have to run. Congrats on the fundraiser's success.

Alex: Thx for your help. Talk later.

I should've told him I'm in London and suggested we meet, but I didn't want to explain what I'm doing here. He probably already left anyway. By the time I'm back in New York and he visits, I'll have a new job, or even better, a bestseller. A girl can dream, right?

CHAPTER TWELVE

ARIANA

T aking in the grandeur of Orion House makes me want to pinch myself. It's one of London's most exclusive private clubs, with its Portland stone facade rising five stories above the street in Mayfair. The door attendant nods when presented with the code "purple sky," and silently tugs the star-shaped, wrought iron handle to open the massive mahogany door.

After stepping from late-afternoon daylight into the dark of night, wooden doors thud behind me. It's not clear if I should be frightened or enchanted by the mysterious atmosphere of this place.

Once my eyes adjust to the dimly lit foyer, I do a double take, scanning the scene before me. It's the entrance to a garden. The only light is from a quarter moon against a star-studded black sky. A gentle breeze brushes across my bare arms, raising goosebumps. My senses are confused. Somehow, they've transformed the inside into the outside.

I'm questioning my eyesight when a tuxedo-clad man appears, offering a slight bow. "Good evening, Miss Montgomery. Welcome to Orion House. My name is Gerald. Please follow me."

Soft lights in the floor reveal a path with stepping stones embedded in grass. I wonder if the grass is real—probably not a good idea to check. As we wander down this garden path, we pass sitting areas, fountains, and beautiful clusters of blooming plants before reaching a wrought iron gate with an arched top. Gerald opens it and indicates I should pass through. Unexpectedly, I find myself alone in a dimly lit elevator sans Gerald. This whole experience is incredibly strange so far.

As the elevator slowly rises, anticipation takes over. Meredith didn't send any info on the guy we're meeting. All she provided was the time, location, and codeword. Curiosity has been getting the better of me. He must be wealthy to be able to afford M-Cubed's services, but why does he need them? Is he shy, unattractive, or awkward with women? Of course, the character in my novel wants to start family, and is simply too busy to date. Does that happen to successful men in real life? Hmm.

He must be anxious about meeting us too. I'll have to ask Meredith whether she gave him bios on the women that will be here tonight. If so, that seems a little unfair.

When the elevator stops, and the doors open, questions are still running through my head. Gazing around the new space, the codeword suddenly makes sense. The most gorgeous purple and lavender sky shines with twinkling stars and floating clouds all around me. Trees in silhouette stand tall in the distance. As my eyes focus on a line of three bright stars in the indoor sky, something else clicks. The owners named Orion House after the Orion constellation.

Meredith's impressive. She certainly knows how to select the perfect place to set a romantic mood. A night sky, stars, the scent of roses and lavender wafting through the air, and soft music. It's magical. Add a wealthy single guy, and she has the stage set for matchmaking.

Speaking of Meredith, she's walking toward me in a plum chiffon cocktail dress with a jeweled neckline that sets off her shoulder-length, silky black hair.

"Maddie—excuse me—*Ariana*, it's wonderful to see you again. You look lovely. That little black dress is perfect, and your hair looks fantastic pulled back on one side. Where did you find that beautiful crystal-encrusted comb?"

"Thanks, Meredith. The stylist recommended it."

With the help of an experienced salesperson, my dress is a sleeveless, black satin dress with a lace overlay, scalloped along the hem. The slightly flared skirt hits a little below midthigh, so it's flirty but classy.

The stylist insisted on heavier makeup than I usually wear. I was worried it would be too much, but in this nighttime lighting, I'm glad I trusted her.

Placing her hand on my elbow, Meredith guides me toward the far end of the "garden" where other women are chatting under the limbs of a tree that's lit with soft yellow lights. "Orion House is a special place, perfect for tonight."

"It's spectacular, Meredith. You've done an amazing job setting the atmosphere for tonight."

"Thank you. Now let me introduce you to the others."

Meredith claps her hands, and the room quietens. "Ladies, welcome to our small gathering. Let me introduce the final addition to our group. This is Ariana."

I'm relieved she used the right name. Now if only I can remember to use "Ariana" tonight. It's still a little new to me.

"Ariana, I'd like you to meet Princess Caroline, Lady Everly, Lady Gianna, Lady Emma, Lady Constance, Miss Olivia, and Miss Jessica."

My eyes meet each in turn as Meredith calls out their names. These women are beautiful, decked out in designer dresses, red-bottomed shoes topped with crystal sparkles, and sporting more jewels than I've ever seen in one place. My black patent stilettos, without the famous red sole, and simple diamond stud earrings my parents gave me for college graduation pale in comparison. Most meet me with ice-cold glares, betraying their upturned lips as they scope out the latest competition for tonight. I can almost see the claws and hear the meows. I'm back in high school. Ugh.

Smile locked in place, I ignore the cool welcome, saying, "It's a pleasure to meet you."

They murmur polite, perfunctory greetings. I shake off the idea I don't belong because it doesn't matter. I'm here to learn and gain inspiration for my novel, not to throw myself into the middle of this cat fight.

Oblivious to—or more likely ignoring—the tension in the room, Meredith explains, "The gentleman you're meeting tonight is Prince Xander of Catalinius."

Exclamations of excitement, awe, and nervous giggles ripple through the group of eligible bachelorettes. Meredith has their attention now. I thought this was going to be a cat fight before I heard the guy is a prince. Now it will be an all-out war. Quite the prize for these royals and aristocrats.

Bringing a finger to her lips, Meredith silences our group. "Ladies, decorum please. He's nearby. Prince Xander is thirty-six years old. He wishes to find someone who will share his interests, work on charitable endeavors to benefit his country, and be his wife when he ascends to the throne later this year."

More muted chatter.

Someone mumbles, "I thought he was marrying Harper Sinclair. What happened to her?"

"He must have dumped her."

"I can't believe it. I could be a princess in a few months, then queen. He's mine."

"No way. He's leaving with me."

Another quips, "You'll have to make it past me first. I'm not letting anyone get in my way of marrying a prince."

"I'm not even sure I want to marry a prince," says another.

They can have their games and catty remarks, I'm here to view how this unfolds and make notes for my novel, not walk away with a husband. Even with that plan, my palms are sweating as it never occurred to me that I'd meet royalty tonight. And now I'm supposed to appear excited about competing for the heart of a crown prince under a twinkling fairytale sky.

Meredith continues, "When Prince Xander enters, I'll introduce each of you to him. Even though you're not from his country, it's considered respectful to curtsy. For those of you not familiar with a proper curtsy, I'll demonstrate."

Thank goodness. I've never curtsied before, except for the semi-curtsies we did at curtain calls for school plays. Something tells me those weren't proper form, so I watch Meredith closely.

"Ladies, simply place one leg behind the other like this. Bend both knees, sinking slightly while bowing your head. Hold for one or two seconds and rise." Meredith's movements are elegant. "Wait for the prince to address you before speaking. Do not attempt to shake hands or touch the prince unless he initiates the contact. Do you understand?"

We all nod, but the royals among the group are rolling their eyes. I guess this isn't their first prince.

"Outstanding. You'll each have group time and one-on-one time with the prince. My assistant and I will coordinate the timing. I'll return with His Royal Highness in about ten minutes. Enjoy a glass of champagne and canapés while you wait."

Meredith has barely disappeared through a black side panel I hadn't noticed when servers appear with silver trays. Some offer crystal champagne flutes, and others hold small appetizers. The other women quickly accept glasses of bubbly and cluster around high-top tables. I veer away from the drinks and stand at a table alone, observing.

No way can I curtsy while holding a glass. With my luck, I'd spill it all over the prince. Champagne will have to wait until after the introductions.

The noise level rises quickly as the women chat about the luck of meeting a prince and how it's no wonder their parents insisted that they attend this reception. And there's further speculation as to what happened to end the relationship between Prince Xander and Lady Harper. Of course, I'd never heard of either one of them, much less their relationship.

While watching the scene unfold, two of the women approach me. "Ariana, I'm Olivia and this is Jessica."

"Hello. Are you excited about tonight?" I ask.

"Yes, but the three of us are the only nonroyals here. That puts us at the bottom, right?" Olivia asks.

"That's rather pessimistic, isn't it? Is he required to marry a royal? If so, I can't imagine Meredith would've invited us," I say, confused.

Would she? Do I care? Meredith did say she needed more candidates. Are we extra dolls dressed up to fill the display window but not really of interest to the prince?

I need to be taking notes so I can ask Meredith later, but how? Meredith and the club prohibit phones, and my tiny clutch only has room for a hotel keycard, credit card, and ID. How am I going to remember all these details? I should have picked a dress with pockets for paper and a pen. I could've escaped to the restroom to jot down notes.

"Even if he's not required to marry a royal, I assume it's preferred," Jessica says. "Besides, I'm not sure I want the restrictions of royal life, much less those that come with marrying the next king of a country."

"Those are interesting points. But there's no way he won't notice you two," I say. "Do you know anything about him?"

Olivia leans in. "Last week he was caught in a London hotel room with Lady Harper. Everyone thought they were getting engaged."

"How do you know that?" I ask.

Olivia downs the rest of her champagne and snags another one from a passing server as she shares a little too loudly, "It was all over the tabloids. Didn't you see it?"

It's none of my business, but Olivia's on her way to an early buzz.

"No, I haven't been in London long."

"Me neither. I flew in from New York yesterday," Jessica says, drawing her eyebrows together as she twirls the stem of her flute.

Before I can ask what she's thinking, the music changes to some sort of march.

Meredith walks in on the arm of a six-foot-tall muscular god in a custom-fitted black tuxedo. His straight chocolate-brown hair is barely long enough to rest behind his ears, and his emerald eyes sparkle with fire as the twinkling lights dance across them.

If this is the prince, something's wrong with the universe. With those looks, he must be fighting off hordes of women. There must be something wrong with him if *he* needs a matchmaker.

I'm staring spellbound, oblivious that the music stopped until Meredith cuts through my brain fog, saying, "Ladies, it's my pleasure to present His Royal Highness, Prince Xander of Catalinius."

As Meredith steps back, in a deep voice, the prince says, "Thank you for accepting the invitation to join me tonight. I'm looking forward to getting to know each of you this evening."

Jessica whispers, "His accent is yummy."

"That's not all that's yummy," Olivia says, bringing giggles from the women at the nearby tables.

"It's the accent. The Brit I know from work sounds just like him." But my eyes are still glued to his face, and I'm looking forward to the excuse to talk with him.

Meredith says, "As I call your name, please come forward. First, I present Princess Caroline."

The princess gracefully moves forward, dropping into a practiced curtsy. Her white chiffon cocktail dress conjures visions of a royal bride.

Lady Everly is next in her shiny silver knee-length dress. I'm watching the royals carefully for pointers on etiquette in greeting a prince. Lady Gianna and Lady Emma follow, and both execute perfect curtsies in their minidresses. I'm not sure how they keep their behinds covered as short as their dresses are. Experience, I suppose. Lady Constance is next in her elegant navy dress, laced with gold metallic threads.

Meredith is introducing the women in order of title, and—Olivia was correct—we commoners will be last. When called, Olivia moves forward in her poofy green dress and stumbles slightly during her curtsy. The prince doesn't miss a beat, though. He reaches for Olivia's hand to steady her as she rises. Skipping the champagne was the right call, but my pulse increases as it's closer to my turn. I don't want to embarrass my mom's friend. Wringing my sweaty palms, I wonder if Meredith will call me or Jessica next?

The air releases from my lungs in a quick escape when she calls

Jessica forward. Jessica is attractive, petite, and exudes class and confidence. The prince is fully engaged as he talks with her.

Closing my eyes, I wait for Meredith's next words. Finally, she says, "Your Highness, I'm pleased to present the final guest, Miss Ariana."

As I walk forward, time moves slowly, my heart pounding with each step. I dip into a curtsy, silently counting to two. When our eyes meet, his head is cocked to the side. He doesn't look happy. Oh no. He's disappointed.

"Why is such a lovely woman frowning?" he asks. "I hope you don't mind sharing your evening with me."

"I've never curtsied before. I was afraid I'd fall flat on my face and make a fool of myself." I blurt out in one breath. Oh no, that was too much. Why can't a trapdoor open and let me vanish now? "I'm so sorry. I didn't mean to share that much." I'm making it worse.

Prince Xander chuckles and takes my hand in his. "You know, I've never curtsied before either, so I'm sure I'd fall flat on my face the first time. You were very graceful though. I'm extremely impressed." He raises my hand to his lips and gives it a quick peck, sending unexpected chills down my spine. "I look forward to talking with you this evening. Something tells me you're a breath of fresh air."

Either I'm blushing or there's a heat wave in here, but the hard part is over. I survived meeting the prince with only a slight hiccup, and unlike the other women, I'm not worried about whether he'll select me. I'm not a real candidate.

It's time for a drink and something to nibble on while taking mental notes on the rest of this matchmaking process. Hopefully, some of the parmesan crisps and mushroom canapés are still left. And where's the damned champagne?

CHAPTER THIRTEEN

XANDER

Eight beautiful women stand before me—a princess, the daughters of two dukes, an earl, and a marquess, plus the daughters of a tech entrepreneur, a hedge fund manager, and a professor. All here, apparently willing to be my wife despite having never met me before.

If this isn't strange, what is? There is, however, a limited supply of single royal men—not to mention that marrying me offers a virtually unlimited expense account with the chance for a significant title upgrade. The commoners can live out the age-old fairytale of becoming a princess. But do they understand what it would mean? I don't have a choice, but they do. One of my goals is to determine who is here for the right reasons. At least tonight I only need to narrow the group to four, not one.

Meredith shows me to a private sitting area with a curved sofa and glass-topped coffee table before returning with Princess Caroline, Lady Emma, and Lady Constance.

Princess Caroline is well spoken and charming, but we aren't clicking for some reason. Maybe one-on-one will be better. Emma's a little distracted. It's not clear she wants to be here. On the other hand,

I'm impressed by Lady Constance's alluring auburn hair and knowledge of Catalinius.

The second group consists of Lady Everly and Jessica. They both stand out. Everly is rather quiet but thoughtful and intelligent. The latter two qualities are excellent for a queen. As for Jessica, she has spunk without being arrogant. I admire that.

After group two leaves, Olivia, Lady Gianna, and Ariana join me on the sofa.

Ariana intrigued me when we were introduced, so I'm looking forward to chatting with her. But Olivia quickly takes over the conversation, asking about Lady Harper and the tabloid stories. Ugh. I don't want to talk about those rags, but it appears Olivia has had a little too much champagne and is oblivious to my attempts to change the topic.

My eyes dart to Ariana. She gives me an understanding nod. Without thinking, I flash her a quick smile and wink in acknowledgment. Her cheeks tint as she lowers her eyes. Charming.

When Olivia finally takes a breath, it's my chance to jump in. "Lady Gianna, tell me about yourself."

She flicks her hair. "My father is a marquess. I'm sure you already know everything you need to about me."

It's no secret that she's a royal, but that's an odd answer. Either she didn't understand my question or she's quite arrogant. Let's hope it's a misunderstanding. "My apologies for the confusing question. I was intending to ask how you enjoy spending your time."

"The usual activities for someone of my position—representing charities, traveling, attending galas, and following fashion. My staff signs me up for events, and in exchange my father provides my allowance. I do what's expected. My parents trained me well for royal life."

Whoa! Gianna's nose is so high in the air, she'd drown if it rained. But the good news is she wouldn't care what I do as long as she receives a sufficient allowance.

Unfortunately, Meredith ends the group chat before there's an opportunity to speak with Ariana, but we'll have the one-on-one time.

As the women walk away, my gaze focuses on the mesmerizing sway of Ariana's black lace skirt. Is she wearing black lace underneath too?

A server draws my attention, presenting a glass of champagne, which I accept, and Meredith escorts me to an expansive balcony for the private talks with each woman. One by one, I'm surprised by how accurate my first impressions were. My thoughts race ahead, impatiently wondering if the same will be true with Ariana. Will she be as candid and charming as she was during our introduction?

She *finally* approaches, stops a few feet away, and says, "Should I curtsy again?"

She's attractive, adorable, and amusing. "No, that's not necessary. First let me thank you for your patience during our group chat. I'm sorry we didn't have much of a chance to talk."

"No need to apologize, Your Highness."

"Please call me Xander. There's a lovely view of the city." Reaching for her arm, we walk to the edge of the balcony. Picking up two glasses of champagne from the nearby table, I hand one to Ariana. "Let's toast to getting to know each other." We clink and sip. "Now tell me something about yourself."

I watch as she takes another drink, slipping the thin crystal rim between her plump red lips. She keeps her eyes locked on mine, trying to read my thoughts.

"I'm a writer, working on my first novel, which is set in London. I want to capture the combination of the city's tradition and vibrancy, so I'm living here for a few months."

"That's fascinating. How long have you been a writer?"

"It's a new direction for me. I was in corporate work but always wanted to write. When given the chance to make a change, I took the leap."

"That's risky. I commend your willingness to try something new."

"Thanks. It's risky from a financial perspective. But I'm single, not tied down, and can afford to give writing a chance thanks to a small inheritance from my grandmother. If not now, when? I don't want to

69

look back on life with regret," she says with a shrug of her shoulders and a wistfulness in her voice.

"Admirable. So how did you end up here tonight? You didn't come to London looking for a husband, did you?"

Laughing softly, she says, "No, I didn't. Meredith is my mother's close friend, and she invited me to this reception when I asked for advice on the matchmaking process for my novel."

"So, I was right. You *were* frowning when we met. You're not interested in a match with me." My shoulders drop slightly. It's disappointing that one of the most interesting women tonight isn't here for the right reason.

Her eyes lock with mine. "That wasn't the case at all. I really *was* afraid of falling on my face."

I laugh, a little hope returning. "Good to know. How is your writing going so far?"

"I have a basic outline finished, but currently, I'm focusing on research. The tiny room I rented isn't very conducive to writing."

"That's too bad. What type of place would be best for your creative work?" I ask.

With a far off look in her eyes, she says, "My dream writing space would have a giant chair I can sink into and a place to prop up my feet. A desk overlooking a peaceful garden would also work. But if those aren't available, then a big bed with overstuffed pillows to lean against and a TV for background noise would be great. Also, I'd prefer somewhere that allows snacks."

"In other words, you want to be able to relax while you write."

"Exactly."

"That makes sense. If you don't mind, let's return to my earlier question. Are you interested in finding a match?" I hold my breath.

She looks into the distance, hesitating. Turning back, she says, "Not really, but Meredith believes people can find love even when they aren't looking. That's why she's a matchmaker. But I hope you're not upset I'm here. I won't divulge anything specific about you or tonight in my book. I promise to honor the nondisclosure agreement I signed."

Taking a small step back and staring at the London skyline, my mind processes what Ariana shared. It wasn't what I wanted to hear, but she appears genuine, which is refreshing. "You are quite interesting. I probably shouldn't believe your promises not to sell me out to the tabloids or your future publisher, but I do. You seem, as they say, to lay all your cards on the table."

"True. I'm not particularly good at hiding things," Ariana admits with a crooked smile that captivates me.

"What did you hope to learn tonight?" I ask, turning my body to rest my arms on the railing but keeping my gaze on her.

"Well, I'm interested in knowing why a wealthy, handsome prince is using a matchmaker. How does someone narrow the choices in a single evening? What happens next? Are you afraid you aren't meeting the real versions of the women tonight? My list of questions is unending. I should stop before I overwhelm you." Her eyes sparkle as she freely shares her thoughts.

Inexplicably, I'm more at ease talking to her than I've felt with any woman before, so I open up further, sharing my dilemma. "In Catalinius, the reigning monarch may retire at age sixty-five. Father has decided he wants to do that, which means I'll need to take the throne on his birthday later this summer. But there's an issue with that."

"What's the problem?"

"Our laws require me to be married to take the throne. If I'm not married when King Louis turns sixty-five, he must remain on the throne the rest of his life. It will be my fault if he misses out on his one chance at retirement."

Her eyes go wide and mouth gapes. "What a guilt trip. That's terrible. Hang on—why the last-minute need for a matchmaker when you already knew about this law?"

In a quiet voice, I admit, "Honestly? I was living in denial. I didn't want to believe my father would go through with his plan to retire."

"Oops." She giggles as she rocks forward to lean against the glass rail.

I smirk. "Oops is right. Now you know why I sought Meredith's help."

"Given your circumstances, you're in good hands. You have seven amazing options here. How will you narrow it down to four?"

"You miscounted. There are eight of you here tonight."

"Seven, when you exclude me."

Frowning, I ask, "Why would I exclude you? That would be disappointing."

"That's kind of you to say, but as I told you, I'm only here for research. Besides, I'm not princess material." She shrugs, palms up.

"I'm not so sure about that, but in answer to your question, I'll select the women based on my gut instinct. They need to be genuine, easy to talk with, and here for the right reasons. I'm also asking everyone the same two questions to help me make my decision."

For some reason, I don't share that I'm only looking for a marriage of convenience, not a romantic match.

"What questions are you asking everyone?"

She's shifting her weight again. Hmm. "First, let's move to the sofa, so you can rest your feet."

"I'm fine. No need to worry about my feet."

"When my sister alternates between ball and heel, repeatedly shifting her weight, it means her feet are tired, and she'd love an excuse to sit. I'm guessing you wouldn't mind that either. Am I right?"

"I'm embarrassed to admit it, but that sounds wonderful. You're very observant. I didn't pack formal attire for this trip, so I bought new shoes for tonight. They are rubbing blisters on my heels."

"That sounds painful." Reaching for her elbow, I ask, "May I?" She nods, so we move to the sofa and sit, leaving a little space between us. "After the first time your sister hits you on the head with her shoe, asking why you didn't rescue her, you tend to pay closer attention."

"She didn't!"

"Well, not exactly. It was my younger brother she hit when she was about seventeen."

"I need to hear every detail of this story. Why did she hit him?"

"It was her first gala as an almost adult, so she was wearing an extravagant yellow ball gown with matching high heels. The problem was my parents expected her to stand all evening and dance every time someone asked. By midnight, her feet were in pain, and she thought my brother and I should've figured it out from the way she was shifting from foot to foot and come to her rescue."

"I gather neither of you understood her pleas for help."

"Unfortunately, we didn't. When it was finally time to leave, we headed back to our rooms. As soon as we reached the private part of the palace, she took off her shoes and started chastising us. Her arms were flailing as she described why we were arseholes, and she accidentally hit Evan in the face and gave him a black eye. That's when we learned some high heels include metal reinforcement, especially the designer brand she had worn. Since then, we've done our best to rescue her feet when she sends up the signal." I laugh.

"No wonder you noticed my feet were hurting. But I promise not to hit you with my shoes," she says, softly giggling.

"That's reassuring. But you're not escaping the questions I'm asking everyone," I tease. "The first one is what are your three best qualities? How would you answer?"

Ariana taps her index finger on her lips. "Hmm. I'm driven and easily disappointed in myself if I don't achieve my goals. That may sound like a negative, but it's important to have goals, so I put it in the positive column. I also love learning new things and care deeply about the people in my life. What are your best qualities?"

"Surprisingly, you're the first to ask me that."

"Tonight, or ever? There had to be some interviewer who asked why you would be a good king."

"No, no one has cared enough to ask. But since you were kind enough to enquire, let's see. I'd say I'm dedicated to doing what's best for my country. I'm passionate about my charities, particularly those that help improve the environment, and I strive to maintain my integrity, despite the lies the tabloids print."

"You mean I shouldn't believe the tabloids?" she offers with a bemused smile.

"Absolutely not! They print pure rubbish." I laugh heartily at her question.

"Don't worry, I discount *most* of what I read. But what about all those articles and photos of you partying that I've been hearing about? There must be at least a smidgeon of truth in those."

"Well, I have done a little partying." I chuckle. "But let's move on to my second question. What do you do for fun? Travel, movies, hiking, sports, something else?"

"Give me a minute. I haven't had a lot of spare time lately." Leaning her cheek on her palm, Ariana stares into the dark night. "It's hard to narrow things down, but I love movies, reading, and watching football —and I mean American football. I also want to travel, and I love horseback riding, but hiking isn't my thing. Oh, and jogging is my favorite exercise. What are your top three?"

"If I'm limited to three, they would be sailing, tennis, and riding. I enjoy travel too, but it's usually for work these days. And like you, running is one of my go-to workouts."

"So, based on the answers to these two questions, you'll pick four women, right?"

"Personality and chemistry matter too."

"Fair enough. Then what happens?"

"Those four women will fly with me to Catalinius for a couple of weeks. That'll give us time to get to know each other, and they can meet my family."

"Do you need your family's approval?"

"Not really. But their impressions matter to me."

"May I ask something personal?" Ariana asks.

I raise my eyebrows a bit. "I thought we were already discussing personal things, but go ahead and ask. I'll try to answer honestly." Of course, if she gets too personal, it could be uncomfortable, but I'm curious to see what she'll ask.

"Doesn't this whole situation bother you?"

"What do you mean?"

"Your country's law requires you to marry now whether you're in love or not. I don't mean to be rude about your traditions, but they seem so arbitrary and unfair."

"I've grown up under these laws, and as a royal, we understand and routinely deal with expectations that those outside the royal family don't have to contend with. There are many royal obligations that outsiders would consider unfair. That's my life, and it'll be my wife's life too," I say matter-of-factly.

She goes rigid. "That leaves commoners out of contention since you don't seem to believe we can understand the expectations." Her tone is sharp.

"Ouch." I recoil as if she slapped me. "My apologies, as I meant no disrespect. Royals are accustomed to following tradition without question, but that doesn't mean one of you untitled ladies couldn't be the better match for me. And I don't have to marry a royal. It's just a fact that my future wife and I will often have to follow various traditions whether we like them or not."

She visibly relaxes. "The rules seem harsh to me, and I feel sorry for the awkward situation you're in."

"Please don't. I have a great life that most would trade for in an instant. But I plan to change the law, so my children won't end up in the same position."

"Why can't your father change the law for you?"

"It's complicated. He could have at a price, but he didn't. It's too late now."

"That's rotten for you."

"In some ways, it is."

Meeting Ariana has made tonight better. Chatting with her is easy, and my guard is down. I've never been this relaxed with other women. Her candor, genuine interest in me, and concern for my situation draw me to her. It's as if we've known each other for ages and are friends already.

But there's more to it.

We have chemistry, and it's not just that I want to take her to bed. Yes, that sounds fantastic. Those inviting red lips could do wonderful things for me. But, for some unexplainable reason, she makes me want to court her, impress her, and make her understand my country is a wonderful place, despite the marriage laws she doesn't understand. Hell, the laws don't make sense to me either.

Meredith approaches, preventing further conversation. It's too bad my time with Ariana is ending, and unfortunately, our paths are leading us in different directions.

CHAPTER FOURTEEN

XANDER

"Your Highness, my apologies for interrupting, but it's time for you to make your decisions. I'll take Ariana back inside and give you a few minutes," Meredith says.

"Thank you, Meredith." Reaching for Ariana to help her up, her soft touch sends an unexpected zing up my arm. I'm not sure where that reaction came from, given she friend-zoned me. "Ariana, I've enjoyed chatting with you immensely."

"I can't explain it, but I have that same feeling. Good luck with your decisions." Her hand slowly slips from my grasp, and I involuntarily squeeze her fingertips one last time as she pulls away. I smile, watching her wavy chestnut hair bounce against her shoulders as she disappears back into the club with Meredith.

At the balcony's railing, I stare over London for a moment before closing my eyes and listening to the street sounds—car engines, the occasional siren, laughter from couples passing below, and music drifting out the doors of nearby nightclubs.

It's time to decide. One of the four women chosen tonight will become my wife and the future queen of Catalinius. No pressure.

Letting out a deep breath, my interactions with each of the women replay in my head. They're all attractive. Most would be suitable for royal life, but who's the best match?

Princess Caroline was interesting and regal, but we didn't have any chemistry. Even in a marriage of convenience, it would be preferable to feel something.

Lady Emma said her parents insisted she show up for this reception. She also dropped not-so-subtle hints that I'd only be of interest to her if I were a woman. We're not a match for marriage, but we plan to stay in touch. She generously offered to help with one of my charity events.

Lady Constance and I know many of the same people. It's surprising our paths haven't crossed before. She's stunning, showed an interest in Catalinius, and our conversation flowed easily enough. She also has the advantage that as the daughter of an Earl, she knows what our life would entail.

Lady Everly is stunning in a muted way, classy, and seems intelligent and thoughtful. But she's a little quiet and meek, so she may be a little boring for me.

Jessica's personality shines, and she is refined. She also wasn't afraid to raise concerns. I respect that.

That leaves three: Olivia, Gianna, and Ariana. Olivia was outgoing but would be a handful. Gianna is snobby but would know how to fill the role. As for Ariana, she excites me while making me comfortable, and banter is easy with her. But she doesn't want a husband. The decision will be harder when it comes to this group.

The click of high heels grabs my attention. "Your Highness, would you join me on the sofa?" Meredith asks.

"My pleasure, but Meredith, please call me Xander. I insist."

"As you wish. I've brought photos of each of the women so you can take a last look as we discuss them." She places a stack of printouts on the coffee table in front of us.

"Thank you. How should we proceed?"

"Let's look at them one at a time so you can share your thoughts with me."

Meredith and I go through the first five photos, and so far, I'm interested in inviting Lady Constance, Lady Everly, and Jessica to Catalinius. Princess Caroline and Lady Emma are in the no stack.

"That leaves three: Olivia, Gianna, and Ariana," Meredith says.

"This group is easy. Olivia is vivacious and outgoing but used poor judgment tonight when she drank too much champagne. She's also too similar to Lady Harper. Anyone that obsessed with the tabloids is a no for me.

"On the plus side, Gianna was raised for royal life and would leave me alone if her financial desires were met. But she's too self-absorbed for my taste. I doubt we'd enjoy each other's company when we need to be together, so she's also a no."

"That leaves the lovely and refreshing Ariana. She's my fourth yes."

"Um. Did Ariana share her reasons for being here tonight?"

"She did."

Meredith raises her eyebrows.

"She was honest with me about her novel. But I want to spend more time with her—take her horseback riding."

"I see. Just friends. You're sure you wouldn't rather have one of the other women as a backup? The others are all *looking* for a match."

"Absolutely not. I'm not marrying someone from the no group. Ariana is my fourth."

If the laws of Catalinius are forcing me to marry now, my future wife should at least be someone I'm looking forward to getting to know better, not someone who didn't click with me tonight.

And yes, Ariana is not looking for a relationship, but I wouldn't be either but for my country's strange requirement. With that and the fact we both enjoy running and horseback riding, she'll understand me. Perhaps she'll love sailing too. It will help to have a friend to relax and escape with while navigating this stressful process.

What doesn't make sense is the chemistry between us. It's so natural even though we just met. If neither of us is looking for a relationship, why would we have an electric connection? It's not merely a desire to take her to bed. Of course, watching her cute behind sway as she walked away *did* give my cock ideas.

She's my fourth because, at the end of my deliberations, the thought of not keeping her around was upsetting.

Worst case, we become good friends, and she helps me through this process.

No. Worst case, she doesn't accept my invitation to join me in Catalinius.

CHAPTER FIFTEEN

ARIANA

D id I hear that right?

He chose me.

My chest tightens as I pace. He's got to be kidding. I made it perfectly clear I'm not looking for a match. Of course, there was a tingle down my spine when our hands touched. Did he experience it too? The timing is wrong though. After Brian, the mere thought of dating, much less a serious relationship, isn't enticing.

Hugging myself, my eyes search the room for Meredith. She's ushering the no group out, but she holds up a finger when she sees me trying to get her attention.

When the disappointed women have left, she meets me out of earshot from Lady Constance, Lady Everly, and Jessica.

"Why am I still here?" My voice wavers as I clutch my throat.

"Calm down, Ariana. Prince Xander understands you're not looking for a husband, but he still insisted you be the fourth candidate."

"Why? It doesn't make sense."

"He enjoyed spending time with you and found you quite charming. He wants to be friends. He also said since you're not trying to win him over, you can help him determine the true nature of the other three candidates. And he wants to help you with your research by letting you see the next phase of the matchmaking process. That would be a fabulous opportunity for you."

Oh. My breathing slows. But did I hear her correctly? "Does he want me to spy for him? That's not okay. And why would he waste one of the four slots on me? He should pick someone else," I say, shaking my head.

Placing her hand on my shoulder, she says, "I don't believe he wants you to spy. And we discussed the downside of only having three *real* candidates, but that didn't sway him. He made his wishes clear. He wants you to spend the next two weeks with him in Catalinius. He could use a friendly advisor, who is not part of the family, to help him through this process. You've signed the confidentiality agreement, so it makes sense for him to have you to confide in. His only request is that you don't tell the other candidates that you're there for research. He's concerned that if they knew, it would stifle their ability to be themselves around you."

Tapping my finger against my lips, I say, "Hmm. That makes sense. I won't lie though."

"Just for my curiosity, what are your thoughts about him?" Meredith asks.

"Oh, he's essentially perfect. Handsome, well-spoken, educated, wealthy, a prince. And he's surprisingly easy to talk with. It pains me though to see him forced to marry someone he doesn't know or love." I smile, remembering our conversation.

She tugs at her ear, watching me. "But you're not interested in him for yourself? He did say you're lovely."

My smile grows, but I wave off the notion. "How sweet, but, of course not, as there's nothing about me that's princess material. I must say, though, I was surprised at some of the comments from the royal women. Did you hear the catty snipes when he was out of the room? If he picks the wrong one, he could be stuck with a real bit—um, I mean bitter one." My jaw clenches.

"Uh-huh, I see. The more I think about this, the more I agree you need to go with him. He's going to need a *friend* close to the process to watch his back."

"He will." I nod. "If he's sure, I'll go."

"Then pack your bags."

Meredith walks away to deal with the other women's questions, leaving me to my thoughts.

What I didn't share with her is how Xander sends shivers through me, the tingly kind, and it's confusing. It's not only his deliciously good looks and hot, captivating accent, but of course those don't hurt. The thought of his strong arms pulling me close while he whispers his desires in my ear makes me tremble.

But that's not all. He's flirty, interesting, and amazingly attentive. He even showed interest in my novel and my reasons for being in London. And we both enjoy some of the same outdoor activities. It never occurred to me a prince would share things in common with me.

Even these things don't explain my strong reaction to him though. We just clicked.

But I've clicked with guys before, and they burned me badly. Brian was proof my judgment about men is terrible. I'm not ready to go there again, but that doesn't prevent me from helping Xander with his tough predicament. No one should be in his situation, and he needs help selecting a woman he can trust.

I'm in. Besides, who wouldn't enjoy a trip to Catalinius and a little more time staring at a gorgeous prince. There's no harm in looking, right?

CHAPTER SIXTEEN

XANDER

E ntering the royal jet, I'm holding my breath, wondering if Ariana accepted the invitation.

So, turning the corner and seeing her in the main cabin, a smile spreads across my face and a sense of relief washes over me. She's here. Why does that matter to me so much? She's not even available to me, but somehow knowing she's here is comforting.

As I move forward, followed by Edmund, Robert, and Darren, the women take note, stand, and curtsy in unison.

"Hello, everyone, Welcome aboard." They return my greeting as I motion for them to retake their seats at the dining table.

"Thank you for joining me on this journey. We're headed to my beach house on the island of Catalinius for some privacy from the press while we get to know each other better."

Based on the women's fidgeting, I'm not the only one finding this situation a tad awkward.

Finding that reassuring, I press on, aiming for a calming tone.

"It'll also give you a chance to see one of the most beautiful parts of my country. Our flight is a little over two hours, so please enjoy brunch while I make a couple of urgent business calls in the office. Hopefully, the calls won't take long, but my assistant Edmund and my security team are here if you have questions before my return. Until then, make yourselves comfortable, and our flight attendants will serve food soon after takeoff."

Glancing back from the office door, my eyes meet Ariana's, and I wink before going inside. Her cheeks turn pink with the charming blush that enchanted me on the night of the reception.

Shaking my head and grinning, I fall into the comfy, high-back leather chair behind the desk to make a couple of calls. Instead, I find myself staring out the window, pondering which of the other three women will be my queen. At this point, it's hard to know, but something tells me Ariana will play a key role in helping me pick the best match. Her candor is exactly what I need right now.

If I'm honest with myself, it's not her *candor* that has her popping into my head all the time. I'd love to capture her inviting lips with mine as my fingers tug on her thick, wavy chestnut hair. That's unlikely to happen though. We're destined to only be friends.

As the plane taxis down the runway for takeoff, my phone chimes, demanding my attention.

"Hey, Evan. How's Las Vegas?"

"It was surprising. But I arrived back home today."

"Did you stay out of trouble?" I'm almost afraid to hear his answer.

"It depends on how you define trouble." He chuckles.

"Ugh. Does that mean I'm going to be reading about you in the tabloids again?" Leaning back in my chair, I rest my feet on the corner of the desk, prepared for the worst.

"It's all good. Nothing to worry about. But forget about my press. What about yours? Your speech made headlines even in the US. Did *His Majesty* lose it?"

My shoulders tighten with the reminder of the fallout from my talk at the conference. Rubbing my neck, I say, "I mucked it up by answering questions from the audience. But, in my defense, the press misrepresented what I said. Apparently, the king's furious, so I've been avoiding him until I arrive home."

"That's going to be a fun reunion. How's your other problem? Have you found a wife yet?"

"Karl's matchmaker made some introductions, so a plan is moving forward. I'm hoping that bringing a potential fiancée home will temper Father's verbal lashing about the conference snafu."

"Don't count on it. He compartmentalizes quite well. He'll deliver the lecture, followed by congratulating you on the engagement. Who is she, by the way?"

Staring at the ceiling, I say, "I'm not engaged—at least not yet. I'm headed home today. We can talk in person."

"Sounds good. I have a surprise too."

"What is it?"

"Be patient, Xander. Life's good now. Really good. Talk later."

That's strange. Evan left for Las Vegas sounding haunted and talking about needing to find himself. He sounds so much happier, which is fantastic. What could have happened to change his perspective in just a few weeks?

CHAPTER SEVENTEEN

ARIANA

"This is Stacey, your pilot," says a strong feminine voice over the intercom system. "My copilot, Stan, and I are pleased to welcome His Royal Highness Prince Xander and his guests onboard Catalinius Royal Jet Two. We have now reached our cruising altitude, so you're welcome to remove your seatbelts and move around the cabin as you wish. We'll let you know when you need to buckle up again. According to traffic control, we'll land in approximately two hours. Your flight attendants will be serving a light brunch and mimosas shortly. Enjoy your flight."

Looking around the dining table, I ask the other women, "Do they have so many royal jets they number them?"

Constance smirks. "No, *dear*. That's not what the number means. It's a designation as to which royal is onboard. The king and queen are always assigned number one. Prince Xander is number two because he's next in line to the throne. Prince Evan is number three, and Princess Briana is number four. But, of course, *you're* not a royal. You wouldn't know these things."

"That makes sense," Jessica says, ignoring Constance's attitude. "In the US, they distinguish between the president's and vice president's flights in a similar way."

Hearing a click, we all turn toward the door where Prince Xander disappeared earlier and see him. Damn, he's gorgeous. And when his hair flops over one eye, I can't help envisioning my fingers brushing it behind his ear.

But I'm only here for research, and until I learn how to pick men who aren't assholes, I'm not getting involved again. Brian's cheating was the last straw.

Can you say trust issues?

I catch myself frowning and clenching my fists under the table. I still can't believe Brian thought he could fit in a quickie with his assistant right before our lunch date. I was only fifteen minutes early when I walked in on their tryst. It crushed me at the time, but in the end it's a relief to be rid of that loser. Whether I could ever put my faith in another man's promises is not clear though.

Xander closes the door behind him and walks to the head of the dining table, asking, "May I join you?"

He catches my eye and lifts an eyebrow. Confused, I tilt my head in question. What is he thinking? Oh no. He must have caught me frowning again.

Damn you, Brian.

"Of course, Your Highness," Constance says.

Prince Xander slides into the swivel chair. "Thank you. And please call me Xander. If we're in the company of others, I must ask you to follow royal protocol. But let's dispense with formalities when it's only us and my immediate staff. Agreed?"

"Agreed," we say in unison.

"Let's break the ice with a few questions for each other," Xander suggests as he accepts a croissant and orange juice from the flight attendant. "Jessica, would you start? What would you like to know?"

I take a sip of the mimosa that materialized, thankful I don't have to go first.

"Xander, I'd love to hear more about Catalinius. I have so many questions. Let's start with some basics. What's the national language? Is Catalinius known for its wine? And what foods are typical there?" Jessica prattles on.

"Let's see if I can remember all your questions. First, English is the national language of Catalinius, although you'll find many Italian and French influences, particularly when it comes to food. We have access to wonderful fresh seafood. As for wine, we're best known for our Sangiovese, but we make several outstanding wines. You'll have opportunities to taste some of them, so you can decide which one is your favorite. Ariana, you're next."

"I'm curious about your accent. It sounds British but you grew up in Catalinius. How did that happen?" I ask.

"My brother, sister, and I had a nanny and a tutor from London before we went to boarding school in the UK. I stayed there for uni, but my brother went to the US, and my sister went to Paris. If you listen closely, we each have a slightly different twist to a British accent from our differing experiences, but most people wouldn't notice. I also still spend quite a bit of time in London, handling various business-related matters for our family, so the British aspect of my accent is routinely reinforced," Xander says.

That explains why his accent sounds so similar to Alex's British one. Interesting. But it's still surprising that their accents aren't distinguishable given Xander grew up on an island several hours from the UK. My ears don't pick up on subtle differences in accents that I'm not familiar with.

Everly asks, "What are the main concerns you have for your country?"

"Such a serious, but important, question. I worry about preserving our environment and finding ways to continue growing our economy in the coming years. For example, I mentioned our outstanding seafood, but if we don't protect the waters surrounding our country, we could lose that resource. However, doing the right thing is expensive, so we'll need to make smart choices."

Constance chimes in, "I understand Catalinius is a very stable country. King Louis must have done an outstanding job with the economy."

"He has." Xander nods.

But I notice Xander's smile doesn't quite reach his eyes. What's that's about?

"Constance, what question do you have for me?"

"I'm somewhat of a foodie, so I'd love to know what your favorite food is."

"If you insist that I pick only one, it would definitely be chocolate." He shrugs. "My turn. Let's start with that same question. What's your favorite food?"

Constance immediately agrees with Xander that hers is chocolate. Everly can't live without cheese and particularly loves Swiss fondue. Jessica loves lobster and pizza but not together. The pizza part isn't surprising. One of the first things I learned after moving to New York City was how much New Yorkers worship their pizza.

I answer, "It's hard to pick only one, but I love éclairs." I savor the thought of how good an éclair would taste right now.

"That's a very specific choice. Why éclairs?" Xander asks.

"Close your eyes and imagine the first bite of the choux pastry topped with chocolate ganache and filled with rich, vanilla cream. My mouth is watering remembering the last one I had. It's a guaranteed foodgasm," I sigh.

When I open my eyes, everyone is staring at me. Not good. That was a little too much. I take a deep breath and exhale slowly. "Sorry. I can get a little carried away over food, and éclairs are at the top of my list." I shrug with a coy smile.

Was I subconsciously flirting with him? Shit, I was. Xander's deep voice reminds me so much of Alex, the flirting is almost automatic.

The table is silent for what feels like an eternity, but it's only a few seconds before Xander smiles. "Many people have strong connections with food, particularly if it's associated with a fond memory."

My cheeks are on fire from the image that comment conjured.

Fortunately, just then the pilot speaks over the intercom, saving me. "This is Stacey. Please buckle your seatbelts for landing. We'll be on the ground shortly. Welcome home, Your Highness."

Xander excuses himself and takes a seat by Edmund, and they start talking, as we buckle the seatbelts built into our dining chairs. Thankfully, he's still within earshot. That's the only reason the women don't tease me for my gaffe.

What's wrong with me? It must be the romance novel I'm writing that has me thinking about food in such a sensual way. That's it. It can't be the steamy prince. Or can it?

CHAPTER EIGHTEEN

XANDER

E xiting the plane, we're greeted by the familiar warm rays of golden sunlight and the clear, cerulean sky. Thankfully, a cooling breeze wafts past as we walk to the waiting stretch limo. Jessica, Everly, and Ariana slide onto the leather bench seat on the far side of the limo, while I join Constance opposite them for our drive to my beach house.

Chilled bottles of champagne, glasses, and chocolate-hazelnut-filled raspberries sit atop the burnished-wood coffee table that's affixed along the center of the limo. Popping a cork and filling the glasses, we start the celebration of our arrival in Catalinius.

I'm one step closer to finding the next queen.

"Everyone, please join me in a toast." Raising my glass, I say, "To new friends and new experiences. May we each find our right path and have a bit of fun along the way. Cin cin." We clink our glasses and sip the bubbly liquid.

As we travel through the city, I point out various landmarks, including our parliament house, restaurant row, the fashion district, and my family's palace on the hill. Traffic thins as we reach the outskirts of the capital, and the lush countryside comes into view.

"Xander, are they raising cattle and sheep in that field?" Everly asks, pointing to the right.

"Yes, and in the distance, you can see citrus orchards." The women, except Ariana, pepper me with questions as we sip champagne, pop raspberries into our mouths, and enjoy the scenery.

Ariana is unusually quiet. I suspect she's embarrassed by the orgasmic éclair comment. But she shouldn't be. She's passionate, which is an admirable quality. Besides, I thoroughly enjoyed watching her describe her favorite food. The look on her face made me envy the pastry. Too bad she's off limits or I'd order éclairs and watch her savor *every* delicious bite.

While I can't do that, I *can* try to put her at ease. "Ariana, are you enjoying the tour so far?"

Looking out the window, she says, "I had no idea what to expect, but it's truly beautiful." Our driver turns left, and Ariana takes a sharp breath. "We're at the coast?"

"Yes. Check out the view behind me."

"It's magnificent," she says.

Ariana's right. We have the perfect view of the glistening azure water dotted with sailboats and fishing vessels in the distance. Surfers are catching waves near the white sand beaches below us.

The water is a source of tranquility for me. If I didn't need to concentrate on finding a wife, I'd sneak away with my surfboard or find Evan and take our sailboat out.

A few minutes later my place comes into view.

"We're here. My home is through the gate on the right. And the Royal Vineyard is on our left." Its rows of grapevines cover the hillside.

The front gate opens, and we pass through, stopping in the driveway near the etched-glass double doors at the front of my beach house.

Standing on the drive, breathing the fresh sea air reminds me how wonderful it is to be back here. It's a place where my movements aren't as restricted due to fewer security concerns. And casual attire is my norm here. It's a relaxed lifestyle compared to life at the palace where my parents require business attire, at least when entering any public spaces.

At The Shores, I'm able to be Alex instead of Xander most of the time. It's a place where the pressures of being the crown prince aren't quite as stifling. That's why I've brought the women here. Hopefully, this environment will make the process comfortable for all of us.

"Follow me," I say, escorting them into the foyer, which is on the top level of my house. Edmund and Darren are already waiting for us, having ridden ahead in a separate car.

"Welcome to my home. It's called The Shores, but to me, it's paradise. Hopefully, you will enjoy it as much as I do. My home has four stories that are terraced into the side of the cliff. The lowest level opens onto a private beach, so you'll have easy access if you want to take a walk in the sand. Edmund is going to give you a tour now and show you to your suites."

"What's the plan for the rest of the day?" Jessica asks.

"Thanks for reminding me. I forgot to mention that a poolside dinner is planned for sunset tonight. Unfortunately, I won't be able to join you because of a family obligation. Please forgive me, but we'll see each other tomorrow."

They murmur their assents but are distracted as they take in my home. The foyer opens directly into a large living area with a solid wall of glass across the back, revealing a coast-side deck with an infinity pool, giving the appearance of water flowing directly into the Mediterranean.

While the women will have an enjoyable evening lounging by the pool, I'm not looking forward to *my* evening. It's time to face the music with my father and to learn about Evan's surprise—whatever it is. If I time my arrival at the palace right, they'll already have had cocktails. That can only help.

CHAPTER NINETEEN

XANDER

My sister is in the library but to my surprise my parents aren't present for cocktail hour. Giving her a quick hug and peck on the cheek, I ask, "Bri, where are their majesties?"

"They had to meet with some visiting dignitary for drinks, so it's just us. Evan should be here any minute. Have you heard about his big surprise?"

"Only that there is one. Do you know what it is?"

"He's bringing ..."

Bri stops speaking when Evan walks in with a big grin on his face and his arm around a lovely, petite woman.

"Xander, Bri, I'd like you to meet my girlfriend, Cassandra Edwards. Cassandra, this is my brother Prince Xander and my sister, Princess Brianna. If she approves of you, she'll let you call her Bri."

Hearing Evan say *girlfriend* and noticing the diamond key around her neck, my jaw drops.

Cassandra starts to curtsy, but Bri waves her off, hurries across the room, and pulls her into a tight hug. "I'm so glad you're here. It's exciting that Evan has a real girlfriend."

"Bri, let her breathe," Evan says.

"You've never brought anyone home before, so I have the right to be excited. I've always wanted a sister," Bri says, eyes gleaming.

"Your Highness, it's wonderful to meet you too, but please call me Cassie. Everyone does—well, everyone except Evan," Cassie says.

"It's a pleasure to meet you. Now I understand what Evan meant when he said he had a surprise for us," I say.

"Hopefully, it's a pleasant one," Cassie says.

Before I can answer, Bri grabs Cassandra's hand, pulling her to the sofa. "Of course, it is, and please call me Bri. Evan, can you and Xander mix drinks for us while Cassie and I chat? I assumed we'd want some privacy, so I sent our bartender away."

"We can manage that. Cassandra, what will you have?" Evan asks.

"A SoCal martini, please."

"That's vodka, a splash of Grand Marnier, and a twist of orange peel, right sweetheart?" Evan asks, scanning the bottles on the bar cart.

"That's it."

"Ooh, that sounds good. Evan, I'll have the same," Bri says.

"Coming right up. Xander, give me a hand."

Evan quickly mixes drinks for us. After handing them around, he and I step onto the outdoor terrace to talk while Bri has Cassie engaged.

"What's up with Cassie? How did you two meet?" I ask.

"I was helping Sean with a cooking competition at the Grand Athena. She was an alternate."

"You love food, so dating a chef's not a bad idea."

"She's actually an attorney, who's also a chef."

"Even better. She's smart, cooks, and is great looking. If you brought her home, you plan to keep her around awhile."

"Hopefully, longer than that. Life's better when we're together. We're connected to each other. There's this electricity ... It's hard to explain."

"Do you realize how ironic this is? I'm the one who needs a wife, and you weren't even looking but fell for someone."

"Yeah. My feelings for Cassandra blindsided me. What's the status of your matchmaking process?"

"It's complicated. The matchmaker introduced me to eight prospects. I narrowed it to four who came home with me and are staying at The Shores. If all goes well, one of them will be my wife soon."

"You have four possible wives living in the same house with you? What were you thinking?"

"I know. It's weird, but I'm running out of time to figure out which one will be most compatible. I couldn't simply pick one at the reception and propose marriage that night, so they came here with me. They understood my situation, so they were willing to go along with the arrangement."

"Is there a frontrunner?"

"Not really. They're all attractive, educated, and interesting in different ways. I'll sort it out over the next couple of weeks."

"Be careful. All of them under one roof is a disaster waiting to happen. Let's go rescue Cassandra. I'm sure Bri's already shared all my embarrassing secrets by now."

Evan pats me on the back as we turn to go inside. No need to share that my strongest connection so far is with the one woman who isn't interested in marrying anyone, much less me. The irony of that would lead to merciless teasing.

It's strange, but when Evan described his attraction to Cassie, my thoughts immediately went to Ariana. Hmm.

CHAPTER TWENTY

ARIANA

E dmund left me at a luxurious ocean-themed suite with its own sitting area. This place is like a fancy hotel in a travel magazine, but it's Xander's *home*, which is beyond my comprehension. My family had enough money to provide almost everything I needed growing up, but I've never known anyone who has a home this grand. It's so beautiful, extravagant, and perfect that I'm also scared to touch anything.

My jaw drops further as I enter the marble bathroom with a massive soaking tub for two. A long, hot, bubble bath is definitely in my future. Plush white towels with an intricate, embroidered, silver crest hang on towel racks with additional ones rolled and stored in baskets. They look too fancy to use; they remind me of the ones mom put on the counter in the guest bath when we had company. I made the mistake of using one once. She wasn't happy.

French doors near the king-sized bed are opened outward, the doorway shielded by sheer-white drapes dancing in the light sea breeze. Pushing aside the drapes and stepping onto the balcony, the fresh scent of salt air fills my lungs as my eyes are drawn to the pristine sandy beach below.

Staring at the small waves lapping against the sand is somehow freeing. The water is washing away bumps in the sand and leaving a smooth surface—a new beginning, which isn't lost on me. The weight of losing my job is a little lighter. The hurt Brian caused is slightly less painful. Is being here a sign that there's something better waiting for me? Nana was right. I need an adventure and a little risk to see what possibilities exist for me.

Sighing, I lean on the concrete railing and look out to sea, enjoying the peaceful water as it transitions from turquoise to royal blue and finally to a dark navy near the horizon. The sky is so clear, I can see for miles.

As my gaze returns to the beach below, I can't wait to curl my toes in the fine white sand and wade in the foamy water that flows back and forth, covering, and uncovering shells as strings of seaweed bob in the gentle waves.

It's the perfect vacation photo—mesmerizing and calming. Xander's right. This *is* paradise. I take a last deep breath of fresh air before going back inside to change. It's time to meet Constance, Jessica, and Everly for a dip in the pool before dinner.

Walking onto the pool deck, three pairs of eyes are focused on me. Thankfully, Meredith took me shopping because these women are dressed to kill, even though Xander said he wouldn't be around tonight.

Jessica is sporting a tiny red bikini dotted with rhinestones under a short, see-through red dress. Constance has her assets on display in an all-white bikini with a white gauzy shirt draped over her shoulders. With her striking, long red hair, she looks fabulous. If it weren't for Everly's one-piece navy swimsuit, my black two-piece, edged in a Greek key pattern with matching black coverup, would be the most conservative outfit here.

Constance's suggestion we change into our swimsuits and meet at the pool had nothing to do with swimming because no one dips even a toe into the inviting water. Instead, everyone is reclining on lounge chairs, sipping white wine, and chatting.

As the sun sets, the staff announce that dinner is ready, but we don't bother to change clothes since we're eating on the outside deck. We dine on a light meal of baked fish atop fresh greens with a citrus vinaigrette. Not surprisingly, Xander is the topic of conversation.

Watching everyone while not revealing my friend-zone status, it's hard to gauge who's genuinely interested in him and would make a suitable wife. Constance is smug and very self-confident. Everly is extremely shy. It's not clear if she'd be comfortable in a public role. Jessica is harder to read. Like me, she's listening more than talking tonight.

When the second—or maybe it's the third—bottle of wine is emptied, Constance drops a bomb, saying, "I'm not sure if Xander will make a good husband."

Jessica asks, "Why do you say that?"

"Rumor has it that he's a playboy. He has the reputation of not being faithful. He's never had a serious girlfriend. And there were those tabloid photos of Lady Harper in his hotel room the week before we met him. But my father insisted I participate in this match-making process, so I'm giving him a chance. I can't imagine marrying someone who's known to cheat though," Constance says.

Jessica finally pipes up with "Me neither. I don't plan to date another playboy. I've had it with those guys. I'm also not sure if I'd want to marry into a royal family. The idea of giving up my freedom and following a bunch of strange rules isn't appealing. I'm not sure it would be right for me."

"Then why did you agree to come to Catalinius?" Everly asks.

"I'm not a hundred percent sure," Jessica says. "When we met at the reception, I didn't know anything about Xander. He was charming and didn't seem like a playboy. I also wouldn't have to worry that he was dating me for my money, or rather my dad's money. Ultimately, I decided this was worth a shot. But if he turns out to be the jerk Constance describes, I'll be on the next plane home."

Everly quietly says, "I never trust those tabloid stories. They make most of that stuff up. I don't doubt that Xander and his brother have lived extravagant, fun-filled lives, but Xander seems serious about settling down and honoring his duty to his family. I can't believe he wouldn't be faithful."

"Don't be naive, Everly," Constance says. "The tabloids may exaggerate things, but Xander's not a saint. He's handsome, wealthy, a prince, and constantly surrounded by willing women. The temptation to play will always be circling and enticing him."

"Call me whatever you want, but for now, I'm giving Xander the benefit of the doubt. He's been a gentleman so far, and I admire the family's work with charities." Everly says with a frown.

"What about you, Ariana?" Constance asks.

"I have no time for cheaters, but it doesn't matter. I doubt Xander is going to marry a commoner who practically orgasms while describing an éclair. He won't consider me as princess material after that, but I plan to enjoy this beautiful vacation at the beach and spending time with all of you."

"I see your point. That wasn't exactly royal-approved conversation," Constance says.

But Everly smiles, quietly saying, "Don't be silly, Ariana. You didn't say it in front of the press. It didn't appear to bother Xander. He laughed. I suspect he thought it was charming. If only I could be like you, men wouldn't find me boring."

"Everly, you are a lovely person. Don't put yourself down that way," I say.

Before Everly can protest, Edmund appears. "Ladies, you'll be riding horses tomorrow morning, so you'll need your rest tonight. The car will leave for the stables at 9:00 a.m. so plan to be dressed in riding gear for breakfast at eight. Proper attire has been placed in the closet in each of your suites."

"That sounds wonderful, Edmund," I say.

I haven't ridden in ages, so this is going to be a real treat.

CHAPTER TWENTY-ONE

ARIANA

C rawling into bed, I start to scan my emails and messages when my attention turns to Xander and how he reminds me of Alex's British accent and fun banter. Yes, Alex. Memories of planning the fundraiser with him bubble to the surface, putting a grin on my face.

Before I met Alex—well before we started talking and texting about the fundraiser—everyone warned me he was very direct and had an uncompromising approach when it came to how he wanted things done. He did have high standards, which I had no problem with, but he was also polite, attentive, and a little flirtatious with me. I miss our exchanges.

His life is so exciting. He's always on a plane traveling to his next exotic locale. It must be wonderful to have the freedom and money to jet around the world. Despite googling him, it's still a mystery how he made his fortune, but he's clearly exceedingly successful at something.

He's also the only client who's made it difficult for me to keep my thoughts professional. His deep sexy voice has invaded my dreams more than once. And after the last couple of weeks, I wouldn't mind hearing him flirting with me again. If nothing else, it would fuel tonight's dreams. I'm sick of the recurring tear-filled nightmares my ex-boyfriend has caused.

Subconsciously scrolling through my texts with him, I'm kicking myself for not offering to meet for drinks when we were both in London. But my emotions were too raw. Maybe I should text him now to see if he'll be there when I return in a couple of weeks.

Reaching the texts about training, I stop to reread them.

> Alex: Got it. Will meet in the lobby. How's your 10K training going?
>
> Me: Not bad. Pulled a thigh muscle running downhill. Taking it easy for a few days.
>
> Alex: Massage was crucial to my quick recovery when I did something similar last year. Ask your boyfriend to help.
>
> Me: We broke up earlier this week. Turns out Brian's a jerk.
>
> Alex: Too bad. You need someone with strong hands to get up in there and really work your thigh muscles.

Mmm. Yes, I do need strong hands. Closing my eyes, I slip my hand beneath the covers and reach between my legs, massaging my inner thigh, pretending it's Alex's fingers rather than mine. Yes, yes, I sigh. That feels soooo good. My core is beginning to pulse with need as I imagine Alex's luscious deep voice whispering in my ear while his palm warms my leg and *really works those muscles*.

Scooting further under the covers, I spread my legs and move my fingers over the damp lace of my underwear. I softly rub up and down as my other hand fumbles to retrieve my rechargeable boyfriend from the bedside table. Pulse quickening, I pull my underwear aside and press my friend against my needy nub. I move the toy in small, slow circles as I imagine Alex begging me to come for him. My body coils tighter and tighter. I need more. Plunging the vibrator deep inside, I fall over the cliff, moaning as the release thunders through my body. Sighing, I savor every pulse until my breathing returns to normal.

As the satiated calmness washes over me, my eyes flutter closed.

I'm astounded at how hot it is to experience the fantasy version of Alex. I wonder if the spark with the real Alex would ignite a blazing fire. But would I even want to take the chance? My track record with intimate relationships is horrible. I've been burned enough. It's not worth the risk to continue our text flirtations. Forget the idea of texting him.

Fantasy Alex won't let me down and is probably better than the real version, anyway.

CHAPTER TWENTY-TWO

ARIANA

I jerk awake panicked. My breathing is ragged as I grab my phone to check the time. It's only six-thirty in the morning. Falling back on my pillow, I heave an enormous sigh of relief.

It was only a dream. It started peacefully. We were planning to ride horses along the beach and watch the sunrise. Then it turned strange and embarrassing. I'd forgotten to set my alarm for the ride and over-slept. Trying to catch Xander and the other women on their horses, I ran down the beach in a see-through, lace camisole and sleep shorts.

But the riders disappeared into the horizon as I slipped on the wet sand. Falling to my knees, I screamed, "Come back!" as I collapsed on the beach from exhaustion.

How ridiculous was that? The dream made no sense.

Giving up on sleep, I yawn my way to the shower where beads of water fall from hundreds of tiny openings in the ceiling. Fresh-rain-scented shampoo and lavender bath gel help me wash away my ludicrous dream.

As the water wakes me, my thoughts focus on my excitement about today. We're going riding! It is going to be an extra special treat for me. The last time I was on a horse was before moving to New York, which was a lifetime ago.

But when I found English rather than Western gear in my closet last night, I knew it's going to be a little challenging too. Not only has it been years since I've ridden a horse, but I've only ridden English a couple of times. And that was at camp when I was 11 or 12 years old. Hmm. Does this explain my dream? Was I subconsciously worried I'll embarrass myself today? I have to hope it's like riding a bike and will come back to me quickly. At least I won't be wearing sleep shorts!

Not wanting to miss breakfast, I quickly dry off, dress, and hustle to the dining room with my riding helmet and purse in hand. The other women are already discussing their experience with horses as they enjoy omelets and fruit.

"Good morning. Is everyone excited about riding today?" I ask.

"Does that mean you already know how to ride?" Everly asks.

"I do, but it's been quite a while and mostly Western. I'm sure you all have much more experience than I do riding English."

"Not me," Everly says. "Part of me wants to skip today. I'm not much for outdoor activities, so I've only ridden a couple of times. I'm not comfortable around horses. They're such enormous, powerful creatures. I'm always worried I'll fall off and be trampled." She shivers.

"The best plan is not to let your horse sense that you're scared. Take control. Otherwise, the horse won't respond well," Constance says.

Everly frowns but nods and lowers her head, avoiding further discussion.

Sensing her discomfort, I try to redirect the conversation. "I hope everyone slept as well as I did. I left the doors open last night. The sea breeze is so calming, don't you agree?" This does the trick, and conversation turns to the panoramic ocean views.

Edmund appears as we're finishing our tea and coffee. "Ladies, it's time to leave for the stables. Your SUV is waiting in the driveway. Prince Xander will be meeting you there."

As promised, Xander is waiting for us after the forty-five-minute drive. "Welcome to the royal stables. This is Peter, our riding instructor. He will be leading our ride today. Are you ready to meet your horses?"

In unison, we say, "Yes," except for Everly. She's silently biting her lip, but Xander doesn't notice.

"Great! The lavatory is through the door to my left. You have time to make a stop. There's also a table inside with reusable bottles filled with water, so be sure to pick up one of those for the ride."

A few minutes later everyone is assembled, except for Constance. She eventually appears, lamenting problems with a zipper.

Xander doesn't waste any time. "If everyone's ready, follow Peter and me," he says, waving us forward.

He must be looking forward to our day too. There's a little extra bounce in his step.

Looking into the distance, six horses are tied to a fence on the far side of an open area, waiting for us.

As we wander among the horses, a stable hand approaches with a basket of muffins. Xander says, "Be sure to take one or two of the molasses muffins for your horse. The treats will ensure instant friendship. I promise."

Everly leans toward me, whispering, "I hope two of these magic muffins will be enough to ensure the horse takes it easy with me. If only I could find a nice guy who hates the outdoors and wants to binge historical documentaries with me."

I pat her on the back. "Don't worry. I'm sure they picked calm horses for us. And who knows, maybe Xander enjoys documentaries."

We end our private conversation when Xander says, "Let me introduce you to your rides for the day. Everly, this is your horse. His name is Cocoa."

"He's a beauty. I'm not comfortable with horses though." Everly frowns.

"Don't worry. Cocoa's very gentle. You two should get along well. Why don't you give him one of the muffins?"

Everly complies, gingerly placing a muffin on her hand and

offering it to Cocoa, He takes it immediately. "Cocoa likes it." She smiles back at Xander.

"You can give him another one before we help you into the saddle. Constance, your horse is Rock Star, which is quite fitting. He knows he's special."

"I'm sure I can handle him," Constance purrs, batting her eyelashes.

"I have no doubt," Xander says. "Jessica, your horse is this magnificent creature, Serendipity. He's refined but a little spirited. You two will be well matched. And finally, Ariana, let me introduce you to Champagne."

"She's beautiful," I say. While I'm gently petting the light gold horse, she nudges me. "I bet you smell the muffins, don't you? Here you go, girl. This is what you want, isn't it?" The muffin disappears in a flash.

"Everyone, as soon as you finish up with the treats, Peter and I will help you mount your horses. It's time to ride."

It only takes about thirty seconds for Champagne to devour a second muffin. Then I clasp her reins, preparing to climb into the saddle, as Xander sneaks up behind me, saying, "May I give you a hand?"

"That would be great." I smile appreciatively, having noticed there aren't any mounting blocks to step on.

Grabbing the saddle, I place my left foot into the stirrup.

"I'll give you a little boost," he says. As he gives my tush a gentle push, I swing my right leg over the saddle and settle atop Champagne. Was the absence of mounting blocks on purpose? Did Xander want to get a little personal with each of the women. I can't say I minded the touch of his strong hands, though.

As I'm adjusting myself on the saddle, Xander climbs onto his horse, which is on my left. "So, what's the name of *your* horse?" I ask.

"Meet Midnight Racer." Xander smiles broadly, leaning forward to pat his horse's neck.

Xander clearly loves this horse, and it's great to see him happy and relaxing a little. "Hello, Midnight Racer. You're quite handsome. And with that powerful name, I bet you prefer gallops to trail rides."

"He does. Midnight is a special horse, but that's a story for another time. Are you ready to go?" he asks.

"Definitely. You probably don't remember me mentioning it, but I love riding. And this is the first time I've had the chance in quite a while."

"I do remember. It's one of the reasons I arranged for this today." He winks as he guides his horse toward the riding path.

Peter reminds Jessica, Constance, Everly, and me to check our helmet straps as he walks by, making final adjustments to our stirrups.

Satisfied with everyone's equipment, Peter climbs atop his horse, saying, "Follow me. We'll take it slowly to give you time to bond with your horses. Let me know if you have any questions or need any help."

The scenery is beautiful, and I quickly bond with Champagne as we ride along the trail for about thirty to forty minutes. I duck to avoid low-hanging limbs as we pass under the branches of a small clump of trees. Distant cliffs above the water come into view as Xander rides alongside Jessica with Peter leading the way. Constance and Everly are not too far behind.

It's easy to fall into a serene trance listening to the clip-clopping of the horses' hooves, the singing birds, and the murmur of Xander and Jessica's conversation next to me.

"Ahhh!"

Suddenly, Cocoa streaks past at a full gallop. Lady Everly is clutching the reins with a white-knuckle grip; one foot having escaped the stirrup. "Help! I can't stop him!"

I catch a glimpse of sheer terror in her eyes as she looks back over her shoulder pleading for someone to stop her horse.

Peter yells, "Pull back on the reins!"

Xander turns to Jessica, Constance, and me, instructing, "Wait here!" as he and Peter take off in pursuit of Everly. From a distance, we watch Cocoa run toward the cliff with terrifying speed.

"Oh no! He's not stopping," I gasp.

We all watch in horror as Cocoa comes to an abrupt halt at the rock's edge, catapulting Everly over the cliff.

"NOOOOOOO!" Lady Everly's blood-curdling scream reverberates as she falls.

"No! This can't be happening." I shudder.

Cocoa rears back, neighing while bicycling his forelegs. As Xander reaches him, Cocoa gallops away.

Xander and Peter dismount and rush to the edge of the cliff.

In stunned silence, we ride toward Xander, stopping well short of the cliff's edge.

A sour taste fills my mouth, but I manage to call out, "Did Everly land in the water? Is she okay?"

Peering over the cliff, Xander shakes his head. In a husky voice, I hear him say, "Peter, call for help. I'll ride down the switchback trail and see if there's anything I can do."

Xander skillfully guides Midnight Racer along the narrow cliffside path.

Climbing off my horse, I yell, "Xander, please be careful."

He nods as he slowly descends toward the water.

I walk to the cliff's edge, wanting to make sure Xander is safe, but my eyes are quickly drawn to the rock ledge 40 or 50 feet below. I cover my mouth to hold in a scream. Spooking Xander's horse while he's on that precariously narrow trail would be disastrous.

I swallow hard, trying to control my emotions as I sense the others approaching. Constance is clutching her throat, and Jessica gasps.

Without saying a word, I step away from the edge, salty tears rolling down my face, wetting my lips. Constance and Jessica follow me, and we silently join in a group hug, knowing Xander won't be able to help Everly. She's gone.

We were wrong. She had every right to be afraid of horses.

CHAPTER TWENTY-THREE

ARIANA

Peter returns with help and insists we move farther away from the cliff's edge as chaos erupts with the arrival of vehicles carrying medical personnel, stable hands, and other staff setting up equipment.

Constance, Jessica, and I scatter. Constance walks into the distance to make a phone call. Jessica said she wanted to see if the medics have something for a headache. I go to check on our horses.

Lost in a brain fog, I absentmindedly pet Champagne and whisper soothing words to her while I try to process what happened to Everly. I'm not sure how long I've been standing beside my horse when a man finally gets my attention.

"Are you okay? You should sit down," he says.

Huh? "Um. I'll be fine."

"I need to take Champagne back to the stables now."

"Oh." I nod. "Sorry, I'm shaken up after ... you know."

"Anyone would be upset. May I get you some water?"

"No, thanks. I appreciate your concern, but I'm fine. Is Prince Xander okay? He rode down the path to check on Lady Everly."

Taking the reins from me, he says, "His Highness is fine. He's standing by the cliff."

"Thanks."

Scanning the area, commotion surrounds me. I catch a glimpse of Xander talking with several people in suits. Emergency personnel are conferring, some are talking on mobile phones, others are preparing to ride our horses back to the stable. When my gaze locates Xander again, he's walked away from the group of suits. He's now standing by himself, facing the sea.

That's wrong.

His back is to me, his shoulders are sagging, and his head is bent forward. It's painful to watch. The emotions of this horrible accident must be eating away at him. Is he blaming himself? It's not his fault. But I'm even feeling a little guilty. We shouldn't have minimized Everly's concerns about horses and kept reassuring her that she didn't have anything to worry about. If we had let her do what she preferred and skip the ride, she'd still be alive.

If he's having any of these same thoughts, he shouldn't be alone now, so I walk toward him on slightly shaky legs. His arms are crossed as he stares at the horizon, which causes me to have second thoughts. I shouldn't intrude on his grief. I'm not sure what to do, so I stand quietly beside him. Neither of us speak.

Time passes slowly, but he doesn't move away. I sense he appreciates my presence. Finally, he asks, "How are you doing?" His voice is husky and even deeper than usual. He's still staring straight ahead.

"I'll be okay. But I can't imagine what this is doing to you. I don't want to break too many rules, but can I give you a hug?"

His nod is barely perceptible. But when he unfolds his arms, it's clearly an invitation. So, staring into his hollow eyes, I wrap my arms around him. After a brief hesitation, he pulls me closer. I lay my cheek against his warm chest, and his chin rests on my head as he gently rubs my back.

"Xander, I can't believe she's dead. She was so quiet, it was hard to get to know her in the brief time we had, but she seemed kind. She certainly didn't deserve to die from such a freak accident."

"No, she didn't. It doesn't make sense. We specifically put Everly on Cocoa because she said she didn't ride much. Cocoa is the gentlest horse we own. I don't understand what happened," Xander murmurs, placing a soft kiss on the top of my head.

"So, Cocoa doesn't have a history of getting spooked easily?"

"Definitely not. It was completely out of character. Cocoa has never been spooked before. They're already talking about sending him to the country and not letting anyone ride him again."

Snapping my head back, I ask, "That's so sad. They can't do that!"

Gently cradling my head, he pulls it back under his chin. "Yes, the palace can do exactly that if they decide the horse is dangerous, and if they need to show they're taking steps to prevent future accidents. But it'll destroy Bri."

"Your sister, Princess Briana?" Thank goodness I'd googled his family.

"Yes, he's her favorite. Cocoa is a member of the family to her."

"Cocoa didn't intend to kill Everly. As you said, it was an accident. You can't let them take him away from your sister."

"Of course, Cocoa didn't kill her on purpose, but we can't let him *accidentally* gallop away with another rider either."

"I spent a lot of time around horses when I was young, and I never saw a docile horse react that way. Something completely out of the ordinary must've happened. We need to figure out what it was. Then you can take the right precautions. Cocoa may need specific training."

"You make an excellent point. His reaction was odd."

"Xander, I have an idea. Are there snakes in this area? Some horses are extremely afraid of snakes and easily spooked by them."

"Some horses are afraid of snakes, particularly poisonous ones. But the only snakes around here are small grass snakes. The horses are usually curious about them rather than afraid. Everly might have accidentally kicked Cocoa, signaling she wanted to go faster. But even then, I can't imagine he would've been that out of control. It doesn't make sense."

"I agree. Where's Cocoa now?"

"You won't believe it, but he galloped all the way back to the stables. They're trying to cool him down now. He's badly overheated. The vet's on the way."

"Hopefully, he'll be okay. It's possible the vet will figure out what caused Cocoa's erratic behavior. He could be sick or in pain."

"Maybe. We'll know soon," Xander says.

"Will there be any type of police investigation?"

"Given Lady Everly died on palace property, the palace police are in charge. They'll interview everyone to verify it was an accident."

As I'm about to ask another question, Lady Constance and Jessica approach. Realizing we're still hugging, I lower my arms and step back, feeling a little awkward. Xander inquires as to their wellbeing and gives them reassuring hugs.

The thump-thump-thumping of a helicopter draws my eyes skyward. Instinctively, I move closer to the cliff's edge as it slows to hover. The engine noise drowns out the voices of the medics, who work efficiently. I stare at the scene in a sad daze, as the basket twists in the wind and slowly raises Everly to the helicopter.

Gathering my thoughts, I look down. The tide has risen enough to wash over the rock ledge where Everly landed, removing the remnants of her tragic fall. All traces of her are gone.

"It's wrong for the evidence of Everly's existence to vanish so fast. She deserves to be remembered," I mumble to myself as tears stream down my face.

The whir of the helicopter subsides as it flies into the distance. Wiping away my tears, I try to compose myself.

As I rejoin Xander, Jessica, and Constance, a man and woman approach. Based on their no-nonsense manner, black suits, dark sunglasses, and earpieces connected to spiral wires that disappear down the back of their collars, my guess is they're akin to our secret service or FBI agents in the States.

The woman says, "Your Royal Highness, please pardon the interruption. If you don't mind, we are going to take the women back to The Shores. They'll be more comfortable there as we take their statements. We have an SUV ready. We also have one ready to take you to the palace. The king and queen await your arrival."

"Of course. Ladies, please go with our palace officers. They'll take care of you. I'll check on you as soon as I'm able."

Xander follows us as we walk in silence. As he helps me climb into the back seat, I whisper, "Take care of yourself. We'll be fine."

He nods and squeezes my hand as he turns and walks toward another idling black SUV.

CHAPTER TWENTY-FOUR

ARIANA

M y hands are trembling as my seatbelt finally snaps into place for our long drive back to The Shores.

The female agent says, "I'm Officer Darcy, and this is my partner, Officer Sorrento. When we reach The Shores, we'll give you time to change clothes and have something to eat. We know this has been a traumatic day for you, so we apologize in advance, but we'll need to ask each of you to give us a brief description of what happened today. We hope you understand. It's our required protocol."

We all nod, sniffling and dabbing tissues on our bloodshot eyes.

Staring out the window, watching the countryside go by, it's easy to avoid eye contact with the others. It was such a peaceful ride until Cocoa came barreling past. In that one instant, everything changed. I never expected to witness something as devastating as that. Unlike in a movie, we watched the tragedy kill someone we all knew. It was real —not some writer's idea of entertainment. What happens next? How do we cope with what we saw?

It's hard to hold back the tears. I want to crawl under the covers and sleep. But I'd just dream about the accident, which sounds worse. Some alone time to gather my emotions might help, but that won't happen for a while.

Unlike the drive to the stables this morning when we were bursting with anticipation of the fun day ahead, the trip back drags on forever with Everly's accident playing on repeat in my head.

A soft humming sound breaks the silence, and a glass partition rises in front of me, separating us from the officers.

Constance says, "That's better. Now we can talk. Ariana, what was up with the cozy hug you shared with Xander? You showed poor taste using Everly's tragedy as an excuse to gain an advantage with him."

"You're out of line. I merely checked on Xander, and we comforted each other. The moment you and Jessica showed up, he hugged you two as well, so drop it." I stare daggers at the snippy version of Constance on display. "Instead of such nonsense, we should be discussing what spooked Everly's horse. Did either of you notice anything out of the ordinary?"

Jessica replies, "I have no idea what spooked her horse. Everly might have accidentally pressed him into a gallop. Or maybe she panicked and froze, forgetting to pull back on the reins. That's all I can think of."

"As scared as she was of horses, she would've done anything to cause the horse to gallop. Constance, did you see anything?"

"Not really. A group of butterflies flew by about the time her horse bolted. Mine was a little skittish when they flew past, but I know how to handle horses. It could have been the butterflies combined with her lack of riding experience that caused the accident." She shrugs.

"That's possible. Butterflies are known to spook horses. This whole situation is horrible. I assume Xander's search for a bride will remain on hold for a while, don't you think?" Jessica asks.

"He can't put it on hold. He's up against the deadline of the king's birthday. He'll have to move forward," Constance insists.

I shake my head, shocked at her lack of compassion and duty-first attitude. "You may be right, Constance, but I assume there will be at least a few days of mourning. I can't imagine going on dates and taking part in group social activities right now."

"You wouldn't understand. You're not royals. We're accustomed to putting on our public smiles and moving forward when duty calls," Constance says.

"I would've thought duty would include honoring the deceased royal," I retort.

Before Constance can rebut my comment, we pull into the driveway at The Shores. The doors open, and we part ways.

My suite provides much needed privacy after this day. It's hard to believe it's already 5:00 p.m., and the palace officers still want to talk with us. At least they gave us an hour to ourselves first. That should give me time for a warm, soothing bath, but first these snug riding boots and tight pants must go.

As the luxurious tub fills, the roar of the water begins to drown out my thoughts. I sprinkle lavender crystals from the goodie basket into the warm water. Let's hope their purported calming effect does its job. Now for some candles and a glass of wine. With the events of today, I need all the help available.

Vanilla candles lit and wine in hand, I slip into the warm water and savor a long sip of the soothing liquid. Setting my glass on the side of the tub and taking a few deep cleansing breaths, I close my eyes, hoping not to relive the day's events yet again. Before long exhaustion sets in and my body relaxes into dreamland.

Leaning against the back of the tub, I hear a noise and look to my right, finding a sexy guy standing within arm's reach of the tub. He's pulling his shirt over his head so I can't see his face, but I stare longingly at his six-pack. I reach my hand toward him, but as he flings his shirt across the room with one hand, he wags a finger on his other hand, signaling me to be patient as he dips his head and slowly lowers his zipper.

Not concentrating on his face, I watch with bated breath as he pushes his pants and briefs to the floor in one swift move. "Do you like what you see?"

His magnificent manhood steals my breath, making me forget the question he asked. Before I can ask him to repeat it, he rests his hand on my back, gently pushing me forward as he steps into the tub built for two, sitting behind me, and nestling me between his outstretched legs. I wiggle my ass against his nakedness, liking what I feel.

Sandwiching my legs tightly between his, he massages my shoulders as his lips caress my ear and slowly moves down my neck, sending shivers throughout my body. I want to kiss him, so I turn, practically purring in contentment. To my shock, I'm staring straight into Xander's mesmerizing emerald eyes.

Bolting upright and splashing water everywhere, I grab a towel. "No! It can't be!"

I look around trying to distinguish what is real from the enjoyable adventure that existed only in my mind. I calm my ragged breathing, saying to myself, "I'm alone. I fell asleep. It was only a dream."

Damn, what a dream it was.

Sighing, I sink back into the tub, sliding down and leaving my head barely above the water. It may have been a dream, but my body's revved up with heat and desire. A wave of disappointment passes over me, knowing it wasn't real. My burning need for relief will not be satisfied by Xander's sexy, hard body.

Damn. Why do dreams always end before the good part?

But why was I dreaming about Xander in that way? What's wrong with me? I'm not interested in him. I'm only here to learn about the matchmaking process. He's going to marry Constance or Jessica. A royal or a wealthy American would be much more suitable for him than I'd be. Besides, he's not interested in me. He invited me along to help him as a friend, and I'm not sure I can ever trust a man with my heart again, much less trust the player Constance described. It's odd though. That description doesn't match the part of Xander I've seen so far.

Shaking my head, I hop out of the tub, dry off quickly, comb my hair, and slip on a casual sundress and flats. It's time to give my statement to the officers. No more fantasizing in the tub. Xander will be an amazing person to have as a friend, but that's all our relationship can be.

CHAPTER TWENTY-FIVE

ARIANA

After talking with the officers late yesterday afternoon, Jessica and I went for a walk on the beach, sandals dangling from our fingers. We couldn't persuade Constance to join us. She wanted to be alone. We respected that. Everyone handles trauma differently.

When we first arrived at The Shores, the idea of curling my toes in the sand was so inviting, but it wasn't the happy pleasure I'd imagined after what had happened. Even so, there was still something soothing about the wet sand oozing between my toes.

As we slowly made our way along the coast, we talked a little, but mostly were silent, processing our own thoughts. It was surreal. Why were we the ones still here? Why Everly? What profound lesson should we learn from her death? The answers eluded me. My eyes were cried out and my mind was numb. When the sun began to set, we instinctively turned around.

Back at The Shores, we requested glasses of wine and sat on the pool deck, toasting Everly as the sun disappeared below the horizon. We discussed how kind Lady Everly was, but we both had sensed an undercurrent of hurt or disappointment in her life. For some reason, she wasn't happy. That wasn't fair and neither was her death.

May she now rest in the peace she deserves.

Despite being mentally and emotionally exhausted, it took hours to find sleep last night. When it did come, my dreams were filled with a confusing combination of unrelated people and events. I don't wake until Constance and Jessica knock on my door, wanting me to join them for breakfast. With my promise to meet them in the dining room, they leave me to get ready.

I manage to wake up enough to slip on jeans and a cotton shirt while questioning why they stopped by my room. They've never done that before. It is already mid-morning. Perhaps they were worried they hadn't seen me yet and wanted to make sure nothing was wrong. They're probably still shaken from yesterday. I sure am.

Jessica and Constance are already eating fruit and croissants when I finally join them for breakfast. We speculate about what will happen today. We assume it will be a quiet day here, waiting for details.

I've barely had time for a sip of coffee when Xander surprises us and takes a seat at the table.

"Ladies, my apologies that I wasn't able to join you sooner. Have the staff taken care of you?" he asks as he reaches for the coffee cup that magically appeared.

We murmur assents.

Staring at the dark circles under his eyes, I wish I could make this dreadful situation better for him.

"As I'm sure you can imagine, we've been busy contacting Lady Everly's family and assisting with arrangements for her return home. We've also been dealing with various paperwork and protocols required when a death occurs on palace grounds, which fortunately is an extremely rare occurrence."

"Will there be a funeral or memorial service for her?" I ask.

Speaking slowly, his voice heavy, Xander says, "Her family will have a formal funeral service in their country. Due to the unusual circumstances under which I met Lady Everly, the king has informed me that Queen Josephine will attend on behalf of our family."

I ache for him, knowing he needs closure. Hell, we all need closure.

"It makes sense the service would be in her home country, but I wish we could pay our respects. She saw the positive in people and was kind to me," I say.

"Me too. She was genuine," Jessica says.

"If there's any way I can help you, let me know," Constance adds.

"Thank you. This has been a shock for all of us."

Jessica follows up, "Xander, should we return to our homes now? I'd certainly understand if you don't want to proceed with the match-making process in light of the tragedy."

"That's very thoughtful of you, but it won't be necessary. You see, it's customary in our country to have at least a three-day mourning period when a royal passes away. Even though Lady Everly was from another country, the king declared that today and the next two days will be days of mourning. That means it wouldn't be appropriate for me to be seen dating during that time, but I'd love to spend time with each of you afterward. So, I need to ask you for a favor."

Leaning in, he asks "Would you be willing to extend your time in Catalinius so we can still try to make this process work?"

"Anything you need, Your Highness," Constance says without hesitation.

After a brief pause, Jessica nods. "I can extend my visit."

"Thank you," Xander responds. Turning to me, he asks, "Ariana, will you stay as well?"

We lock eyes. "If you'd want me to, I will."

He blinks slowly. "Thank you. I would. I very much want all of you to stay, so I appreciate your willingness to change your plans. Please forgive me, but I need to attend to some business matters. I'll see you again soon." He departs with a quick nod.

The atmosphere is subdued and awkward, but we stay and chat about changing our arrangements, rescheduling events back home, and how we'll fill our time for the next couple of days, and various other topics as we finish our breakfast. Ready to escape to the privacy of my room, I'm dabbing my mouth with a white linen napkin when Edmund approaches me.

"Miss Montgomery, this mail arrived for you. It appears to be personal," he says, handing me a sealed ecru envelope.

Two pairs of eyes are staring at me like hawks, waiting for me to open the letter. Looking down, I hesitate, rubbing my fingers over the textured envelope. Hmm.

"My mother is quite formal at times, so I'm sure it's just a boring note from her. I'll save it for later," I say.

Jessica and Constance nod, turning back to their morning coffee and burying their heads in their phones.

But my mother doesn't have this address, so it's not from her, and I didn't see a return address. It could be from Meredith, but it's the thick paper used for fancy invitations, which is strange. Hmm. Who in Catalinius would invite me to a party?

Excusing myself after a last sip of coffee, I disappear to my suite to find out.

CHAPTER TWENTY-SIX

XANDER

Taking the women riding was supposed to be an ideal group event. It should have been the perfect way to get to know everyone in a casual environment and see how they interacted with each other and with me. Not to mention, Ariana said she loves riding. It was supposed to be a way to thank her for helping me with the matchmaking process, and I thought it would put a smile on her face. She lights up the world when she smiles.

But instead of a successful group date and a special day for Ariana, it was an epic disaster. And it was my fault. While I may not be directly responsible, it was me who put Everly in danger. If we hadn't gone riding, she would still be alive. The guilt is weighing me down, and I don't know how to handle it.

There's a hollowness inside me that I've never felt before. It's because she's still supposed to be here but is missing.

Everly and I barely knew each other, and it's doubtful she was the one for me. My preference for a wife would be someone outgoing and independent. Everly would have been an acceptable queen though. Now it doesn't matter. She's gone because of me. And we were all forced to watch it happen.

What must the women be thinking right now? Understandably,

they were quiet and sullen this morning. Everyone knew Everly was inexperienced at riding. For all I know, they're upset with me for what happened. At least they were kind enough to agree to stay, but is the matchmaking process doomed at this point?

Pacing the room, I'm not sure what to do next. Normally, Evan would be my sounding board, but he's in a love trance, spending every minute with Cassie. Bri is so worried about Cocoa's future, she doesn't need me to dump my problems onto her. Besides, my job as the oldest is to look after her, not the other way around.

Father is essentially useless when it comes to dealing with emotions. As far as he's concerned, Everly's death is a matter of state business rather than something personal. Of course, he's horrified she was killed and wants to determine what happened. But he didn't know her, so it's not personal to him. As king, he'll do the right things, including showing respect by sending Mum to the funeral, but Father is not someone to turn to for emotional support in such matters.

And Mum is busy helping me on another front. She's doing every-thing she can to prevent Father from selecting a bride for me. She's allowing me time to give the matchmaking process a chance to work. Even though she's skeptical about it, she agrees it's best to see if one of these women is the right choice for marriage. If she's going to keep Father at bay, I can't let her see me falling apart or giving up on the process, so talking to her won't work.

I'd rather talk with someone other than family anyway, someone trustworthy—*Ariana*.

That thought makes me shake my head. It's extremely unusual that she's gained my trust so quickly. There's a sense we've known each other for so much longer. But the basis for the trust is that she tried so hard to dissuade me from being interested in her. She flat out told me she wasn't looking for a match.

A skeptic might argue that if someone were scheming against me, reverse psychology might work to capture my attention. A person might push me away, hoping that would make me want them. But it's too far-fetched to imagine she orchestrated this friendship, or what-ever it is, based on turning me down at a matchmaking reception. No one could expect an invitation to join me in Catalinius after friend zoning me. The probability of success for that type of scheme would be exceedingly low. Of course, she did exactly that, and I invited her here. What does that mean?

It's both comforting and exciting to have her around, which doesn't make sense if she isn't interested in more than friendship. I keep asking myself, why there is such a spark between us when we're in the friend zone. And it's inexplicably stronger each time we're together.

She puts a silly grin on my face and eases my stress each time we're together. And she makes me want to please her. The horseback riding *was* for her. And I'd planned to invite her for a run on the beach this morning, but that was out of the question after yesterday. Hopefully, seeing her again will help me sort out these feelings, and even more importantly, maybe she can help make sense of what I learned today.

"Your Highness, you have a visitor," Edmund's voice says through the closed door of my study.

"Come in."

"Miss Montgomery, sir."

"Have a seat, Ariana. Will you join me for a cocktail? Rum is your favorite, right?"

"Yes, but I'm confused," she says as she sits on the edge of the leather sofa facing the fireplace, ankles crossed. "I followed your instructions and didn't tell anyone about your note asking to meet at 8:00 p.m. tonight. But why did Edmund sneak me down the back hallways to meet you in secret? What's going on?"

Pouring rum, fresh-squeezed lime juice, simple syrup, and a splash of my secret ingredient into a cocktail shaker, I answer, "Sorry about the subterfuge, but I wanted to talk with you about the investigation into Everly's death and didn't want Constance and Jessica to know. I'm not ready to reveal that you took yourself out of the matchmaking mix. And they might get the wrong idea about our relationship if they knew we were meeting privately."

Ariana is staring out the side window.

"Are you okay? You're not mad, are you?" I ask.

She turns back, shaking her head. "No, of course not. I was remembering … you know, Lady Everly."

Her eyes are dull, which pains me.

"I know. I'm sure we're all haunted by what happened. I can't get it out of my head either. Hopefully, this will help. Meredith's match-making bio said rum is your favorite, so I looked up a recipe. It's my twist on a lime daiquiri," I say, handing her a drink.

I sit, leaning back against the sofa, watching her. "Let me know how it tastes."

"How did you know that I love rum. There's a hint of something unexpected, though." She takes another sip, looking at me over the rim of her glass. "I can't quite place it. It's not an herb. What is it?"

"A splash of vanilla. Do you like it?"

"That's it! It's delicious. Tart but a little sweet. The vanilla rounds out the flavors. It's perfect. You surprise me. You're very thoughtful."

For some reason, it's easier to remember her preferences than those of Constance and Jessica. Her bio was shorter than theirs. I also tend to pay more attention to my friends than my dates. My friends tend to be around longer. After my disastrous college girlfriend, it's been difficult for me to emotionally invest in a romantic relationship. But I have the sense that Ariana and I will become close friends. Perhaps that's why details about her are already cementing themselves in my memory.

"Outstanding. I'm glad you are enjoying it. You need to relax, though. You're sitting on the edge of the sofa. This isn't a formal tea with my mum."

"I'm sitting with a prince." Her body remains rigid.

"Relax, we're in private. Tonight, I'm just Xander—a normal guy, having a drink with a new friend. If it helps, pretend I'm not a prince for now. Can you do that for me? Please."

"I'll try." Ariana slides against the back of the sofa and faces me as she takes another sip. "Mmm. If I don't put this down, it'll be gone in an instant. So, what did you want to talk about?" she says, placing her glass on the coffee table.

"Remember I mentioned the vet was going to check out Cocoa?"

"Yes. What did you learn?"

"Based on the examination, she decided to do a blood test. We received the results this morning and were shocked to learn they found drugs."

"Drugs? How would drugs have gotten into his system?"

"We don't know. He had a significant level of stimulant in his blood. It's the same drug that people take for ADHD. It's possible that Cocoa ate pills someone accidentally dropped. It's the vet's opinion that someone purposefully drugged Cocoa. Her reasoning is that the blood levels indicate a much higher dosage than one or two dropped pills would cause, and the timing is suspicious."

Her eyes widen. "That's terrible. Would the drug have caused Cocoa to take off?"

"The vet says it would've caused anxiety, and anything could've spooked him at that point."

She scoots closer and places her hand on my forearm. "Does this mean Cocoa can stay at the palace stables? They won't send him to a pasture far away from Bri, will they?"

Covering her hand with mine, it's hard to ignore the now familiar zing, but I try, saying, "I hope not, but a final decision won't be made until the investigation is complete. That could take some time because now they're treating Everly's death as a homicide."

She pulls back in shock. "You mean someone intended to kill her?"

"We don't know whether Lady Everly was targeted, or someone didn't care which one of us was harmed. It's also possible they just wanted to scare us."

"Why would anyone want to do that?" Her eyebrows draw together in confusion.

"The palace police don't know yet, but I'm going to the stables tomorrow to ask a few questions myself. I want to find out who had access to the horses and talk with the vet when she stops by to check on Cocoa. I need to know how long it would have taken for the drug to take effect."

"Would it be okay if I tag along? I can help, and I'd love to spend time with your horses, particularly Cocoa."

"I wouldn't mind the company and would appreciate a second set of eyes and ears, but what about Constance and Jessica? How would you explain disappearing with me for the morning without them being suspicious?"

"Edmund arranged a spa day for us tomorrow. They won't give it a second thought if I stay behind because of a headache."

"It's set, then. After they leave for the spa, you and I will go to the stables."

"I'm not sure if this is the right time, but should we also talk about how I can help you through your matchmaking process?"

"It's hard to find time for the two of us to talk, so now's a good time. What's your opinion? Which woman is the best match for me?"

"It's too early to tell. But it would help if I knew what qualities you find attractive and how you want a wife to fit into your life," she says.

I sigh and explain, "This will sound rather cold, but you can't help me if I'm not honest with you. I suspect my wife and I will lead rather separate lives, except when we need to appear together. So, I'm not interested in anyone who will be clingy. It would be helpful if we have some interests in common so we're compatible when we're together. She'll need to have proper manners, of course, but royal lineage, while preferred, is not legally required in Catalinius."

"What about chemistry, love, passion? Aren't those important?"

I shake my head. "I gave up believing in true love a long time ago. It's not going to happen to me. At this point, I'll be content with a marriage of convenience and companionship," I say.

"That's sad. I'm not sure love is in the cards for me either though." Her voice is quiet as she looks away, wiping her eyes.

Some asshole did a number on her. She deserves better.

Hoping to comfort her, I say, "I could use some fresh air. Will you walk down the beach with me? I could use the company. And by the way, I'm starting to think you're right about the merits of rum. Let's take a refill with us."

CHAPTER TWENTY-SEVEN

XANDER

Rising early, I escort Constance and Jessica to the limo for their trip to the spa, which is on the other side of the island. Thirty minutes later, Ariana meets me in the foyer of the beach house to begin our fact-finding mission.

As Edmund ushers us out the front door, confirming he cleared my schedule for the day, my eyes and thoughts are focused elsewhere —on the way Ariana's tight jeans hug her squeezable little ass. While helping her into the saddle, it grabbed my attention, but the accompanying thoughts were left unspoken. Again, I'm suppressing the temptation to act, but nothing prevents appreciating the view when it's directly in front of me.

Oblivious to my thoughts, Ariana stares ahead at the only vehicle in sight, saying, "Don't tell me we're taking a golf cart all the way to the stables? It took us at least forty-five minutes by car." She laughs.

"No. We're taking the golf cart over there," pointing to the helicopter that's waiting in the field to our left. "I don't want to waste the time driving to and from the stables. We can use the time we save more productively at the stables. It'll also ensure we're back before Constance and Jessica return in the limo."

"Smart plan. I've never ridden in a helicopter before. The views must be spectacular."

In the chopper, we pull on headphones so we can talk over the engine noise.

"Look to your left. I grew up surfing at that beach. It has the best waves on the island."

"It's beautiful. Do you still surf?"

"Not as much as I would like. My full schedule makes it tough, but I love any excuse to be on the water. My brother and I are avid sailors, so we take the family boat out when we're both in town."

"I love to relax on the beach, reading a book or staring at the hypnotic ripples in the water. You're so fortunate to live here."

"I am. We're turning inland. You can see the palace in the distance now. My apartment is in the left wing. I split my time between there and The Shores." Leaning closer with one hand on her upper back and pointing with the other toward the left side of the palace's expansive structure, I get a delightful whiff of her perfume—orange blossoms.

"I'd get lost living there. It's so enormous and magnificent. We have the perfect view from the air. But I'm surprised we're allowed to fly so close. Aren't you worried about security?"

"Our pilot informed the palace we were going to do a flyby, so they know it's me. Any unidentified aircraft would be in serious trouble, though. We'll take a turn to the right soon and head to the stables," I say, pointing to a structure in the distance.

"I hadn't thought about it earlier, but won't the noise of the helicopter startle the horses?"

"You do care about them, don't you. Well, rest assured, the landing pad is far enough away not to bother them."

With no more interesting landmarks in sight, I force myself to pull away from Ariana, missing the warmth from touching her. And her scent—I miss that too. Walking through our citrus groves when they're in bloom is heavenly, and she smells just like them. I wanted to nuzzle against her neck and … Never mind, that's not happening.

Peter is waiting for us at the landing pad. "Welcome, Your Highness. And you too, Ariana. I didn't realize you were also coming today," he shouts over the noise of the helicopter, motioning for us to climb aboard the nearby golf cart.

Before Ariana can answer, I say loudly, "She knows quite a bit about horses, so I thought it would be helpful to have her join us." There's no need to share more details about our relationship, whatever it is.

"Wonderful. Dr. Capelli said to let you know she's on her way."

"Excellent timing. I have quite a few questions for her."

We ride the short distance in silence, watching the horses graze in the lush green pastures. It looks so peaceful, which is surreal and eerie given what happened last time we were here.

My first destination is Cocoa's stall. Peter follows, keeping stride.

"Your Highness, as you can see, Cocoa's doing much better today."

"That's a relief. Ariana, do you want to pet Cocoa?"

When Ariana doesn't answer, I look around for her. She's lagging behind, stopping to pet each of the horses along the way. It warms me that she's genuinely interested in the animals, and they respond well to her. Animals usually have excellent instincts, so it's a reassuring sign that my trust in her is probably not misplaced.

Peter draws my attention, saying, "Everyone is upset and doesn't understand what caused Cocoa to bolt. Do you have any ideas?"

Joining us, Ariana starts to answer, "It must—"

But I interrupt, "I agree with Ariana. Something must've spooked him." I'm not ready to share the results of the blood test yet. Fortunately, she gets the message.

"I doubt we'll ever know." Peter shakes his head.

"Ah, Peter, there's Dr. Capelli. Would you mind giving me some time to talk with her?" He nods and walks away with a quick bow to me.

"Dr. Capelli, thanks for meeting us today. Let me introduce my friend, Ariana. She shares my love of horses and was present when Lady Everly fell."

Exchanging greetings with Ariana, Dr. Capelli says, "It's such a tragedy."

"It was horrifying to watch. I've never seen a horse react that way," Ariana says.

"Your Highness, may I speak freely?" Dr. Capelli asks with a heavy sigh.

"Yes, Ariana knows about the drugs in Cocoa's blood, but no one else here does. I'd prefer it to stay that way, so let's keep our voices low. But you may speak frankly."

"You're correct. Cocoa was drugged. Specifically, we found a form of amphetamines in his bloodstream. Doctors typically use this drug to treat ADHD in children."

"Why would someone give that to a horse?" I ask.

"Twenty or thirty years ago, these drugs were used in horseracing to enhance performance. It was illegal, but they were hard to detect, so unscrupulous trainers got away with it for a long time. Fortunately, now race officials routinely test for these drugs, so the practice has virtually disappeared. But people in the industry would know about the effect of this type of drug on horses."

"How was the drug administered?" Ariana asks.

"We can't be sure. The drug is injectable, and it can be difficult to detect an injection site. It also comes in pill or liquid form. My professional opinion is that Cocoa swallowed pills."

"How did you reach that conclusion?" I ask.

"Liquid doesn't make sense. It's hard to force a horse to drink something without anyone noticing. If someone gave Cocoa an injection, it would have had to be moments before the ride started. That would've been difficult to do without being observed. If it had been given to him earlier, the drug would've taken effect much sooner instead of during the ride. That leads me to the conclusion it was pills," Dr. Capelli says.

"How long does it take for pills to take effect?" Ariana asks.

"It depends on several factors. It could be ten or fifteen minutes if it was a fast-acting version. It could be thirty minutes, sixty minutes, or even longer if the drug was in regular pill form, depending on Cocoa's metabolism at the time. That's why I'm leaning toward the conclusion he ingested several pills less than thirty minutes before your ride began. Under that scenario, his anxiety level would've peaked thirty to forty minutes into the ride."

"Would that have been enough to cause him to react the way he did?" I ask.

"The pills alone probably wouldn't have caused him to gallop off. But we suspect something spooked him while his anxiety level was high. Given his drug-induced state, it wouldn't have taken much— even something that usually wouldn't bother him could've caused him to bolt."

"How's Cocoa doing now? Have the drugs cleared his system?" Ariana asks, gently stroking him.

"The combination of the drugs, heat, and overexertion caused him severe distress, which could've been fatal. But fortunately, he returned to the stable where the staff were able to cool him down and rehydrate him. I'll do another test today, but the drugs should be completely out of his system within another forty-eight hours. He's doing much better, but I'm going to monitor him for a few days."

"Thanks, Dr. Capelli. We appreciate your help," I say.

My palm resting on Ariana's lower back, we walk toward the stable manager's office. Knocking on the doorframe, I ask, "Mr. Hamoncourt, do you have a minute?"

"Of course, Your Highness," he says as he rises. "Please come in."

"My friend, Ariana, and I are following up on the accident. I'm mystified as to what could've spooked Cocoa. Can you tell us if anyone other than the employees and family were at the stables that day?"

"Sir, I don't recall anyone out of the ordinary that day but let me double-check our registration log." Typing on his keyboard, he opens a spreadsheet. "Here it is. The only people listed are your four guests. Oh, and Lady Harper was here earlier that day."

"Did you say Lady Harper? What the bloody hell was she doing here?" I ask through gritted teeth.

"She comes by from time to time to ride. Your father put her on the family list ages ago, but we still log her name when she arrives."

I shake my head at Father's attempt to make Harper part of the family. At least her stunt in London dimmed his enthusiasm for that match, but I'm not sure he has given up on the idea entirely. Making sure she's removed from the list is for another day though.

Refocusing, I ask, "Why was she here that specific day? Did she ride?"

"No, she arrived when we were saddling the horses for you and your guests. She was looking for you, but security told her we had a special event that day, so she'd need to come back another time. She was disappointed, and if I may say so, a little pouty."

"Did she leave right away?"

"Actually, she didn't. She insisted on helping us lead the horses to the outer fence, and she fed them some treats."

"What kind of treats?" My body tenses. He's got to be kidding.

"Carrots. We were saving the basket of muffins for your ride, so we told her not to give them to the horses."

"About what time did she leave?"

"Let me see if I can remember. You arrived about fifteen minutes before the ladies. Lady Harper left about fifteen or twenty minutes before that. So, she was nowhere near here when Cocoa was spooked if that's what you're asking."

I bite my upper lip, keeping my response short. "That's helpful. Thank you."

"I have one quick question. Did anyone find anything unusual that day? You, know, something out of place or unexpected?" Ariana asks softly.

Rubbing his chin, Mr. Hamoncourt stares forward. "Hmm. I don't recall anything out of the ordinary. Oh, there was something unusual, but it can't be important."

"What was it?" I ask.

"I found a pile of small envelopes in the trash near the refreshment station. They were made from greaseproof paper, which was strange. I don't see how that would be related to Lady Everly's death," he says.

"What's greaseproof paper?" Ariana asks.

"It's used for baking. You call it parchment paper in the US," I say.

"Oh. My grandfather used to store the stamps he collected in those envelopes," she says.

"Hmm. That's interesting. But I've never heard any of the stable hands mention collecting stamps," Mr. Hamoncourt says.

"Did you happen to save one of the envelopes?" she asks.

"Nah. I thought about it but couldn't think of a use for them."

"No worries. I can't imagine how they would be relevant anyway. Thank you for your time. Ariana and I will let you get back to work."

Walking away, I whisper to her, "You know, Harper may not have spooked Cocoa, but she could've fed him the drugs in a treat. She also clearly had access to the muffins and could've tampered with the ones we fed the horses."

"Why would she do that?"

"She threatened to make me regret not marrying her, and she's pulled some outlandish stunts before."

But sabotaging the horses seems a step too far even for Harper. As much as she knows about them, she would realize that drugging one could injure a rider. I'd hate to believe she would have taken that risk for revenge.

"Would she have had access to the medication? Does she have ADHD?"

"I don't know, but I'm going to find out. The vet said Cocoa must have been given the drugs shortly before the ride started. That gives me an idea. Let's search the area where the horses were tied up."

"What are we looking for?"

"According to Dr. Capelli, Cocoa consumed several pills. It's a long shot, but let's look for a medicine bottle or extra tablet on the ground. Hell, anything we find could be a clue."

Outside, Ariana and I divide the space in half and search for anything out of place, eyes glued to the ground. After twenty minutes, we've found a couple of hair clips, a few coins, and an earring, but nothing of real interest.

I'm about to give up when Ariana exclaims, "Xander, look at this."

I jog over. "It's a chunk of a muffin treat. But that's not surprising. It must have fallen out of the basket, or someone dropped it," I say.

"Someone stuck a finger into it," Ariana says, pointing to the side of the muffin.

Before I can stop her from tampering with what may be evidence, she breaks it in half revealing ... absolutely nothing. Our shoulders sag in unison.

CHAPTER TWENTY-EIGHT

ARIANA

"Are those rain drops?" Xander asks.

"Yes! We better go inside."

The rain begins to pour, and he shouts, "Run!"

Taking off at a sprint, we're almost back to the stables when my shoes slip on a muddy patch. Suddenly, I'm yanked by the back of my shirt. The buttons pop off the front, and it slips off my arms. Pitching forward, I plop face down in a muddy puddle.

Quickly rolling onto my back, I hastily wipe the wet mud from my eyes as Xander kneels above me with my legs between his knees. He leans over, placing one hand beside my head while his other tenderly cleans my face with the torn white shirt.

As rain continues to pelt us, Xander asks, "Are you okay?"

I stare back in shock, and after a pause, say, "I'd heard you're a player, but I didn't expect you to actually rip my clothes off in public."

In a gruff voice, he retorts, "It was an accident. I was trying to prevent you from falling."

I hesitate, and then grin. "Sorry, but I couldn't resist teasing you. You've got to admit this is hilarious. I'm lying in the mud, wearing only a thin-lace bra, with a prince on top of me." I laugh.

"Our situation is rather amusing, isn't it?" He joins me in soft laughter as he continues to hover above me.

I smear a little mud on his nose, catching him by surprise. He reaches for a handful in playful revenge. Wrapping my arms around his torso, I catch him by surprise and roll us over before he knows what's happening. Straddling him, we can't stop laughing.

"While I'm the last one I thought you'd try to undress, It's good you practiced on me first. Your technique is a little messy and muddy," I joke.

Suddenly stilling, it's become obvious he's packing some substantial heat in his trousers, and it's growing by the second. Before I can decide what that means and why it feels so amazing, he flips me back over. His fingers gently brush wet strands of hair off my face as the rain continues to pour.

Xander's eyes go dark and hooded, locking on mine. His voice husky, he says, "I promise if I were making a move on you, it would be smooth as silk and melt you to your core. Perhaps, a demonstration is in order."

I lick my lips as he lowers his body and presses his chest against mine. I'm overwhelmed by an irresistible desire for him to kiss me that draws my mouth toward his. Right before our lips touch, Peter shouts, "Your Highness, are you okay?"

Xander softly growls, "Fuuuck," as he jumps up, pulling his shirt over his head and tossing it to me. He shouts back, "We're fine. Please go to the stables and find some towels."

I quickly put on his shirt, looking around. "Xander, have you seen my other shoe?"

We don't find it. It must be buried in the mud.

Suddenly, Xander picks me up and pulls me against him as he carries my water-soaked, mud-covered body toward the stables. Wrapping my arms around his neck, I can't resist resting my head against his warm bare chest.

I wash as much mud as possible in the lavatory, and gratefully, change into the slightly too large, but dry, work clothes Peter offered.

But I'm overcome with frustration. It's already mid-afternoon. We haven't found any clues or anything out of place. And my stomach's churning. I must be hungry. Or is it my unexpected reaction to Xander's touch and the almost kiss that has it tied in knots? No, it couldn't be that. We're just friends.

CHAPTER TWENTY-NINE

XANDER

Over the years, I've often found peace gazing across the lawn from the top of the palace steps. Looking for that solace, I'm here again because the meeting with my parents and palace security this morning shook me. I'm still reeling from their shocking news.

The motorcycle incident in London was intentional.

No one can tell me who wants to harm me or why. The security officer repeatedly assured me I'm safe on the palace grounds, but that's of little comfort when Everly died from sabotage on palace grounds. What if she died because of a target on my back? That's a startling thought. I'm at a loss as to what to do to protect myself and those around me. All I know is that Robert and Darren won't be letting me out of their sight any time soon.

Breathing in the fresh air for another five or ten minutes, my head starts to clear. Unexpectedly, thoughts of Ariana fill my head. My mood improves, remembering how she was playful and sexy when the rain was pummeling us at the stables. We laughed like teenagers while rolling in the mud. It felt so freeing. I haven't had that level of fun in ages. Not to mention the almost kiss ...

Damn Peter's timing.

Looking into the distance, I wish we'd met under circumstances where we could've explored the spark between us. But she's not looking for a relationship now, much less a royal one. And the king still believes my future bride should be versed in our way of life to handle her future role as queen. Deep down, I know he has a point. How could I ask someone to take on my life who wasn't born into this twisted mess of rules and protocols? Look at all the royal marriages that have failed even when the couple knew before walking down the aisle that this life would put an immense strain on their relationship.

For some reason, I'm no longer smiling when Edmund approaches.

"Your Highness, Her Majesty Queen Josephine has left for Lady Everly's funeral. She asked me to let you know she'll convey your regrets."

Biting my tongue, I nod. There's no reason to take my frustration out on Edmund. It's not his fault my parents won't let me pay my respects in person.

"Will you need my assistance today?"

"No, I'm having lunch with Evan and Bri. Take the rest of the day off. I'll be back at The Shores this evening."

On my walk to Evan's apartment, I contemplate my latest frustration with Father. It's ridiculous he won't let me attend the funeral service for Everly, but he and Mum argued it wouldn't be proper. They're concerned that if I attend, the matchmaking process will leak, and the tabloids will report I'm part of a reality dating show. They're also worried the tabloids will say Everly was my first choice, making my future wife appear to be a backup bride. That's preposterous, but the king resorted to a little-used tactic. He directly ordered me to stay in Catalinius. I'm stuck here because the earth would quake if the crown prince disobeyed an order from King Louis.

I twist the knob on Evan's front door, but it doesn't yield. Hmm. He was annoyed the last time I burst in without warning, but I wouldn't have thought he would resort to locking his door.

Eventually, Evan greets me with a smirk on his face, clearly amused with himself for having made me wait. "Everyone's in the kitchen. Bri and I are having a drink while Cassie prepares lunch. She wants us to try one of her new recipes."

"Sounds good. I could use a drink."

Bri gives me a quick hug and hands me a glass of white wine.

"How are you doing?" I ask.

"I'm worried about what's going to happen to Cocoa, but I'm trying to be strong," she says. "So, let's talk about something happy. I want to hear all about your reality show. We hear you're holding a contest to pick a bride."

I sputter, almost spewing wine over the group. "Where the hell did you hear that rubbish?"

Bri and Cassie share a conspiratorial look. Shrugging, Bri says, "If that's not right, let's hear your version."

"It's simple. I hired a matchmaker. She introduced me to the four women I invited to join me here. The best match will be my bride."

Laughing, Bri asks, "Other than no cameras following you around, how does that differ from reality TV?"

My jaw clenches. "The dates are real dates, not setups. It's quite respectable. I'm not sleeping with them. It would be much too boring for television, so give me a break here. You've had your joke. I'm doing my best to find a wife and uphold my duty."

"Lighten up. We're just having a little fun. But on a more serious note, were you close to Lady Everly?" Bri asks.

"She was nice, but we had just met. And she was especially quiet. I didn't have enough time to learn much about her. But, in our limited chats, she was pleasant, and being a royal, she was familiar with our life."

"What are you going to do now? Are you going forward with dating the other three?" Evan asks.

"I don't have a choice. After the mourning period, we'll resume the process. I still need to marry before Father's birthday."

"Will that give you enough time to pick the winner?" Bri asks with a smirk.

"Bri, I'm hoping one of these women will be a match. I'm not picking a *winner* of some contest. But yes, there should be sufficient time because it's down to two, Constance and Jessica."

"Tell us about them. How did they impress you enough in one evening to invite them here?" Cassie asks as she stirs something on the stovetop.

"That's a good question," I say, taking a couple of sips of wine to consider my answer. It also gives me time to realize how easily Cassie is melding into our group. Evan's a lucky bastard.

"They both have desirable qualities. Constance is a royal, attractive, and knowledgeable about Catalinius. Jessica grew up spending time in New York and London and comes from a wealthy family. She's sophisticated but pleasantly spunky."

"What's wrong with the third woman?" Bri asks.

"Nothing's wrong with Ariana!" My voice rises unintentionally. "She's fantastic—smart, fun, beautiful, easy to talk with—the whole package—but she's not looking for a relationship. I invited her here as a friend."

Bri tilts her head as our eyes meet. "The look on your face says you wouldn't mind Ariana being more than a friend," she says as I catch Evan and Cassie exchanging questioning glances.

"There's no look on my face. It's been helpful having someone who's part of this process to talk with openly."

"What's she getting out of this?" Evan asks.

"She's writing a novel that involves a matchmaker, so she's doing research. She's also been helping me investigate who may have drugged Cocoa."

Bri gasps. "Someone drugged my horse? Why didn't anyone tell me when I went to check on him?"

"We're trying to keep the information about the drugs quiet for now, so we didn't tell anyone at the stables. If the saboteur believes they got away with it, we'll have a better chance of catching them."

Cassie's eyes widen, "That means Lady Everly was murdered. Are all the women in danger?" Evan moves closer and wraps a protective arm around her shoulder.

"After the motorcycle incident in London, and now this, the palace is increasing security for all of us as well as for Jessica, Constance, and Ariana."

"What motorcycle incident?" Evan asks.

I tell them what happened and add, "Originally, our security thought it was an accident, but I just learned it was intentional. They finally finished analyzing video from the security cameras outside the convention center in London. It showed the motorcyclist idling a short distance away, watching the exit. They surmise he timed his approach to hit me when I reached the limo."

"But why were you a target when so many important leaders were there?" Evan asks.

I chuckle. "Thanks for putting me in my place, little brother. But as to your real question, they don't know yet. They're still trying to track down the logo on the rider's jacket. It was an angry purple leopard, or maybe a jaguar, baring its teeth."

"Hmm. A purple jaguar sounds familiar. I've seen something similar to that before, but I can't remember where. It will come to me later. If you weren't so popular with the people, I'd think someone was trying to prevent you from taking the throne," Evan says.

Cassie visibly shivers. After a short silence, she softly says, "I hate to interrupt, but lunch is almost ready. Would you help me take our plates to the table, so we can talk while we eat?"

"Of course, sweetheart. I'm starving and this looks fantastic. What is it?" Evan squeezes her shoulders as she finishes plating the food.

"Prawns with a light garlic, lemon, and white wine sauce over homemade fettuccine. The salad and rosemary dinner rolls are already on the table."

"Damn, Evan. I'm jealous. You found someone who cooks even better than you. I'll be stopping by for dinner more often," I say.

"And I'll make sure to keep my door locked so you remember to knock. No more barging in like you did before I left for Las Vegas. Better yet, call first. I have a girlfriend now. We might be busy," he says as he playfully punches me in the arm.

After a few moans of food-induced pleasure, we all compliment Cassie.

"You said you and Ariana are investigating Lady Everly's death. What have you done so far?" Cassie asks.

"We met with the vet. She believes Cocoa ate something with amphetamine pills shortly before the incident. They would've made him anxious. At that point, anything could've spooked him."

"Someone wanted to frighten a rider. It's not clear they intended to kill anyone though," Evan says.

"I agree. Ariana and I searched the area and didn't find anything unusual, but we suspect that someone spiked at least some of the horse's muffin treats with the pills."

"If the muffins were tainted, does that mean all the horses were drugged?" Bri asks.

"We can't be sure because Cocoa was the only one given a blood test. It's possible they were all drugged, but that Cocoa ate more of the muffins, receiving a higher dose of the drugs."

"Do you have any idea who could've done this?" Evan asks.

For a moment, I debate whether to share my suspicions before sharing, "I can't believe I'm saying this, but it could've been Harper."

"She's a little outrageous when it comes to her publicity stunts, but would she do something that malicious?" Evan asks.

"I wouldn't have thought so, but unfortunately, the facts point in her direction. When I tossed her out of my suite in London, she threatened to make me regret not marrying her. More importantly, Mr. Hamoncourt confirmed Harper was at the stables shortly before our ride. She had ample opportunity to drug Cocoa or sabotage the muffins. And the timing fits."

"How would she have obtained the drugs?" Bri asks.

"Amphetamines are commonly used to treat ADHD, so it wouldn't have been too hard," I say.

"Did anyone else have access to the muffins?" Cassie asks.

"Other than the employees at the stables, the only others would be the palace's kitchen staff. They supplied the muffins," I say.

"Maybe I can help. I've been invited to bake with the chef tomorrow. Queen Josephine suggested your pastry chef and I exchange favorite dessert recipes. That will give me a chance to find out who made the muffins," Cassie says.

"That would be great. But be careful. Don't let on that we suspect there was an issue with the muffins."

"Don't worry. I'll be careful," Cassie says.

"Perfect. Let me know what you learn."

Checking her phone, Bri says, "I need to hurry back to my apartment to change. I'm substituting for Mum at an event this evening. But let me know what I can do to help, and don't let them send Cocoa away."

"I'll do my best. Until we find out who's behind these attacks, be extra cautious and don't ditch your security team like you've been known to do."

Waving, Bri walks out the door and calls over her shoulder, "Don't worry, I'll be careful. And set something up so we can meet your bride contestants." She laughs.

"They're not effing contestants!" I huff.

CHAPTER THIRTY

ARIANA

I lost track of time writing and am running late for tonight's gathering by the beach. Instead of hurrying, I leisurely take in the scene. From a distance, it's clear that Xander has created the perfect setting for a romantic evening. The firepit is nestled in the sand, surrounded by swivel chairs with blankets and small tables for drinks. Who wouldn't want to cuddle with him next to the glowing embers, staring at the starlit sky? His warmth wrapped around me would ward off the cool sea breeze. I'm glad that tonight is a group date because otherwise I might accidentally fall under his spell, and that can't happen.

From everything I've seen, Xander is a fantastic guy, but Constance and the tabloids say he's a player. No way will another guy with roving body parts mess up my life. Some men are better as friends than boyfriends.

Slowly meandering closer to Xander's beach party, I can't help but wonder whether I'll ever be ready to put myself back in a situation to fall for someone. Most people would label me an intelligent woman, except when it comes to men. What happened with Brian confirmed that. He played me, as did the two before him. It's embarrassing not to have figured it out sooner, but my radar is clearly off when it comes to picking men. The last three guys were decently attractive, had stable jobs, and were attentive at first. It's not like they were ultra-hot billionaires who were out of my league.

You'd think those guys would have been dependable boyfriends, but no. They turned out to be liars, cheaters, or both. There must be something wrong with me. Otherwise, why would three guys treat me that way?

Is it my long hours at work? They expected me to be able to drop everything at the last minute to accompany them to various events, which I couldn't do. It's odd that they weren't available to be my plus-one even when given plenty of notice. Clearly, they didn't appreciate or respect the importance of my career.

Regardless, my work conflicts weren't a license for them to cheat. In my heart, I know those men would have cheated anyway, despite their attempts to blame me. My busy work schedule merely meant I was too slow to pick up on the clues.

"Hi, Ariana," Jessica calls out over the music, drawing me back to the present,

She's wrapped in a plush blanket, sitting in one of the swivel chairs surrounding the fire and clutching a mug in both hands.

As I reach the firepit, Xander's talking to Constance but turns to pull me into an embrace, whispering, "We'll talk on our *date* in a couple of days. I'll have more to share then."

Smiling weakly, I nod as we separate. Why is he making me wait two days to discuss what's happening? Unfortunately, I can't ask now.

"Let's join Jessica by the fire," he says, moving toward the chairs.

Constance maneuvers to take the empty chair next to where Xander stands, and I sink into the comfy thick navy cushion on the remaining chair between the two women.

Blowing across the top of my mug, I notice the server place a small plate of inviting cookies on the table next to me.

"Xander, I'm surprised at the marshmallows in the hot chocolate. I've heard they aren't popular in Europe," I say.

"They aren't, but that's one of the traditions my brother, Evan, brought home with him from his college days in the States. He's also planted many American sayings in my head that make their way into my daily conversations. I sometimes forget and use them in situations where people have no clue what I'm saying."

We all laugh softly, but it's awkward and quiet as we adjust our blankets and sip our drinks, waiting to see what happens next. It's our first social event with Xander since Everly's death, so the mood is a bit subdued.

Xander finally breaks the ice after dismissing the servers. "It's so good to see all of you again. I know it's been a stressful time, which has made this process difficult. It must be as uncomfortable for you as it is for me. But thank you for being here."

"We're here for you," Constance says with an extra dose of sugar added to her aristocratic voice.

"Again, thank you. I appreciate that. If you don't mind, let's start with a toast to Lady Everly," Xander says. We raise our mugs in unison. "To Lady Everly. Your time with us was far too short, but you won't be forgotten. May you rest in peace."

The look on her face as Cocoa rushed by haunts me as we drink to her. Neither the hot liquid nor the fire is sufficient to stave off the chill that runs through me.

The uncomfortable silence returns. I stare at the flames intently, studying nature's fire art. I sneak a glance at the others; they are all in a daze. I should say something to lighten the mood. Xander needs this evening to work if he's to learn enough about Constance and Jessica. Unfortunately, nothing comes to mind.

Xander finally suggests we each share a little-known fact about ourselves. It works. The awkwardness slowly fades as the conversation turns to food, hobbies, and vacations.

I study Xander's interactions with Jessica and Constance, watching for clues to their personalities in their body language and word choices. My degree is in creative writing, so I've learned that word choice can communicate more than people realize. Unfortunately, I'm having trouble reading which one he connects with the best. Constance is more aggressively seeking his attention, but that doesn't necessarily show a natural chemistry between them.

Xander turns to me, saying, "You've been quiet tonight. Are you enjoying Catalinius so far?"

"My apologies. It is such a peaceful night, I found myself lost in the moment. And I can't stop devouring these cookies. They're yummy."

"I'll give my brother's girlfriend and the pastry chef your compliments."

Constance rolls her eyes as she says, "Your brother is dating the pastry chef? That's *unusual*."

"I'm not sure about the unusual part, but no, he's not. My brother's girlfriend wanted to learn about local desserts, so she and our pastry chef baked these today. They were kind enough to share some of their creations with us when my personal assistant returned from a meeting at the palace."

It pleases me that Xander is annoyed by Constance's snobbishness.

"I hate to bring this up, but it's been bothering me," Jessica says. "I overheard someone say that Everly's horse may be sent away. That's not true, is it?"

"I hope not. Cocoa is my sister's horse, and it would devastate her to not have him near and not be able to ride him," Xander says.

"Your poor sister. I can't imagine what she's going through," Jessica says.

"It might help if we can figure out what spooked him. Are you sure none of you saw anything?"

Xander gives me a quick look to make sure I go along with his story that Cocoa isn't safe from exile. But his plan is a good one. If Constance or Jessica saw anything they forgot to share with the police, sympathy for Brianna and Cocoa could trigger a memory.

Xander looks pleadingly at each of us in turn.

Jessica says, "I didn't see anything. I wish I had. Other than the low branches we rode under, nothing was in our path. Constance, you were closer to Everly. Did you see something?"

"As I mentioned before, several butterflies flew close by," Constance says.

"That could've been the trigger. Butterflies can spook horses. It's that small, fast flash of color that can frighten them," Jessica says.

"You know a lot about horses. Where did you learn so much?" I ask.

"As far back as I can remember, during my school breaks, my parents sent me to equestrian lessons and sailing lessons. I fell in love with both. You see, I was overly energetic as a child. Mom always joked I'd bounce off the walls if that was possible. The physical activities helped me burn off the extra energy."

Xander says, "Well then, you're going to enjoy our next group event. I've planned a day of sailing."

"I can't wait." Jessica claps.

"You won't have to wait too long. But first, it makes sense to go on individual dates, so that's the plan for the next three days. Don't worry, you won't be bored. The house manager can organize other events for you. You can go on shopping excursions, spend time at the various beaches, experience our local cuisine, or take tours of the island. I want you to enjoy your time in Catalinius, but please be careful not to reveal the reason you're here."

I've spent too much of my "sabbatical" budget already, so I'll opt out of the shopping excursions and instead use some alone time to work on my novel. I'm early in the writing process and already way too far behind.

CHAPTER THIRTY-ONE

ARIANA

Grabbing my laptop, I head to the main floor of the beach house, hoping to catch Xander before he leaves on his date with Jessica. Something she said by the firepit last night has been bothering me, but I didn't connect the dots until now.

Constance is already in the living room whipping through the pages of her magazine with a scowl on her face.

"What's wrong? Did something in the magazine upset you?" I ask.

"No, it's not the magazine. It's ridiculous that Xander is taking that New York party girl on the first real date. Surely, he doesn't think *she'd* be a suitable wife for him. I'm the royal here, so he should've taken me out first. It's a sign he's not serious about this matchmaking process. I'm tempted to have the maid pack my bags and go home."

Whoa. That's a little over the top. "Why are you calling Jessica a party girl?"

"She's been all over *Page Six* and the American tabloids, on the arm of one celebrity after another. What else would you call her?"

"I don't give much credibility to those publications, but Xander's done his fair share of partying too, according to the tabloids. Doesn't that make them a good match?" I hide my grin behind my hand.

"That's ridiculous. He can't marry a party girl."

She's unreasonably upset and a little irrational, so I try another approach to calm her down.

"I'm sure you're correct. Xander must have something particularly special planned for your date with him tomorrow. As you pointed out, you're the last royal here, so I assume you're the frontrunner."

"I hadn't thought of it that way. You must be right, but it's still not the proper order," she says as Jessica walks into the room.

So much for catching Xander alone before they leave. I had wanted his opinion on my theory that Jessica may have ADHD since she was an overly energetic child.

"Hi," Jessica says as she sits on the other end of the sofa from me.

"Where's Xander taking you on your date today?" I ask.

"I have no idea, which makes me a little nervous. I was only told to dress casually and meet him at 3:00 p.m. in the foyer."

"You'll have a great time, I'm sure," I say as Constance goes back to flipping the pages of her magazine, ignoring us.

I can't avoid shaking my head. One minute she's the consummate, superior royal, and the next minute she's an immature, jealous child.

My attention shifts from Constance's histrionics to determining whether Jessica is the source of the drugs given to Cocoa. I know ADHD has something to do with having trouble concentrating, but I'm not sure what else it entails, so it's time to google for answers on my laptop.

My internet searches answer the factual questions about symptoms and treatments, but they can't help with other questions. Does Jessica still suffer from hyperactivity? Does she take medication for it? If so, is it the same medication that was used to drug Cocoa? And why would she drug Cocoa? Does she want to end the competition? I'm not even sure she wants to marry Xander.

There's only one way to start answering these questions. We have to find out if she's taking pills for ADHD, which means searching her room while she's on the date with Xander. The trick is not to get caught.

CHAPTER THIRTY-TWO

XANDER

T he conversation with Evan, Bri, and Cassie replays in my head as I dress for my date with Jessica. It's disturbing. I staunchly defended that this matchmaking process isn't a reality TV show, but is it really that different? Multiple women are dating me; we're living in the same house; we're going on dates and group outings; and one will receive a proposal after the last date. Except for the lack of sleepovers and cameras, it's not so different, which horrifies me. I have no choice at this point, but the press will rake me over the coals if they ever learn this is how the next queen was selected.

At 3:00 p.m., I find Jessica with Constance and Ariana in the living area next to the foyer. She greets me with a wide grin that I instantly return. Her sparkling eyes and glossy straight black hair hold my gaze captive. "You look lovely. Are you ready for our adventure?"

"Absolutely, I can't wait to see what you have planned," she says as a muffled huff comes from Constance on a nearby sofa.

Constance is flipping through her magazine so hard I hear a whish with each page turn. Edmund already warned me she's pissed that she wasn't invited on the first one-on-one date.

Even Ariana looks a little sullen as she's typing on her laptop. I've heard writer's block can be frustrating. That could be why she's frown-

165

ing. Regardless, this is awkward as hell. Am I supposed to talk to them, say goodbye, or pretend they aren't here? As I open the door for Jessica, I opt to wave and call out, "Have a nice afternoon. See you soon."

Sliding into the waiting limo, I say, "Jessica, I'm sorry about the strangeness of this, but I'm looking forward to our day together."

"Thanks for addressing the elephant in the room." She laughs. "I'm glad to know I'm not the only one that finds this situation bizarre. But I'm excited we have time for the two of us today. Let's forget the weirdness for now."

"I'm on board with that plan. Here's to a day that takes us soaring to new heights," I say with a mischievous grin while handing her a glass of champagne and taking one for myself."

Raising her eyebrows flirtatiously, she says, "Before I drink to that, you should know there are limits to what heights I'm up for today. But cheers to testing those boundaries."

"I like how you think. I gave you a clue as to what we're doing. Care to guess?" We clink glasses as I admire not only her beauty but also her spunk. That's why today's date is the perfect one for her.

"You mentioned soaring. Are we flying somewhere?"

"You're close. It's a hot air balloon ride. Are you up for it?"

"Definitely. It sounds like fun."

Ten minutes later, we arrive at the field where a partially inflated, multicolored balloon is connected to a large wicker basket. "That's our ride."

The ground crew is working on the balloon as an older man turns to greet us. "Welcome, Your Highness. I'm Randall. I'll be your pilot today."

"Thank you, Randall. You have taken me up a few times before. This is my friend, Jessica."

"I'm honored you remember. And I'm pleased to meet you, Jessica. Follow me to the basket, which is also called a gondola. Don't be confused if you hear that term too. It's time to climb in."

"Did you say climb? I'm not sure my sundress was the right outfit for this adventure."

"Your dress is perfect. It won't be a problem," I say.

With Randall waiting in the basket, I ask Jessica, "May I lift you in?"

"That would be great. Thanks."

For the second time this week, I hoist a beautiful woman into my arms. But it's strange how holding Jessica is not as exciting. Of course, we barely know each other.

"Jessica, give me your hand, so I can steady you," Randall says as I place her over the edge of the basket and climb in myself.

"Hold on to the side. It's time for lift off," Randall announces as he sends blasts of heat into the balloon.

We wave to his ground crew as they release the ropes anchoring the basket, and away we go. We slowly rise above the field and begin floating forward with the wind.

"It's perfect, Xander. What a beautiful way to see the island," Jessica says.

"I don't get to do this often, but I love the quiet, peaceful ride. And fortunately, our weather conditions are perfect today. Some days are too windy, and the balloons can't go up."

It's a little disconcerting that Constance believes she was slighted by not having the first date with me, but she has the weather to blame, if anything. Today is the only day this week that isn't predicted to be too windy for a balloon ride, which is a better match to Jessica's personality. I have something else planned for Constance that she'll prefer.

"Where are we going?" Jessica asks.

"That's in the wind's control, but predictions say the wind will take us toward the palace," Randall says.

A few extra blasts of fire, and we rise enough to barely clear the trees ahead.

"In the distance, you can see the citrus groves we're known for, and on our right, those are peach trees. Peaches are in season now," I say.

"I'd love to sample the peaches."

"I suspect we'll have some with dinner tonight. I've asked the chef to prepare local favorites."

"I can't wait, but until then I'm enjoying the view. We can see forever, and it's so tranquil. The hustle and bustle of the world have disappeared, and I'm watching from the outside."

"It is. Balloon rides help me clear my mind and reset."

"I can see that. Living on an island so far from the mainland, are you ever claustrophobic?" she asks.

"That is often called island fever, but I've never suffered from it. Of course, I travel extensively. Often, I find myself wishing for more time here rather than less."

Before I can ask if she's worried about living on an island, Randall says, "Are you ready for a quick splash?"

While we've been staring ahead, Randall has been letting the balloon descend as we approach an inland lake.

Jessica grimaces as the bottom of the basket skims the surface of the water. "Are we landing in the water? Isn't that dangerous? Will we get wet?" she exclaims.

Randall gives a quick blast of fire, and the balloon rises above the lake's surface.

Jessica lets out a deep sigh, clutching the basket. "Thank goodness. I thought we were going to fall in the water."

"Don't worry, I would've warned you if that were the case. But I thought that you enjoy outdoor adventures, such as sailing. Haven't you been splashed with water on boats before?"

"Of course, I have, but I was expecting it then. I prefer to have the right clothes, the right equipment, and a plan in case something goes wrong, don't you?"

I'm not sure what to say. There must be a story behind her overreaction. For me, too much of my life is planned, causing me to crave the opportunity for spontaneity. Thank goodness *she* wasn't stuck with me in the unexpected rainstorm at the stables.

"There's the palace. The plan is to land behind it. If we're lucky, we'll end up not too far from where we're having dinner," I say.

Floating in silence, we enjoy the last few minutes of our ride as we watch the rapidly setting sun paint the sky in varying shades of orange, yellow, and red. Randall couldn't have timed this better.

He clears his throat, "Your Highness, we should be right on target this afternoon. I've radioed the ground crew, so they'll be in place."

As we make our final descent, a truck and car come into view. Randall masterfully guides the balloon down and two crew members grab the basket to stop us right before we touch the ground. As we climb out of the gondola, a third crew member offers a silver tray with champagne for the toast.

"This is a tradition dating back to the 1780s in France where balloon flights originated," Randall explains.

After we thank Randall and his crew, our driver transports us to a remote palace garden with a gazebo, where the staff have arranged for a candlelight dinner for us.

As we sip wine and dine on local fish with a spicy peach sauce, we talk about growing up, university, and our families. None of it explains the contradiction between her supposed love of adventure and her reaction to a harmless dip in the water today. Trying to solve the mystery, I say, "Tell me about your sailing lessons."

"I spent summers learning about sailboats at our yacht club in New York. The juniors' program taught us how to sail and about boat safety. We even practiced racing against each other in Sabots and Lasers. It was lots of fun."

"Then I'm sure you'll enjoy the day of sailing I have planned. What else do you enjoy most about living in New York?" I ask, hoping to learn whether Jessica would fit into life on Catalinius.

"What's not to love? We have spectacular nightclubs, Broadway shows, fantastic restaurants, art museums, and unlimited business opportunities. As they say, it's the city that never sleeps. There's always something to do. Don't you love big cities?"

"I do. Of course, I also enjoy island life here. Have you spent much time on islands?"

"Yes, we've often vacationed on various islands. I've always loved the beach and other outdoor activities. But I'm naturally cautious after the incident in the Caribbean."

"What happened?"

"I'm sorry. It made the headlines in New York. I thought you already knew about it. Someone tried to kidnap me."

I jerk my head back. "I had no idea."

"We were driving, and a car hit us as a distraction while another car pulled up beside my door. One of the men yanked me out of the back seat. Fortunately, I'd just bought a heavy carved swordfish as an inside joke for a friend back home. I was holding it when the kidnapper pulled me from the car, so I came out swinging and nailed the asshole in the groin."

I swallow hard, involuntarily cupping myself under the table. But damn I'm impressed.

"He let go, and by then, our driver, who doubled as a bodyguard, tackled him. It was pure luck I'd bought that souvenir. If not, I would've been whisked away before anyone could stop the guy. Since then, I try to be better prepared for everything."

"I had no idea. No wonder you avoid certain types of surprises. My family has always been concerned about the possibility of a kidnapping. The fact you defended yourself is incredibly impressive. With your family's wealth, I'm sure you still have bodyguards. Why didn't you bring security with you?"

"You're correct. I usually have a bodyguard, but my family decided a prince's security would be even better than mine. Besides, I've done a lot of training since the attempted kidnapping. I can take care of myself quite well."

"You proved that even before your training," I say.

Conversation turns to less serious matters as we finish the chocolate cheesecake, which is one of my favorite desserts. Afterward, I hug Jessica good night and have her escorted back to The Shores.

I've decided to stay at my palace apartment tonight to save time tomorrow morning since my early meeting with Father is here. As I walk to my place, I consider whether Jessica is the right match for me. She has many admirable qualities, but it's not clear island life will be enough for her, not even a busy royal version.

On the positive side, we're certainly compatible. We share some interests. She doesn't need my money, and she already has experience handling the press in tough situations. She's also tenacious, beautiful, and brave.

But Catalinius doesn't offer the glitz and glamour of New York. She may get bored. And where's the chemistry with her? Picking her up, I expected to crave a kiss with her. I'd felt that desire when holding Ariana. Not that kissing Jessica at the end of our date would have been bad, I didn't care one way or the other.

Aside from the opening banter in the limo, the date wasn't romantic, despite the setting. We mainly spent time talking as casual friends would do. But given my situation, there are worse things than marrying a friend. After all, other than producing an heir, my wife and I can lead rather separate lives as long as we're in agreement.

CHAPTER THIRTY-THREE

XANDER

Evan warned me there would be issues having all the women under one roof. I should have listened then, but after the date with Jessica I learned the lesson. Do not begin individual dates at The Shores. Never again. Instead, I've arranged for Constance to join me at our destination today, I should've been on my way to meet Constance half an hour ago. Unfortunately, I'm stuck in a meeting at the palace with the clock ticking down too fast, and the royal adviser is still droning on about mundane policy issues.

Sneaking yet another a peek at the time, it's clear that if I don't leave soon, I'll miss my lunch date. Constance is already pouting that she wasn't invited out yesterday, so standing her up today would be a disaster. Surreptitiously, I text an SOS to Edmund and take my phone off silent mode, which is taboo in a meeting with the king. But I've no choice at this point.

Sixty seconds later, my phone rings.

"Why is your phone turned on?" The king shoots me a sharp look.

"My apologies, but I'm expecting an important call. Please pardon the interruption." I answer quietly, "Hello, do you have the results yet?"

"I can only imagine what His Majesty is saying now. But I'm calling as requested," Edmund says.

"Yes, I understand. I'm on my way," I say, ending the call.

"Your Majesty, please excuse me. I must go now. It's urgent." I stand and bow.

"This is highly irregular, but I'll take your word that it cannot be avoided. Go. We'll talk later."

It *is* important to meet Constance on time. After all, it's the king who is insisting I find a bride.

As I'm rushing to the town car, Edmund joins me along the way, lengthening his stride to keep up. He reminds the driver we're running behind schedule.

"Edmund, please call ahead and let them know we'll be a little late. Perhaps you can arrange for Constance's driver to slow her down a little too."

"I'll see what I can do."

Fortunately, Edmund's exceptional at his job, so Constance's car pulls up as we do. I offer her my arm and escort her inside, saying, "Let me be the first to welcome you to the Catalinius Royal Winery. This is a special place for me, and I'm excited to share it with you."

"I'm looking forward to it," she says.

"I've arranged a tour with one of our winemakers."

"It must be beautiful here at night. Will we also be having dinner together?" Constance asks.

"This experience is much better during the day. Trust me. You'll enjoy the lunch I have planned."

"Of course, I trust you. I'm thrilled we have the day together." She smiles.

"I've been looking forward to spending time with you as well," I say as Ms. Bartoli approaches.

"Your Highness, Lady Constance, I'll be assisting with your tour today. Our winemaker, Ms. Chastain, is waiting for us. Please follow me."

As we walk, I explain, "Ms. Chastain comes from a long line of winemakers in France. A few years ago, she decided to explore opportunities to make wine outside her family's business because her family wasn't interested in pursuing some of her newer ideas for crafting wine."

"It must be rather unusual to abandon one's family, particularly when it has such a long tradition," she says.

I shrug, not sure what to say. "Um. Times change. And we were fortunate she chose to join us. She's in charge of making the smaller batches of wine we produce, whereas our other winemaker oversees the larger volume wines."

"Oh, you have two winemakers. Isn't that unconventional?"

Rubbing my chin, I say, "Perhaps, but we wanted to continue our traditional winemaking while exploring a new direction for smaller batches. So, it made sense for us. Fortunately, the two winemakers have a high level of respect for each other." I'm quickly learning that Constance values tradition over innovation. That's a useful trait for a royal though. Father would be happier if he could say the same about me.

Ms. Bartoli announces, "Here we are. This is the first stop on the tour. This is Ms. Chastain. She will be your host today."

"It's my pleasure," Ms. Chastain says. "Let me walk you through our process. After the grapes are harvested and crushed, they're placed in these vats." She points to a large tank to her left, "That is where we add yeast to begin the fermentation process."

As she guides us through the facility, she gives a detailed tour, explaining the types of wine she focuses on for the small batches and how the process differs from making wine in large volumes. As she finishes, she says, "Please follow me downstairs to the barrel room. We arranged a tasting for you."

"It's so much cooler down here," Constance says.

"It is. We must keep the temperature carefully controlled so the wine ages properly," Ms. Chastain says as we sit at a table set with five wine glasses for each of us and a black slate plate with crackers, cheese, nuts, dried fruit, and olives.

Ms. Chastain explains each wine we taste, along with recommendations for foods they pair well with.

When we finish tasting the last wine, Constance says, "Your wines are exceptional. The second white one was outstanding. Xander, which is your favorite?"

"The last one. I tend to gravitate toward our full-bodied red wines." I respect that everyone has different tastes, so there's no need to share that her favorite is my last choice. It doesn't matter. "Perhaps we should have lunch before we're too light-headed to enjoy it."

"That sounds divine," she says. "Where are we eating?"

"I'll show you. It's up the second staircase on the far side of the wine cave."

I thank Ms. Chastain and guide Constance to the stone stairway that leads to one of the private patios overlooking the vineyards and the sea in the distance.

"This view is spectacular. Where is The Shores from here?" Constance asks.

"That's The Shores over there. You can see a small portion of the red tile roof." I point a little to our right.

She squints. "There it is. I expected it to be closer given we can see grapevines from the front of your home. I didn't realize the vineyards were so large."

"The vineyards are quite expansive. We have a front row view of the Sangiovese grapevines from here. We can stroll through them after lunch," I explain while pulling out her chair at the black wrought iron table draped with a white linen cloth.

"That would be wonderful. I'd love to see the grapes."

"They're small this time of year, but there are plenty to see. Let's look over the menus. They designed a special lunch for us today. Let's see what Cassie and the chef have planned."

"Who is Cassie?"

"My brother's girlfriend."

"Oh, she made the cookies we had at the firepit. It's very quaint that she cooks. Like you, I've never had the need to learn," Constance says.

It didn't matter whether we *needed* to learn, my mum made sure all three of her children could prepare a meal. But that's irrelevant, so I don't bother responding.

"The menu sounds delicious. It says the recipes are compliments of PinotAndPie.com. What's that?" Constance asks.

"It's a food website belonging to Cassie's friend. Pinot & Pie is also the name of a restaurant Cassie is opening in Las Vegas," I explain as the server arrives.

"I'm surprised your parents are allowing your brother to date the kitchen help, but they know it's temporary since she's going back to the States to run a restaurant."

Constance is extremely judgmental and flippant when she doesn't even know Cassie, which is surprising and off-putting.

But before I can respond, we're interrupted by our server saying, "The chef created a delightful mango-kiwi sorbet to cleanse the palate after your wine tasting. Please enjoy."

"This is very refreshing and such a thoughtful touch," Constance says.

"I agree. It will smooth the transition from that last full-bodied red at the tasting to the white wine paired with our main course. But if you don't mind a change in topic, I'd love for you to tell me about yourself. Did I understand correctly that you're active in charity work?"

"I am. My primary focus is raising awareness about heart disease. As you may know, my father died from a sudden heart attack when I was eight. I've learned that it could have been prevented had he made lifestyle changes at an earlier age," she says.

"I'm sorry I didn't know about your father. That must've been devastating to lose him when you were so young."

Our server arrives with our main course, explaining, "The chef prepared garden greens and potato slices, tossed with a lemon vinaigrette, along with grilled salmon and roasted tomato and kale relish. The main course is paired with a sauvignon blanc. Please enjoy."

"Your chef should be commended for such a heart healthy menu. But back to our discussion, it *was* devastating to lose my father. I'm trying to help others learn from it. Tell me about your charitable work. I know you're a fierce warrior for the environment."

"I wouldn't have described it in such a graphic manner, but I *am* dedicated to making the world a cleaner, safer place for our people and those who follow."

"What is the most important policy to change? For example, I've heard about the controversy over offshore drilling. Should it be ended?" she asks, giving me her full attention.

"That's the king's decision. But if we're speaking just between the two of us, I'm genuinely concerned about the problems it can cause in the ocean."

"You'll be king soon, so you can do whatever you want. Will you end it?"

"We'll see. Perhaps. Ending the drilling completely could make a significant difference to the environment, but we'd need to evaluate the economic impact further. A compromise may make sense."

"What else would you change?'

"Trash disposal is a problem, particularly for islands. I'd reduce the use of single-use items. What are your thoughts on environmental issues?"

"Saving the environment is a noble cause, but I don't know too much about the tradeoffs. I've spent most of my time learning about my charity's issues. You'll need to teach me what needs to be done on the environmental front. I'd love the opportunity to help make a difference."

"By the way, how is your salmon?" I ask.

"It's a healthy choice and perfect for a warm summer day. The crisp white wine goes well with it too." She smiles charmingly as she places her hand on top of mine.

"I'm glad you approve, but I suspect the final course may not win your heart-healthy stamp of approval unless you push the cream aside," I say as one server clears our plates and another presents the strawberry and chocolate crepes topped with a dollop of cream.

"We can't be good all the time. I'm okay with a little naughtiness from time to time." She winks and giggles.

I laugh at her innuendo, but it's a little forced. Constance is hard to read. One minute she's extremely traditional, a little snobby, and slightly abrupt. The next she's charming, flirtatious, and something else I can't quite identify. She's confusing.

With lunch finished, we stroll among the vines, holding hands, as I point out the various varietals and answer her questions until it's time to part ways.

"I'm sorry to end our date now, but I'm required to return to the palace for a family event."

"That's too bad. I'd love to spend all evening with you, but of course, I understand the obligations of royals."

"I appreciate your understanding. We'll see each other again very soon," I say, helping her into the car that'll return her to The Shores. Her lips are still pouty despite her stated understanding, but I ignore her reaction.

Watching her car leave, it's clear my marriage options aren't perfect, but at least they're viable.

Constance is the best match on paper. We share our love of charity work, she's extremely attentive, and she's a royal. She's even willing to please me with a little naughtiness. I chuckle to myself, wondering exactly what she had in mind.

All the boxes should be checked, but I'm still not sure. Something is a little off, and it's not just that she's a snob because that's common among royals, particularly when they're trying to impress other royals. Perhaps she's too perfect on paper.

CHAPTER THIRTY-FOUR

ARIANA

X ander has spent the last two nights at the palace, so there hasn't been a chance for us to talk. I'm relieved it's finally my turn to go on a date with him because I want to share what I've learned.

When the car comes to a halt, the driver escorts me inside, where Xander is waiting in khakis and a polo shirt. "Welcome to the children's wing," he says while giving me a hug.

"If this is the children's wing, I can't imagine what the adult one looks like. Where did that name come from?" The elegant furnishings and museum-quality artwork scream anything but a place for children.

"Evan, Bri, and I have our apartments and offices here, while my parents have their living space and offices on the other side, so this became known as the children's wing. By the way, you look great. I'm so glad you're here. We're going to movie night with Bri, Evan, and his girlfriend Cassie."

"That sounds fun. But will we have time to talk about the murder? I have news."

"Yes, I also have news. Evan and Cassie say they have information to report as well. This will be the perfect opportunity for all of us to share what we have learned."

As we walk down a never-ending passageway, I ask, "Where are we going?"

"Evan's apartment. We have a larger palace movie theater, but it requires a staff member to operate the equipment, so we decided it would be better to watch at Evan's place. That way, no one will be eavesdropping."

We pass through double doors, emerging outside on a path in a garden area. On the far side, we stop and Xander knocks on the door.

The quiet is broken by the gurgling of a water fountain and the tapping of Xander's foot.

"Are you sure they know we were coming tonight?" I ask.

"Evan thinks he's teaching me a lesson making us wait." Xander laughs.

"Have you been bad?" I ask with a giggle.

"That's a loaded question," Xander says as a tall guy with dark wavy hair opens the door.

"Good to see you, Xander."

"Did you have trouble with the lock?" Xander asks with a straight face.

Evan chuckles, "Are you going to introduce your *date?*"

"Ariana, this is my wiseass brother, better known as Prince Evan."

"Your Royal Highness, it's a pleasure to meet you," I say, starting to curtsy.

But Evan reaches out to shake my hand, saying, "No formalities tonight. It's good to finally meet you. Follow me. We're in the kitchen preparing the food. What do you usually eat while watching movies?"

What has Xander told him about me?

"Popcorn and chocolate-covered raisins. Any chance you have those?"

"You and Bri are destined to either fight it out or be best friends because she loves those too. But we always start with pizza," he says with a welcoming smile.

"You can't go wrong with pizza, popcorn, and chocolate," I say.

In the kitchen, first one and then a second striking woman hug me, the latter thrusting an old-fashioned glass filled with chilled amber liquid into my hand.

Xander places his arm around my shoulder, pulling me out of their welcoming clutches.

"Give her some breathing room."

Sipping the cold drink, I close my eyes, surprised at its smoothness. "Mmm. This is excellent."

"She fits in already," Evan declares.

Xander whispers in my ear, "Just so you know, the first attacker was my sister, Princess Brianna. The second was Evan's relatively new, but apparently very serious, girlfriend, Cassie."

I nod.

"Thanks for letting me join the party. What am I drinking? It's silky smooth going down, but I'm guessing it's dangerously intoxicating."

"It's my brother's favorite drink, a Boulevardier, and yes, it's quite strong. Be careful," Xander warns.

"Time to start the film. Load up on food and let's go," Evan says.

The kitchen counter is covered in junk food—it's a movie theater concession stand, but free.

Snacks in hand, we enter Evan's jaw-droppingly cool home theater. Xander and I settle onto the first of the three sofas facing the screen. Evan and Cassie take the center one, and Bri sits next to the most adorable Yorkie on the third sofa.

"By the way, Ariana, this is Princess. She's addicted to attention, so she goes from sofa to sofa seeking ear scratches and belly rubs. Don't be surprised if she ends up in your lap at some point."

"She's so cute, and I love little dogs. Princess is welcome to spend time with me," I say.

"What are we watching?" Cassie asks.

"We usually watch action films or something scary. Those are the only ones we all enjoy. I don't remember what's next on our list," Bri says.

"Isn't it the one where the stalker attacks the campers stranded on an island? I can't remember its name, though. But before we start the film, should we share the info we've collected about Everly's death?" Xander says.

We nod, so he continues. "Okay. Ariana, what did you learn?"

"Remember Jessica mentioned she was an overly energetic child?"

"She did say that, but aren't all children overly energetic?" Xander asks.

"To some extent, but I started wondering if what she described is a symptom of ADHD, so I did some research and confirmed that it is. But hyperactivity may decrease with age, and there are conflicting reports about using amphetamines to treat adults. I thought it would be too risky to ask her. The only other way to find out if she's taking medication for ADHD was to search her room."

"You searched her room?" Xander questions, rubbing his forehead.

"I did. And before you say anything, I know it was a huge invasion of her privacy, but I didn't know what else to do. I'd hoped to talk with you before your date with Jessica. I couldn't find an excuse for us to be alone. With Jessica out of the house and Constance resting by the pool after you left, it gave me the perfect opportunity to check out her room."

Bri leans forward. "Did you find anything?"

"I did. She has a small bottle of bright yellow pills in her bathroom, but I couldn't read the label. It had been drenched with water, so the lettering was smeared."

"How can we find out what they are?"

"That's the problem. I Googled for photos of amphetamine pills on my phone, and some were yellow. But I couldn't match them up, and I didn't want to linger in her bathroom longer than necessary."

Reaching into my pocket, I pull out a plastic bag and hand it to Xander, saying, "I decided on a direct approach. She won't miss one pill. You should get this tested."

"You shouldn't have taken this," Xander chastises.

"I decided it was better to take one than risk someone else getting hurt if Jessica murdered Lady Everly."

"Point taken, but even if it matches, it's possible that someone else took her pills, or that the pills came from another source. I'll have it tested, though. Evan and Cassie, what did you find out?"

"I spent a day in the palace kitchen with the pastry chef. While I learned to make His Majesty's favorite pizzellas, I found out that the palace kitchen buys the horses' muffins from a supplier. They arrive in a sealed package and are delivered directly to the stables," Cassie says.

"Then it's doubtful the muffins were sabotaged in the kitchen," Xander says.

"Agreed, but I did overhear something else that's interesting. One of the women working nearby was complaining she couldn't get a reusable water bottle clean. Another guy asked what the problem was, and she said, 'One of the bottles from the prince's ride is filled with bugs.' It sounded gross. Then the guy walked over to look and said, 'Those aren't bugs, they're wings from a butterfly.'"

"How would butterflies end up in a water bottle?" Bri asks.

"I don't know, but it caught my attention because it was one of the bottles used on the ride the day Lady Everly died."

"I'll let the palace police know about it. Constance thought butterflies might have been what spooked Cocoa, but I don't know how that would relate to butterfly wings in a water bottle. It's a strange coincidence. I'm concerned that the police aren't close enough to the people involved to solve the crime quickly enough. I appreciate everyone's help with this." Xander says.

"By the way, what's the deal with this family and butterflies?" Cassie asks. "Evan still won't tell me what was so funny about staying in The Monarch Suite at the Grand Athena or why the fountain in front of the palace has butterflies, not to mention the monarch bedroom on the royal jet."

Xander and Bri double over laughing while Cassie looks mystified. When Bri finally catches her breath, she says, "Oh, Evan will never live that story down. It's hilarious."

"Bri, stop it. You know it's not that funny. Let's watch the film," Evan says.

"Oh no, someone has to tell me the story now," Cassie says.

"Xander should tell it. He remembers the incident firsthand. I was too young, but I've heard the story for as long as I can remember," Bri says.

"It's only fair for Cassie to know," Xander chuckles.

Evan rubs his hand over his face as we wait for Xander to continue.

"You see, when Evan was five, his teacher decided to teach him about butterflies by setting up a science project. Over the course of about a month, they watched an egg turn into a caterpillar, the caterpillar turned into a chrysalis, and then a monarch butterfly emerged. He was mesmerized by how the tiny egg changed into a butterfly. He even named it Orange Wings."

"In all fairness, it's a rather amazing transformation," Evan says.

"It is, but the transformation was somewhat spoiled for five-year-old Evan. You see, when we each turn five, it's a milestone in our royal life. That's when we're told about what it means to be a royal. So, dressed in a suit, Evan was escorted to the throne room to see our parents. They explained to him that he's a royal, and specifically, he's a prince. And that means he's part of the monarchy of Catalinius. They also told him that his big brother would be the ruling monarch one day. He started crying. At first, no one knew why he was so upset. They thought he must've wanted to be the king and get to sit on the throne, which at that time he called the big chair," Xander says.

"I'll pick it up from here. It's my story. I might as well finish it," Evan says. "I can promise you, I never wanted to be king, even if I did have fun sneaking onto the big chair when no one was looking. But my parents had this talk with me the same week the butterfly emerged, so I thought a monarch was the same as a monarch butterfly. And I didn't want Xander to turn into a butterfly and fly out the window like Orange Wings did. I also thought we were all going to turn into butterflies and fly away, each going our separate ways. Not to mention the teacher told me that butterflies only live two-to-six weeks. In short, I thought they were telling me we were all flying off to die alone in a matter of weeks."

186

"How horrible! No wonder you were upset. That's worse than showing a horror movie to a child," Cassie hugs Evan.

"It took at least two weeks before we could convince him we weren't all going to turn into butterflies and fly away," Xander says.

"And they've never let me live it down."

"Is that why your friend Sean assigned you to The Monarch Suite at the Grand Athena? How did he know the story?" Cassie asks.

"Yes, that's why. I have Bri to thank for that. She shared the story with Sean when he visited Catalinius one summer during college," Evan says.

"And the butterflies on the fountain. Are they related to the story?" Cassie asks.

"They are. When I complained to Mum about being teased about my butterfly debacle, she told me the story showed how much family meant to me. A few days later, she took me to see the fountain and pointed out the new butterflies. She said every time I see them, I should remember that I'm special to my family."

"What an incredibly kind way to deal with your childhood trauma," Cassie says, placing her palm over Evan's heart.

"It was. Mum is a special person. She's always doing something unexpected to ensure things turn out well. Now, may we watch the film?" Evan asks, pointing the remote control at the screen.

I lean into Xander, whispering, "So what's your funniest childhood story?"

"That'll have to wait for another time. The film's starting." He grins, resting his arm on the back of the sofa behind me.

As we watch the movie, Xander and I whisper back and forth about gaps in the plot and corny gimmicks. It's so natural. If I didn't know better, I'd say we've been friends forever.

Tension builds as the campers sit around a campfire under a moonless sky, talking about the rumors that others have disappeared on the same mountain, never to be found.

Some swear it's ghosts, some blame robbers, and others are convinced it's an ax murderer. Creepy music plays as rain starts to pour, dousing the fire. They look for their flashlights, but of course, they're gone. One guy goes to turn on the truck's headlights. Surprise —the battery's dead. Leaves rustle as we hear the thump, thump, thump of approaching boots hitting the ground.

My heart pounds, waiting for the attack that happens in all horror movies. I'm clutching a blanket against my chest with one hand, and I'm tightly gripping the armrest with the other as the music turns ominous. I jump, squeezing harder, when the campers scream, "Don't hurt us!" as a hulky creature waves a knife and shines a blinding flashlight in their eyes.

"Why would I hurt you? I'm Officer Hadley. I'm checking out the report of a bear sighting. Do you need help?" he asks.

Letting out the breath I was holding, Xander wraps his arm around my shoulder and pulls me closer, asking, "Are you okay?"

I nod.

"Then maybe you could ease your grip on my thigh now." He laughs softly in my ear.

"Oh no. I'm so sorry," I say, pulling my hand away. Shit. I bruised a prince. But how would I know his legs were that hard. He must do intense workouts.

"Not a problem. I'm relieved it was my thigh you squeezed with that killer grip. A little to the right, and you would've damaged the royal jewels. I'd hate to have to handcuff you and haul you to the dungeon for mutilating the next king," he whispers, his voice a little hoarse.

My cheeks grow hotter by the second. I'm not sure what I'm most mortified about—having bruised his leg, almost grabbing his cock, or savoring my latest fantasy. "Is there a dungeon here?"

He leans toward me again, his lips gently brushing my ear, sending a shiver down my spine. "I'm not sure either one of us could manage you finding out," he says in a gravelly whisper.

Leaning away, he puts a little distance between us on the sofa. He must be having non-friend-zone thoughts too.

After the movie, Xander walks me to a waiting car and hugs me goodnight.

"I had a wonderful time with your family. Everyone made me feel welcome. Thanks for including me."

"It was a perfect evening," he says.

"Except for when I almost destroyed the royal jewels," I tease.

"Well, yes. Fortunately, they are most definitely still intact."

CHAPTER THIRTY-FIVE

XANDER

Looking forward to a day on the water, my bodyguard Robert accompanies me to our family's sailboat at the yacht club. *The Crown Pearl* is a sixty-five-foot sloop. Her dark blue hull and natural teak deck are impressive. She's perfect for our group date.

As we reach the cockpit, I do a double take. Shite.

"Robert, please tell me that's not Harper on the foredeck talking with Evan and Cassie. What the bloody hell is she doing here?" First, she showed up at the stables before our ride. Now she's at our sailboat when I'm taking the women out.

"Do you want me to take care of it, sir?"

Sighing heavily, I say, "No, wait here on the dock. Let me handle it. But stand by in case she resists. We only have about thirty minutes to get rid of her before the women arrive. I have no desire to deal with questions about Harper."

Stepping from the dock into the aft cockpit, I call out, "Hello, everyone."

Cassie and Evan wave, but Harper runs to me. In a loud voice, she exclaims, "Xander, it's so wonderful to be in your arms again," throwing herself at me before I can step out of her path.

Robert is in the background yelling, "Get out of here. No photos!"

191

Bloody hell. This is another one of Harper's stunts to link us together in the tabloids. If there weren't paps nearby, I'd be tempted to toss her overboard. But, of course, that photo on the front page wouldn't do. Instead, prying her fingernails off my shoulders and gently pushing her away, I say, "Harper, I thought I made it clear in London. You can't just show up uninvited. We're taking the boat for a sail now, so you'll have to leave."

"What a beautiful day for sailing. I'd love to go with you. Thanks for the invitation," she shouts, ensuring the paps hear.

Attempting to control my voice, I say, "Harper, you are leaving now."

Evan joins us and places himself between me and Harper. Wrapping his arm around her, he escorts her off the back of the boat where Robert takes over on the dock.

Shaking my head, I go downstairs into the main saloon of our sailboat, out of view of the cameras. Cassie follows.

"What the hell was she doing here?" I ask.

"She was waiting on deck when we arrived. She had heard we're taking the boat out today and wanted to know if we had room for her."

"She won't give up. She didn't mess with anything, did she?"

Before Cassie can answer, Evan returns. "While she talked with Cassie, I checked. The cabin was still locked, and all the equipment is in order. As far as we could tell, she waited in the cockpit until we arrived."

"Okay. That's a relief. Even though the palace police believe it's unlikely she's to blame for drugging Cocoa, I'm not convinced. She wants to marry me and was at the stables that day. That's motive *and* opportunity."

"How did she get so near a royal yacht in the first place?" Cassie asks.

"It's simple. She's royal and her family's boat is in a slip at this yacht club. She has access," Evan answers.

"That's scary," Cassie says.

"She's gone for now. Robert will take care of her, and he'll wait on the dock while we're sailing to make sure she isn't here when we return. I hear the palace staff boarding to set up our food and drinks for the sail. Let's finish rigging the boat," Evan says.

"Let's get to work. Ariana, Jessica, and Constance will be here soon," I say.

We finish prepping the boat right before the women arrive. I hurry to meet them on the dock. "It's so good to see all of you. Welcome to our family's yacht, *The Crown Pearl*. Come aboard. It's a beautiful day for a sail."

Giving Constance a hug, I wave her onto the boarding ramp. Evan and Cassie are in the cockpit, ready to greet her.

"I'm so excited we're sailing today. This boat is much larger than the ones I've been on before, so I'm not sure I'll know exactly what to do. But I'd love to help if you'll let me." Jessica says.

"Fantastic. We're thrilled to have another experienced sailor on board today."

Ariana approaches the boarding ramp, smiling. Pulling her close, I whisper, "Please pretend this is the first time you're meeting Evan and Cassie. I don't want the others to know you met any of my family before they did."

"No problem. I haven't mentioned anything about our *date* other than that we had a lovely dinner."

With my hand on the small of her back, we join the others in the cockpit.

After introductions, a quick tour of the boat, and a safety orientation, Evan starts the engine. Robert releases our docking lines from the cleats and gives us a salute as we pull away.

"Now that we've motored out of the port, we have room to hoist the sails," I say.

"How do we do that?" Ariana asks.

"First, we turn the boat to point the bow into the wind. Then we can raise our mainsail," I explain.

"Does someone need to go to the mast to hoist it?" Jessica asks.

"On many smaller boats, we'd have to send someone. But we're doing it the easy way with the electric winch on the cabin top."

When the sail reaches the top, I say, "Next, we need to unfurl the forward sail. It's called the jib. Jessica, can you pull on the blue sheet to bring it out?"

"Happy to." Jessica wraps the blue rope around the winch and yanks, unfurling the jib and pulling it taut.

As the wind fills our sails, the boat glides forward along the coast.

"I'm reasonably good at trimming. Would you mind if I handle the jib for a while?" Jessica asks, sporting a broad smile.

"It's all yours. Let us know if you need a break."

Turning to the others, I ask, "For those of you new to sailing, trimming refers to pulling the sail in or letting it out to match the wind conditions. Ideally, we would have two people assigned as jib trimmers. Who wants to help Jessica?"

"I'd love to, but you'll have to teach me how," Ariana says.

"Me too. I'm happy to help," Cassie adds.

"I'll show you both. We can take turns." Jessica offers.

"Great. Evan's at the helm, steering for us today, so I'm trimming the mainsail. Constance, would you like to help me?"

"I'll sit nearby and keep you company. Where are we sailing to?"

"We'll follow the coast until we reach my favorite spot, Heavenly Cove. We can anchor there for lunch," I say.

We chat and enjoy the views along the way. Constance nudges closer to me with each passing mile, while Jessica, Ariana, and Cassie take turns trimming the jib, laughing, and talking. As we near Heavenly, Evan restarts the engine, and we douse the sails, readying to anchor in the pristine cove.

After we anchor, Constance suggests they take photos of each other, so she, Jessica, and Ariana take turns striking various poses. Evan and I double-check that the anchor is secure, and Cassie goes downstairs to inform the servers they can bring lunch up when it's ready.

Using the tablet, I turn on the stereo to create a party atmosphere, but Evan grabs it from me, as usual complaining about my choice of music. Our brotherly bickering is interrupted by simultaneous screams of "Help!" followed quickly by big splashes and a hard thud against the hull.

My head jerks to the water. Constance is overboard flailing and splashing. Jessica is pointing down frantically. Following her finger, my eyes lock on Ariana. She's sinking.

"Fuck! Evan, get Constance!"

I dive in after Ariana, watching as she continues to sink. Shit. She's going to drown. I swim as hard as I can, my own lungs screaming for air. Time is passing too quickly. She floats farther and farther from the boat as she sinks lower. It seems like an eternity before I'm close enough to grab her. *Finally*, she's within reach. Diving down and grasping her arm, I secure her against my body. She's so limp—hang on, Ariana! With all my strength, I kick us toward the surface.

We break through the water's surface. I gasp for air, while making sure Ariana's head is above water. It's not clear she's breathing. I'm a strong swimmer, but I'm fighting the current that pushed Ariana away from the boat in the first place. I've got to get her help. She can't die too.

Using all the strength in my arms and legs, we pull closer to the boat, and Cassie throws us a life ring. With its support, I keep kicking while pressing breaths of air into Ariana's mouth. Cassie pulls the rope attached to the life ring, bringing us to the boat.

Evan's waiting on the swim platform and immediately takes Ariana from my arms. "Help her. I don't think she's breathing." They start checking on her as I hoist myself up onto the platform, panting. "Is Constance safe?"

"A little bruised and shaken up, but she will be fine. Jessica took her downstairs to change into dry clothes and bandage a few cuts. The kitchen staff are helping. She's in excellent hands." Cassie says.

"Ariana has a weak pulse. We've already called for help. She wasn't under that long, but we need to make sure she's getting enough air," Evan says as he turns Ariana's head to drain water from her mouth.

"I'll do it. Monitor her pulse." Tilting Ariana's head back, I pinch her nose and press my mouth to hers, delivering four powerful breaths down her throat. Placing my ear near her nose, I detect a faint breath, but it could be wishful thinking. I deliver another breath, counting one, two, three and then a weak hand touches me as Ariana starts coughing up water. Thank fuck.

Evan helps me roll Ariana onto her side again. When she finally catches her breath, I help her sit up, "Are you okay? What happened?"

"I'm not sure. The last thing I remember is standing on the deck taking photos. Next your lips were on mine," she says in a hoarse whisper, smiling weakly.

"You and Constance fell in the water, but you immediately started sinking. Don't you know how to swim?"

"I'm a better-than-average swimmer. But my head hurts, and my leg is sore. I must've hit something when I fell over. Ouch." She winces as she rubs her head. "There's a huge bump. I don't feel well." Ariana slumps against my chest.

Shite. The thud earlier must've been Ariana's head hitting the boat's hull. Gently, I pull her closer against me, pressing a soft kiss on her forehead, murmuring, "I've got you now. You're going to be fine. Help is on the way."

"She has a big bruise on her leg too. I'll find some ice, towels, and blankets." Cassie says.

Finally, a medic boat pulls behind *The Crown Pearl*. Evan and Cassie help Robert and the palace doctor climb aboard. "Dr. Rousseau, thank you for coming," I say.

"I came as quickly as I could. Are you injured?" he asks.

"No, but Ariana and Lady Constance are."

The doctor checks Ariana over as I describe the accident to him. There's that word again—*accident*. We thought the motorcycle in London was an accident. It wasn't. Then we thought Everly's fall was an accident. It turned out to be intentional. I can't help but worry this may not have been an accident either.

Constance and Jessica join us on deck as the doctor says, "Ariana, the good news is your vital signs are okay now. But you may have a concussion. We need to take you to the hospital where we can do further tests." He turns to me. "Your Highness, we need to carefully move her onto the medic boat."

"Of course. Can you also check on Lady Constance?"

"That's not necessary, Xander. I'm fine. But I'd be happy to accompany Ariana to the hospital."

"Thanks for offering, but I'll go with her. You should rest in one of the cabins below. I'll check on you after we know how Ariana is doing. Jessica, can you help Evan and Cassie get the boat back to the yacht club?" I ask.

"Of course. Don't worry about us. We'll be fine. Take care of Ariana. We'll look after Constance and the boat."

With Ariana's neck braced to prevent further injury, we lay her down on the padded bench of the medic boat and motor to the nearest port.

Ariana almost died.

That would have been more than I could handle.

She's the first woman who doesn't care I'm a wealthy prince. She grounds me. I want time to laugh with her, tease her, share problems with her, and show her my favorite places on the island. Is that love?

I bite my lip hard. It can't be. She's special. She's my friend—it's okay to care deeply for a close friend, right?

CHAPTER THIRTY-SIX

XANDER

I'm rolling my head in circles and rubbing the taut tendons in my neck, waiting for Evan. It's late, but I'm knocking on his door anyway. I need to talk to him.

Evan slowly looks me over from head to toe. "Come in. You're a mess. Is Ariana okay?"

"Yes, she'll be fine. Fortunately, the head injury is not as bad as the doctor originally thought. He was particularly concerned because she passed out, but the tests show it's only a mild concussion. He wanted her to stay at the hospital overnight, but she refused."

"What are you doing here if she went back to The Shores?"

"The doctor vetoed The Shores. He offered a compromise. She's staying in the palace infirmary tonight so he and his staff can keep an eye on her. If she's doing okay tomorrow, she can move to a guestroom in the palace for the next few days. He says she should make a full recovery."

"That's a relief."

Rubbing my fingers through my already oily hair, I sigh. "No kidding. When I grabbed her, she was completely limp. I was petrified she wasn't going to make it. By the way, where's Constance? How's she doing?"

"She was shaken up at first but settled down after a glass of wine and some food. I was impressed with how calm Jessica and Cassandra were through the whole ordeal."

"Did you have any problem returning the boat?"

"Of course not." He scoffs. "I've spent more time at the helm of that boat than you have. It was a quiet trip back. We motored slowly. Jessica and Cassie helped with docking. Then Constance and Jessica insisted they wanted to go to The Shores to wait for you. They assumed you'd be joining them tonight with news about Ariana."

"I had Edmund relay a message to them with an update. But I'm staying here tonight. Ariana doesn't have any family nearby. I want her to know I'm near if she needs anything."

Evan gives me a strange look but doesn't respond, so I continue, "I'm sorry to burst in on you so late tonight, but I couldn't sleep. I can't figure out how they both fell off the boat, much less how Ariana hit her head."

"I'm glad you stopped by. We need to talk. I'll make us drinks."

"As long as it's not another glass of vodka disguised as water. I'm not falling for that again. And do you have ibuprofen? My head is pounding." I follow him to the living room and sink into his burgundy leather sofa, trying to rub the exhaustion from my eyes.

Frowning, he hands me a glass. It's clear he's worried about me, which isn't necessary. I'm fine but need answers.

"Did you see what happened?" I ask.

"No, but we asked Constance for details after you took Ariana to the hospital. She said that she and Ariana leaned against the 'wire fence' that goes around the boat as Jessica took their photo. I explained that the wire fence is called the lifelines." Evan chuckles.

"It hadn't occurred to me before that the two horizontal steel cables running around a boat resemble a wire fence. But what does that have to do with them falling overboard?"

"Constance said that the top lifeline suddenly gave way, causing them to fall backward and plunge into the water. She said it happened so fast she couldn't grab anything."

"I didn't notice that the lifelines were broken after they fell, did you?" I ask.

"No. They went overboard where the lifeline clips to the stanchion, forming the side gate. After you left with Ariana, I noticed the top wire cable of the gate was hanging open. I assumed someone was careless and didn't completely close the pelican hook. You know how we always double check the gate when we close it because it won't lock if the pin doesn't catch?"

"Of course, but we rarely open it in the first place."

"Right. Honestly, I don't remember the last time it was opened. Since we back the boat in, we always use a boarding ramp and enter at the aft end instead of from the side. I wouldn't have thought to check the side gate."

"Me neither. It could have been an accident. One of our maintenance guys may have left it open."

"Originally, that's what I thought. But there's more to the story. I asked Cassandra to close the gate before we left Heavenly Cove, but she said it wouldn't latch. I warned everyone to stay away from it, planning to check it when we got back."

"So why wouldn't it close?"

"The spring was missing from the hook, so it wouldn't lock. It had been held closed with clear tape that broke when Constance and Ariana leaned against the lifeline."

"Would one of our maintenance guys do a temporary fix until they could replace the broken hook?"

"No. I don't think so. We need to check, but I can't imagine our maintenance team would leave a faulty hook in place, much less use clear tape to close it. They would've used a thicker weather-resistant tape that's white or black. I suspect someone removed the spring on purpose. It's unlikely the fall was an accident."

"Damn!" I groan, burying my face in my hands. "Who is trying to kill the women I'm dating?"

"I hate to say it, but Harper is at the top of my list. She was at the boat before we arrived. She could've removed the spring from the hook. It's easy. Just take off the safety ring and pull out the pin and spring. Toss the spring in the water, and then replace the pin, put the safety ring back, and tape the hook closed. Harper also had access to Cocoa on the day Everly died."

"And she essentially threatened to make me regret turning her down, but I never thought she'd go this far."

"Do you suspect anyone else?" Evan asks.

"I do wonder about Jessica. She grew up taking horseback riding lessons and learning to sail. She would've been able to disable the gate hook, and she would've known what would happen if you feed a horse treats laden with amphetamines."

"I had no idea she knew that much about both horses and boats. You could be right."

"But everything else about her tells me I'm off base. Nothing I've seen indicates she would do such horrible things."

"You barely know her. She could be a phenomenal actor. What about Constance and Ariana?"

"Ariana has no motive. She knows about horses but not sailboats. And most importantly, she took herself out of the running to marry me from the start. Besides, no one would give themselves a concussion and almost drown to throw suspicion on someone else. And we both know she wasn't faking the almost-drowning part."

"No, she wasn't. I agree, it's highly unlikely she's involved in whatever this plot is. But what about Constance?" Evan asks.

"She knows how to ride but appeared to know next to nothing about sailboats and showed no interest in learning how to sail today. She only wanted to enjoy the view and sit close to me. I don't know when she would've had time to sabotage the gate hook with so many people on board. But something Ariana said was odd. When they fell over, she vaguely remembers being kicked. And she has a giant bruise on her leg, which is unexplained."

"As for the bruising, Constance may have accidentally kicked her. Constance panicked when she hit the water and was flailing her arms and kicking as hard as she could."

"That would explain it. It's common for people to panic in the open water even if they're comfortable swimming in pools. Would Constance have had time to disable the gate hook?"

"I don't know when she could've done it. I didn't see her go near it, but I'll ask Cassandra tomorrow."

"Let me know if she saw anything. We need to do something before anyone else is hurt. I'll start with the palace police. They need to assign a security guard to shadow each of the three women. We need to keep them safe, and so far, our security plan has not worked. I don't want to frighten them, but we need to warn them that the boat incident wasn't an accident."

CHAPTER THIRTY-SEVEN

ARIANA

Tentatively opening my eyes, daylight filters between the curtains. Where am I? This isn't my room. When I touch the sore bump on my head, it dawns on me. They brought me to this guestroom in the palace yesterday.

Xander and the others checked on me from time to time, but I was too exhausted to talk much and slept away most of the day. Now, I'm torn between wanting even more sleep and needing food to ease my grumbling stomach.

After splashing cold water on my face, I find a robe and am about to go in search of food when someone knocks softly on my door.

"Come in."

"You're up. How are you feeling?" Xander smiles.

"I'm starving." I blurt out the first thought on my mind.

"That's a good sign. And I have the solution. Would you prefer to eat at the breakfast table or have breakfast in bed?"

"I'm tired of being stuck in bed, but there isn't a table in here."

"It's in the kitchen. Take my arm."

We walk slowly down a hall and through a couple of rooms until we reach the kitchen. Xander helps me into a chair and places a steaming plate of food in front of me. My stomach growls again.

"Xander, where are we?"

"You don't know where you are? I better call the doctor."

He looks worried.

"No. I know I'm in a guestroom in the palace. I didn't notice it was part of a whole apartment. Is this how all the palace guest quarters are set up?"

"Of course not. You're in my apartment. Didn't anyone tell you?"

My mouth drops open. "Why am I in your apartment?"

"Where else would you be? You don't have family here, so I want to be close if you need anything. And it's easier to check on you here."

"That makes sense. My brain's still a little foggy. Forgive me for not offering my thanks first. I appreciate everything you've done to take care of me. Dr. Rousseau said you rescued me from the water and resuscitated me. It's overwhelming, but I owe my life to you." A tear rolls down my cheek.

Wiping it away with his thumb, Xander says, "Don't overthink it. You inhaled a little too much water. You'll be fine."

"I have a lot of questions. Why did we fall overboard? Was it an accident? Did someone kick me? Have you learned any new details about Everly's murder?"

"Slow down. We have plenty of time to talk. Eat first."

After a few bites, I set my fork down. "Xander, the questions keep running rampant through my brain. They haunted me every time I woke up yesterday, but I was too tired to deal with them, and my head hurt too much to process them. Can we please talk now?"

"Of course. I understand. Let's start with your first two questions. Someone sabotaged the boat's lifeline. When you and Constance leaned against it, the lifeline gave way, plunging the two of you into the water. It was *not* an accident."

"You can't be serious! Are you suggesting someone is trying to kill all of us?"

"Unfortunately, that's a possibility. Whoever leaned against the lifeline would've fallen in, so it's not clear you and Constance were the targets. On the other hand, Harper was at the boat before you arrived, and she'd be happy if all three of you disappeared. And Jessica grew up around sailboats and horses. She would've known how to disable the hook and drug Cocoa."

"I don't know Harper, but it's hard to believe Jessica would do that. Are there any other suspects or motives?"

"There's a possibility that someone, or some group, is trying to keep me from taking the throne. There was another *accident* before I met you at the reception in London. That time, I was the target."

"What happened?"

"An out-of-control motorcyclist tried to run me down after my speech about offshore drilling at an economic conference in London."

"Did they catch him? Do you know who was responsible?"

"They didn't catch him. When I mentioned the guy was wearing a leather jacket with a purple jaguar emblem, Evan thought that sounded familiar. It's not much of a lead, but at least it's something."

"If you get me my phone and laptop, I can research the logo."

"Dr. Rousseau said you must avoid screen time for twenty-four to forty-eight hours. Besides, our palace police are looking into it."

"It's been two days already. Please check with the doctor. I'll go stir-crazy with no phone, laptop, or television. And before I became a budding novelist, I was one of the best googlers in the world. You can't imagine all the things I had to figure out in my old job. Let me try."

"Okay, I'll ask. He said you needed to stay still a couple of days. Doing research on your laptop may be the best way to keep you from overexerting yourself."

"Perfect. I could kiss you." I lean forward, kissing him on the cheek and sending a shock of electricity through me. Oops. Hopefully, he doesn't take that wrong.

"You just did." He chuckles as he touches his cheek.

But his expression turns wistful when our eyes lock, sending a chill down my spine.

He must've noticed because he asks, "Are you cold?"

Ignoring the tension in the air, I say, "No, I'm just a little weak. I better finish breakfast. What about my next question? Did Dr.

Rousseau say whether he thought I'd been kicked or hit by something?"

"He said the backs of your calves were bruised by the lower lifeline that didn't give way. When you fell backwards, it would've cut into your legs as it tried to hold you up. He said you may also have been kicked by Constance when she was flailing in the water. Evan even has a few bruises from rescuing her. So, unfortunately, you were collateral damage from her panic."

"That explains it. Is she okay?"

"Yes, Constance is fine. Initially, she was quite shaken, but she was lucky and managed to escape with only a few cuts and bruises."

"Thank goodness."

"I'm relieved that you're doing so much better. You gave me a scare."

"I didn't mean to," I say softly.

Coughing, he stands abruptly. "Unfortunately, I need to go now, but I'll check with the doctor about your phone and laptop. If he approves, I'll have them brought to you."

"What are you doing today?"

"My schedule is full. I'm meeting with the palace police this morning for a progress update. Then I've invited Jessica to lunch in the palace garden and Constance for dinner."

"Have you decided which one to propose to?" I ask, fidgeting with my napkin.

"It's complicated. I'm not sure yet. Which one would you select for me?"

"They're both amazing women from what I've seen. Well educated, refined, accustomed to life in the spotlight. But as for which one is right for you, I'm the wrong person to ask. You need to follow your heart."

"That's harder than it sounds. Let's hope today will help me decide."

I look down. "I'm sure it will."

"I'll check on you later tonight. Get some rest."

My feelings toward Xander are confusing. I told him I don't want a relationship. Then when we're together, it's like we're already a couple. We share our thoughts. He sends chills through me when we touch. I miss him when we're apart.

In my fantasy world, he follows his heart to me. Unfortunately, this is the real world, and knowing he will marry someone else shatters me.

Rest may heal my concussion. It won't mend my broken heart.

CHAPTER THIRTY-EIGHT

XANDER

M y meeting with the palace police was frustrating to say the
least. They are no closer to knowing if I'm having lunch with
a viable candidate for marriage or a villain. It's going to be awkward.

When I reach the veranda, Jessica is standing near the top of the
garden steps with her back to me. Stopping short, I take a moment to
appreciate her beauty. No man would mind waking up next to her
each morning. She's not only pleasing to the eye but she's also inde-
pendent-minded and shares my interest in horses and sailing. Even
her lack of spontaneity fits the role of a future queen. Her schedule
will be planned down to the minute each day.

If only there was proof that she's not behind these horrible
incidents.

Shaking my head, I move closer to her, plastering a smile on my
face. Her head turns, and instead of returning my smile, her expression is painful. Quickening my steps, I wrap my arms around her in a
soothing hug, but her arms remain at her sides.

Pulling away, she averts her eyes.

"What's wrong, Jessica? Are you okay?"

"Physically, yes, but we need to talk."

"Lunch is being served at the center of the maze. We'll have privacy there." Such an isolated location may not have been smart given my concerns about Jessica. It's too late to change the plans now though.

"Won't there be staff?" she asks.

"I'll have them step away. There's even a shortcut to the center."

"Okay. Thanks."

Arriving at the table at the maze's center, I dismiss the staff, knowing my security will stay hidden but within reach as a precaution. "Please have a seat. May I pour you a glass of wine?"

"That's not a bad idea. Thank you," she says.

"You have me concerned. I've never seen you this subdued. What happened?"

Jessica takes a sip of wine. Setting her glass down, she lets out a deep breath as she finally looks me in the eye. "I've thought about this for the last two days. I haven't slept well since Ariana almost died. Everyone has been getting hurt, or, worse, dying. What if I'm next? I used up my luck when I survived the attack in the Caribbean. The stress of so many frightening surprises is too much for me. The bottom line is, I'm sorry, but I'm done."

"What do you mean?"

"I'm taking myself out of this matchmaking process. I never should've let it go this far in the first place. It has reconfirmed that being a royal is not for me. Despite my reputation in the tabloids as a party girl, I studied business in college, and my dad has taught me how to run his company. I want to follow in his footsteps and lead our family business when it's time."

"If you planned to pursue a corporate leadership role, why did you agree to attend the matchmaking reception in the first place?"

"I didn't know the man I would meet that evening was going to be a prince. Ironically, my father said he knew, but he didn't want to tell me until after you and I met. He wanted me to go into it with an open mind. He didn't want me to regret missing an opportunity."

"When you accepted the invitation to come here, you knew who I was."

"I did. You were interesting, and I enjoyed our conversation. It made me question my goals, so I decided to see it through. But now that I've seen your life, which would be wonderful for the right match, it's not for me. And while I was trying to stay until the end, I can't after the accidents. It's the kidnapping nightmare all over again."

"I understand and appreciate your candor, but I'm also disappointed. I've enjoyed our time together."

"Me too, but we're not meant to be. Please forgive me."

"There's nothing to forgive."

"I want to go home now, but Edmund said the palace police *highly recommend* that I stay until their investigation into the accidents is complete. It sounds suspiciously like a requirement. I feel trapped and in danger."

"It should only be a few extra days." At least that's what I hope. "We'll assign twenty-four-hour security to be with you until you leave for home. On my honor, I promise to keep you safe."

After Jessica leaves for The Shores, I'm not sure what to think. Does the fact that she wants to leave mean she's completely innocent, or has she done her damage and wants to escape? Regardless, time is running out.

CHAPTER THIRTY-NINE

ARIANA

I spent today in complete boredom. The doctor said no to my phone and laptop until tomorrow. After unsuccessfully trying to sleep, I took a shower and dressed. That filled about forty-five minutes. Meals took up another hour or so. The rest of my time was spent making notes about what to research for Xander, working through plot ideas for my novel, and looking forward to when he would stop by so we could talk.

That didn't go as planned. He barely popped in to make sure I'm still alive. My enquiries about his dates garnered only simple answers. He said dinner with Constance was okay, but Jessica had decided to go home. It wasn't like him to use such mundane descriptions. When I asked for details, he practically growled that he didn't want to talk about it. Then he ducked out, saying he needed to be alone but promising to see me tonight.

He's never been short with me before. We haven't known each other that long, but my questions were no more personal than our other conversations. I don't understand why they caused that reaction.

If Jessica is no longer an option, then that means Constance is the one. Oh, he may be upset I'm staying in his guestroom. He probably wanted to bring Constance to his apartment after dinner last night but couldn't with me here.

My emotions are all over the place. Disappointment. Confusion. Dread. They don't make sense, and I don't know how to sort through them. Although we may have become friends, I'm in his way now and that stings.

My time here is ending.

Hugging a pillow to my chest, tears rain down my cheeks.

CHAPTER FORTY

XANDER

Everly's death weighs heavy on my conscience. If not for the invitation to join me in this matchmaking journey, she'd still be alive. That will forever plague me. In addition, my lunch with Jessica and dinner with Constance didn't go according to plan yesterday.

Given my resulting foul mood, it was a mistake to check on Ariana last night. It's not her fault my personal life is falling apart or that people I've gotten close to are being frightened, hurt, and even killed. She didn't deserve me taking my anger and frustration out on her.

Not only is Ariana my new confidante and an anchor of support through this debacle, but also she almost died too. Instead of making her feel better last night, my snippy, rude attitude when she asked about my dates clearly hurt her. An apology is in order, but my arse is stuck in meetings all day.

Regardless, with Edmund's help, a plan is in place to make it up to her. Thanks to his quick response to my texts, her phone and laptop were delivered this morning so she can have something to entertain herself with today. By now, she'll have received a giant bouquet of roses with a card inviting her to have dinner with me tonight. Evan promised to ask Cassie to work with the palace chef to plan something that'll remind Ariana of home. If Edmund can arrange it, she'll also have a couple of additional surprises this afternoon.

Unfortunately, the day is passing in slow motion for me. Making one last attempt to sway the king's advisory committee, I present updated data in hopes of convincing them to reconsider recommending limits on offshore drilling. It didn't work. Once again, the committee rejected my proposal, rebutting my argument with their same tired response; they can't risk the economy for a long-term concern that may never actually harm our country. They left out that my proposal would harm their personal investments in drilling ventures, which surely is the real driving force behind their recommendation.

Having failed to reach any compromise, I'm on the way to my daily status briefing with the palace police. They sent a message that they had located additional video footage from surveillance cameras at the dock by *The Crown Pearl*.

My hope for progress is short-lived—the palace police say it was another dead end. I still insist on watching the video myself in case they missed something. Staring at a monitor, the video shows Harper arriving at our boat, but even zooming in, it's too fuzzy to determine exactly what she did on board. She wandered around the boat and eventually sat in the cockpit staring at her phone. No camera angle gives a clear view of the gate though. They're correct. There's no way to tell whether she sabotaged it or not while she was walking around.

The only potentially useful information they share is something new that they learned about Jessica. There's evidence that her family's business has had some recent setbacks, so she may be looking for an infusion of money. That would give her motive to eliminate the other women to reduce the competition and gain access to my funds.

If that was the plan, why does she want to leave now? Does she want me to beg her to stay? Was this all her father's idea? Is she leaving because she's fearful of being caught or because she regrets her involvement in the sabotage? And most importantly, how do we prove or disprove any of this?

While the palace police follow up, I'll brainstorm with Ariana tonight, but right now it's time for Evan's meeting about his new charity. Cassie's presence in his life has helped him work through some of his concerns about his role in the monarchy. And now he has plans to set up a new charity to combat hunger and wants my endorsement before taking his proposal to our father for approval. He's got my support already. I told him I don't need to see the presentation. But he insists he wants my feedback as well as my moral support. That means two long hours before there's a chance to see Ariana.

By 6:30 p.m. I'm finally walking to my apartment. Hopefully, Ariana will be in a forgiving mood after my screw up last night.

Ariana is beaming when I enter my living room. She sets her laptop on a side table, watching me loosen my tie and shed my suit jacket. She looks phenomenal in the short blue dress that was one of the afternoon surprises. "You look fantastic. Have you had a fun day?" I ask, wrapping her in a hug.

"I have. Almost every hour a delivery arrived—my phone and laptop, flowers, an invitation to dinner, this dress, and then a manicurist to do my nails. It was a wonderful day, but why all the special treatment?"

"Because I messed up. I'm so sorry about last night. You never should've experienced the fallout from my frustration. Please forgive me."

"I assumed you were tired of having a houseguest that needed so much attention."

Ariana is pulling away from me with her uncharacteristically soft and reserved voice. Does she believe she's not welcome here? That's almost worse than me hurting her feelings. She deserves an explanation.

"That wasn't it at all. My anger and exasperation got the best of me. Neither I nor the palace police have been able to determine who is responsible for the attacks on you and the other women. We've hit one dead end after another. I am supposed to be selecting either

Constance or Jessica to marry, but no one even knows if I can trust Jessica. Then suddenly she decides to go home. Dinner with Constance was fine, but I cut it short when she again made snide remarks about Evan dating a cook. After telling her never to mention it again, I left. It was annoying when she made derogatory comments during lunch at the vineyard. I let it go then, but last night, I was too tired to put up with the petty comments. Why does she care whom Evan dates? He can date whomever he wants. And Constance didn't even take the time to learn anything about Cassie. Not that it should matter, but she's an accomplished chef and a successful corporate attorney. By the time I saw you, my level of annoyance was off the charts."

"I don't know what to say. No wonder you were upset last night. I have news that may help, though. I did some research today and may know who attacked you in London—well, at least whose jacket he was wearing."

"You're joking. Who was it? How did you figure it out?"

"Remember, I told you I'm somewhat of an expert at internet searches. Checking trademark databases for company logos paid off. Let me show you what I found, and tell me if it's what you saw."

Add dedicated and forgiving to the lengthy list of descriptors for Ariana. After I treated her horribly last night, she spent all day doing research to help me. She's amazing. On the other hand, I'm a real arse.

She grabs her laptop and sits on the sofa, patting the cushion beside her. I lean in as she points to an image on the screen. It's a photo of a deep purple jaguar baring its teeth.

"That could be it based on the description our driver gave, but I didn't see it myself. Who's logo is it?"

"It's the logo for a company called JagFire. And look at this photo. They give leather jackets with the jaguar logo as a reward to their construction workers."

"Brilliant! You *are* good. I'll have Robert get in touch with our driver in London to verify this is the logo he saw, but I'll be surprised if it's not. What does JagFire do?"

"At first, it appeared to be an independent construction company, but I dug deeper and found that JagFire is linked to an energy corporation. And get this, the energy corporation invests heavily in offshore oil and gas drilling. Is that helpful?"

"Bloody hell." I let out a deep breath. "Many people assume I'll discontinue the offshore drilling when I take the throne."

"Will you?"

"I'll limit it going forward. It's endangering our environment. I haven't explicitly shared my plan because the king disagrees, and it would be disrespectful for me to take a public position that contradicts his."

"Unless I'm mistaken, someone involved with this corporation used one of the construction workers to try to kill you, or at a minimum, scare you." She shivers.

"I'll have my team follow up on this. Did you find out who's running the company or who's on their board of directors?"

"Franco Romano and Gerald Martin were the only corporate executives that turned up. Have you heard of them?"

"No, and unfortunately, those are rather common names, but I'll ask Edmund to check."

"I'll be interested to hear what you find out. On another topic, what did you mean last night when you said Jessica's leaving?"

"At lunch yesterday, she said she's afraid she'll be the next victim and doesn't want any part of royal life."

"That's too bad. I guess that means you'll be marrying Constance, which isn't a surprise. She's the only royal remaining."

"Yes, it appears Constance is the last remaining option." I sag against the back of the sofa.

"You don't sound happy about it. What's the problem? Constance is attractive, well-mannered, dedicated to her charity, and a royal."

"I'm not sure how happy a life with Constance will be. She's certainly acceptable, but she's such an elitist. I'm not sure our people will be big fans. And there's no spark. We're missing anything close to the chemistry Evan and Cassie have. Is it horrible that I envy them?"

"I'm so sorry, Xander. You never should've been put in this position. And no, you're not wrong to want what they have."

"It'll be okay—essentially a marriage of convenience. We can lead somewhat separate lives. It's probably for the best. I've avoided relationships ever since my college girlfriend betrayed my trust. She taught me an early lesson. Falling in love is not worth the risk."

"What did your college girlfriend do?"

"We met my third year and instantly clicked. She was fun, clever, and shared many of my interests. I even brought her home to meet my family. I thought we were in love. We'd been together several months when one day, the palace's PR team sent me evidence that she was the source of several salacious articles about me in the tabloids. I didn't believe it at first. I thought there was a mistake, so I asked her."

"What did she say?"

"When she couldn't look me in the eyes, I knew something was wrong. Eventually, she admitted that she was financing her way through college by selling stories about me, my family, and intimate details of our relationship. She tried to convince me that she cared about us but desperately needed the money. I knew that if she loved me, she never would've shared details about our private moments. And not that selling one story would've been forgivable, but she continued selling stories long after she had enough money to pay for college. The entire relationship was a setup and a lie for her financial gain. We were done."

"How horrible. What type of person would fake a relationship for money? That's cruel."

"It was. After that, I vowed to never be in that position again. My promise to myself was to have fun, date whoever interested me at the moment, and avoid relationships altogether. And that's exactly what I've done."

"I understand more than you might think. I showed up at my exboyfriend's office fifteen minutes early for our lunch date a few weeks ago and walked in on him screwing his assistant on his desk."

"Ouch."

"No kidding. I should've figured it out sooner. There were signs, like the day he showed up smelling of women's perfume. He said he'd stopped by a department store to buy some perfume for me but didn't find one that reminded him of me. It sounded off, but I was buried with work and let his lame excuse slide. When I caught him buried balls deep in someone else, it was the last straw, not only for that relationship but also for relationships in general. I already had a track record of falling for the wrong men and vowed he would be my last bad choice. Instead, I'm focusing on my novel for now, and it's unclear if I'll ever be in a place to put my faith in a man again."

"We both have trust issues after our bad experiences. At least my problem of whom to marry is solved, though, and I was fortunate to gain what I hope will be a life-long friendship with you. So, tonight is for celebrating that. No talk about sabotage, cheating and betraying exes, or my upcoming marriage of convenience. Are we agreed?"

"If that's what you want, agreed."

On cue, the doorbell rings. "That'll be our dinner. I hope it will remind you of the comforts of home."

We talk about everything except the topics we designated as off limits as we enjoy the best fish chowder I've ever eaten, followed by tenderloin medallions, lobster, potatoes au gratin, and grilled asparagus.

"This food is spectacular. It must be amazing to be spoiled by such incredible chefs."

"I am extremely grateful for them and learned at an early age the demanding work that goes into well-prepared food, thanks to Mum. When Evan and I were young, she sent us to the chef for cooking lessons. The lessons started as a punishment when she overheard us telling one of the cooks that they had to make us chocolate cookies because we were princes. We were about twelve and ten at the time."

"You didn't really order them to make cookies, did you?"

"Oh yes, we did. Mum was furious. She told us our rude, entitled behavior was unacceptable, and she wouldn't stand for it. In response, she arranged for us to *assist* Chef Sebastiano in the palace kitchen to learn to appreciate the hard work, creativity, and precision that goes into the preparation of fine food. We washed dishes, chopped vegetables, stirred sauces, and learned to read recipes every afternoon for three weeks. To her surprise, we both enjoyed the lessons and begged for more. As a result, we learned to love a variety of foods at a young age and became rather accomplished cooks, which often surprises our friends."

"What a wonderful story. And your mother must be very clever to have come up with such a creative and successful punishment for two mischievous young boys."

"She is an incredible person. She reads people and situations extremely well and instinctively knows what to do."

"I would love to have that talent, especially when it comes to reading men and dating."

"You'll figure out how to avoid players and cheaters in the future."

"As a player yourself, maybe you can tell me what to look out for?"

"Calling me that hurts. Despite what the tabloids say, I'm not a player or a cheater. A player is someone who lies about their situation and makes promises they don't intend to keep. *I do not lie.* After my college girlfriend, I have always made it clear to every woman I've been with that there is no possibility of a relationship with me—that is, until this matchmaking process."

"Forgive me. I shouldn't have made assumptions based on the tabloids and rumors, particularly when they conflicted with my impressions of you."

"Assumptions go with the territory."

"But they shouldn't come from friends. I truly am sorry. It won't happen again."

"It's already forgotten. Let's finish our meal before it gets cold," I say, placing a reassuring hand on hers. Warmth spreads through me from the contact.

"I'll need an extra hour or two in the gym after this decadent meal, but I'm not leaving a bite behind. I'm going into a food coma," Ariana moans.

"Save room for something sweet."

"I may need to wait a little while before dessert."

"Then it's the perfect time for a film. Let's go to the theater."

"Is Evan's apartment nearby?"

"I have my own theater. You see, it's difficult for princes to attend regular cinemas, so Evan, Bri, and I all had small theaters installed in our apartments."

"That's convenient."

She means that's extravagant. It is, but a little privacy is worth it.

CHAPTER FORTY-ONE

XANDER

W e sit on a sofa, sharing a blanket and sipping wine, as we watch the film Ariana picked. My arm ends up around her shoulder, and she snuggles closer when it gets to a scary part.

When the villain is about to emerge from the shadows, I cradle her head against my shoulder, whispering in her ear, "Hold still. Don't jostle your head." She nods, and I kiss the top of her head. My lips tingle. If only there was a fraction of that spark with Constance, I wouldn't be dreading the marriage as much.

Ariana doesn't notice when my chef discreetly places a small tray of miniature desserts on the table beside the sofa. Reaching for one, I say, "Ariana, close your eyes and open your mouth."

"You're kidding, right?" She laughs.

"Don't worry, I guarantee you'll love this."

I feed her a bite and wait for her reaction. She gasps when she figures out what it is but then takes the rest of the mini-éclair in her mouth, moaning, "Mmm, it's incredibly delicious. But I can't believe you fed me that. I'm so embarrassed."

"Why are you embarrassed? I wanted you to have your favorite dessert. I wouldn't have missed seeing that look on your face again for anything."

She turns and stares at me with a look of surprise. I feel the need to make her smile all the damned time.

"Here, you've got a little cream and chocolate on your mouth. Let me get it for you." I rub my thumb across her bottom lip but manage to smear the chocolate rather than remove it. "That didn't work but maybe this will." I lean even closer, kissing her softly, my tongue tasting the chocolate and something distinctly Ariana.

At first, she doesn't respond, but when she parts her lips, allowing me to deepen the kiss, I relish the opportunity. She tastes like chocolate and vanilla, soft and luscious. We're both breathing heavy as I pull her onto my lap, massaging her perfectly round cheeks as I tilt her toward me, gently holding her against me. Her arms are wrapped around my neck, her mouth begging for more. Her nipples are so hard they press through our clothing, revealing her desire to me.

"We can't do this here. It's time for bed," I say, eventually, coming to my senses.

She pulls back and nods. "Yes. It's for the best."

Lifting Ariana into my arms, I head for the bedroom.

"I can walk, silly," she says, patting me on the arm.

"I'd rather carry you. Hang on." I growl, looking anywhere but her eyes. This woman is driving me over the fucking edge tonight with how much she sees right into my soul. If I keep looking back ... I'm not going to lose it—at least not yet.

She relaxes into my arms, and I hasten my pace.

"Xander, this isn't the way to the guestroom. It's on the other side of your apartment."

"I'm taking you to my bed," I say in a husky voice, pushing the door open.

"When you said we needed to go to bed, I thought you were ending things before they went too far."

"Just the opposite. Please tell me this is what you want too." Laying Ariana gently on my mattress, like a porcelain doll that might break, I gaze into her eyes.

"Oh, Xander, it is. But you're marrying someone else. We can't do this. We never should've kissed."

"I'm not marrying anyone tonight. I'm not in love with Constance. And most importantly, I'm not engaged. Tonight, it's just us—two consenting adults who are drawn to one another. If you tell me to stop, I will. But I've never wanted any woman as much as I want you. Please let us have this one night together."

She reaches for me as she searches my eyes. After what feels like an eternity, she nods, pulling my lips to hers.

"All I can promise you is this one night. I need to know you're still sure you want this?"

"I want tonight for us, too. I'd regret never being with you."

"Thank fuuuck." Our lips lock, our tongues tangle, our hands explore, and our hearts race. Then I remember her concussion and move to her ear, whispering, "We need to be careful with your head. I'll be gentle."

"I don't want gentle. If this is the one time that I live out my fantasies with you, I want all of you."

"You've been fantasizing about me?"

"I didn't mean to share that. It must be the head injury."

"I didn't hit *my* head, but you've still invaded my dreams. Our declaration of friendship confused the issue, or I would've acted on it sooner."

"Then stop talking and start acting out your dreams."

"Whatever you say." I pull her dress over her head and unclasp the front closure of her bra, pushing it away from her luscious breasts. I stop to stare. "You're magnificent, Ariana."

"Your clothes have to go too," she says. I happily begin undressing, watching her eyes follow my movements as my fingers slowly free each button.

"Can't you do that any faster?"

"Patience. We need to make this last."

She licks her lips when I finally toss my shirt to the side and begin unfastening my trousers. Pushing them down, along with my boxer briefs, reveals the elevated state of my desire for her.

"Damn!" she gasps as I climb onto the bed.

"Does that mean you like what you see?"

"You'll do," she teases, which earns her a playful pinch of her nipple. She laughs through a moan, and I yank off her knickers.

Parting her legs, mine slip between them. I kiss my way from her chest to her stomach, sliding my body slowly down hers. Moving lower, my mouth presses against her slick folds, my lips and tongue exploring. She rocks into me, moaning as I drive her desire higher.

"You're amazing." I growl, continuing to worship her, feeling her fingers tangle in my hair and pulling me even closer until her body tenses in impending release. With a cry of my name on her lips, she explodes in delicious ecstasy.

Slowly, I kiss my way up to her belly button, then to her beautiful breasts. With my mouth on one and palm on the other, I massage and tease her rock-hard nipples as she writhes under me, begging, "Please, Xander. I need more."

Aiming to please, I hastily roll on a condom from the bedside table and press into her. "Fuuuck! You feel so good. You're so tight."

I start moving slowly, wanting to make it last, but she's in control, pulling me back with demands to go faster as she wraps her legs around me.

I'm not going to last long with Ariana surrounding me with her entire body, making this feel more intimate than just a single night together.

"I'm coming now. Yes, yes, yes!" She groans.

We explode together, our bodies pulsing in harmony as if we were made for each other.

Collapsing on her, I carefully roll us onto our sides.

When our heart rates return to near normal, Ariana says, "That was incredible, but I need to clarify something. When you said we only had tonight, was that limited to one time tonight?" She grins the most beautiful smile ever, full of sarcasm and glee.

She truly is perfect.

With a hug and a little tickle, I roll us over and demonstrate exactly how unlimited one night can be.

The. Best. Sex. *Ever.*

Ariana is nestled against me, sleeping soundly as I run my fingers through her long curls and stare at the ceiling, filled with regret. Why did Ariana have to take herself out of contention to be my wife in this matchmaking adventure? My feelings for her are a thousand times stronger than they'll ever be for Constance.

Even though neither one of us wants a real relationship, wouldn't it be better to at least have a connection with the person you marry? And after tonight, we know the sex would be off the charts.

Maybe if I explain my thinking to Ariana, she'll reconsider her position. I will try to change her mind in the morning. I can't think of any woman but her now that we've crossed this line.

So much for just one night.

CHAPTER FORTY-TWO

ARIANA

A noise awakens me from a deep sleep. Attempting to stretch my arms, they don't move. It makes me panicky to wake up frozen in place.

Experience has taught me to use relaxation techniques, so I take a deep breath, count to ten, exhale, and try to stretch again. I still can't move.

Realization hits me. It's not because I'm half-asleep. It's because Xander's muscular arm has my torso pinned to the bed, and one of his legs is intertwined with mine, holding them in place.

My memories of last night weren't a dream. They were real. And based on the hard-as-steel erection pressing against my thigh, he's up for another round.

But last night was a one-time thing. A pleasure we both agreed to indulge in while the moment lasted. When Xander wakes up, I need to tell him it's time for me to move back to The Shores and stay there until the doctor clears me to fly home. I can't live in his apartment with my desire to be with him. It will be too painful for me to go through the motions now.

How did I end up so emotional over him? It doesn't make sense.

My goal was to avoid men and relationships and concentrate on my book. It's time to refocus on my writing. Distance from him will help.

Lost in my rambling thoughts, I don't notice that Xander is staring at me until he says, "You're beautiful in the morning."

"I doubt that but thank you." Looking at him, I'd swear steam is rising from him. He's so hot—bulging biceps, solid chest, tight ass, mischievous smile, tousled hair, and his desire for me on glorious display. Not to mention he is an amazingly generous lover. I'll never forget him. He's ruined me for everyone else.

"We need to talk, Ariana."

"Xander, it's okay. You will always be extraordinarily special to me, and last night was beyond fantastic. But you don't need to worry. I fully understand that there won't be a repeat. We don't need to talk." My phone buzzes.

"Ariana, last night was unexpected."

Buzz.

"We *do* need to talk, but maybe you should check your phone first," Xander says as he props himself up against the headboard.

Sitting up, he pulls my back against his chest, wrapping his arms around my waist as I open my messages.

My eyes go wide, and my body stiffens. "The nerve of her!"

"Ariana, what's wrong?" Xander asks, planting a soft kiss on my shoulder.

"Can you believe my former boss is asking me to help her after what she did?"

"What did she do?"

"After effectively firing me, Shelly expects me to help her out of a bind with a client's fundraiser. See." I hand him my phone.

"Ariana, take another look. This message was intended for someone named Maddie. It's not for you."

I repeatedly point to the screen. "No, that's me. I use my middle name Maddie for most work things. I've decided to use my proper first name for my writing career to separate the two. What's the big deal?"

Xander pulls back, turning to face me with narrowed eyes. "What's the big deal? You've been hiding the truth from me since day fucking one."

"What are you talking about? My name is Ariana Madison Montgomery. I grew up being called Maddie. It's all the same name. What are you going on about, Xander?"

"Bloody hell! It's all becoming clear now. How did I let myself be so royally deceived? You're Maddie from Platinum International. You worked with Shelly."

"I used to work there ... wait. How do you know the company's name is Platinum International?" I scrunch my face, turning to stare at him.

Xander pushes me away and climbs out of bed, waving his hands as he paces. "You know exactly how. Clearly Shelly told you who I am, and you orchestrated all of this."

"I do not understand a single word coming out of your mouth! You aren't making sense," I shout back.

"For fuck's sake, we worked together for over a year on the Clean Oceans fundraiser. We even casually flirted over the phone. How dare you pretend this whole time that you didn't know who I was? I must admit, you're one hell of an actor."

"Are you saying you're Alex Leonardo?" I ask as my hand flies to my mouth.

"You know damn well I'm Alexander Leonardo Constantine, Prince of Catalinius. Now get out!" He points to the door.

Yanking the sheet off the bed and clutching it to my chest, I shout, "I didn't know about your fake name. How dare you accuse me of lying, you two-faced bastard. You're the one who spent a whole year pretending to be Alex Leonardo. No wonder you wouldn't provide a photo for the fundraiser. You didn't want anyone to know your real identity. If anyone has been deceptive, it's you, Prince Xander!"

Fuming, but on the verge of tears, I turn and walk out of the room, head held high. Sprinting, I barely make it to the guestroom before the waterfall of tears flows down my cheeks. I'll be damned if he's going to see me cry after what he said to me.

CHAPTER FORTY-THREE

XANDER

I'm staring out the window in my bedroom when Edmund finally
appears in response to my text.

"Arrange for Ariana, or Maddie—whatever her name is—to leave
immediately."

"Sir, what are you talking about?"

"She lied. She's not who she said she was. Her presence here was
all a setup. I want her gone now."

"But sir, the doctor hasn't cleared her for travel yet, and the palace
police are insisting that all the women stay until the investigation is
complete."

"Fine. Have her removed to The Shores until she's allowed to
leave. I want security watching her at all times. I don't trust her."

"Forgive me, but are you certain this isn't some misunderstanding?" Edmund asks.

"You know I have zero tolerance for deception. Do as I say. Now!"

"I'll take care of it, sir." Edmund leaves.

Tossing my phone onto the bed, I pace. How the hell did I let
myself be tricked yet again? The last fifteen years were spent
protecting myself from exactly this type of deception. Then when my
defenses inadvertently fall, and I genuinely connect with someone,

she wasn't who she pretended to be. Hell, I came within a few minutes of trying to talk her into marrying me. That was too close.

Now there's no question about what must be done. It's far from ideal, but I'll marry Constance, provided she accepts the terms of my proposal.

Retrieving my phone, I text Mum to see if she can meet me this afternoon. She responds in the affirmative.

Rather than text my brother, I call.

"Evan, would you accompany me to the jewel vault this afternoon? I need to pick out an engagement ring."

"Congrats! Who are you proposing to?"

"Lady Constance." I sigh.

"Hmm. Despite the insistence that you two are only friends, I thought you might eventually end up with Ariana."

"She lied to me, so I threw her out. She's packing her bags now."

"What happened?"

"I'll tell you another time. Will you go with me to the vault or not?" I huff.

"Of course. Would you mind if I bring Cassandra? She'd love to see the jewels and will know more about what a woman would want than I do."

"Cassie's welcome to join us. It sounds like you're looking for a ring too."

"We're not there yet, but I'll win some points by giving her a tour of the vault. She loves jewelry." Evan chuckles.

There's one additional matter for me to attend to: texting Shelly.

Me: I'm transferring our account to another firm. When we retained Platinum International PR, I made it explicitly clear that my identity was to be protected from everyone involved, including your employees. It has come to my attention that you revealed my identity to Maddie. This breach of trust and unethical behavior is completely unacceptable.
Therefore, your services are no longer needed for fundraising and marketing for my charities. Please send a final invoice and cease all work.

Another minute here while Ariana is still in the guestroom is too long. Maybe working up a sweat in the gym will improve my current mood.

CHAPTER FORTY-FOUR

XANDER

At the jewel vault, I'm met by two black-suited guards stationed on each side of the steel door. Footfalls break the silence while I'm signing the register. And Mum, Evan, and Cassie join me as the guards enter their codes and open the heavy steel door.

Mum leads the way, explaining that each set of jewels is in its own case. The rings, bracelets, earrings, and tiaras are meticulously displayed on black velvet and satin stands in the chest-high glass displays.

A few steps in, I hear a gasp from behind me. Cassie is wide-eyed, her hand over her mouth.

"I'm sorry. I had no idea what to expect. This is so magnificent. It makes the jewelry exhibit at the Smithsonian Natural History Museum look small by comparison," she says.

"Tell Evan if you see anything you like." I wink.

She looks up at Evan. "What does he mean by that?"

"He's teasing me. Come on, Mum's going to explain the history of the various jewels to help Xander decide which ring to select."

Mum points out rings and tiaras with diamonds, emeralds, sapphires, rubies, pearls, and other stones that I know nothing about.

My mind spins, missing half of what she says. The thought of proposing is so foreign to me. It's surreal.

Trying to focus, I rub my face and take a few deep breaths.

"Xander, the jewelry sets with pearls are not available because they're my favorites," Mum says.

"Don't worry, after you named our sailboat *The Crown Pearl*, I know you want the pearls for yourself. Are there any others I should avoid?"

"There are a few other pieces, such as the ceremonial crowns, but I suggest you look around and see which ring would be your first choice. Then ask me. Keep in mind Lady Constance will wear the matching tiara for your wedding."

"I'm not sure where to start. Evan and Cassie, do you have any advice?"

"I've always heard that bigger is better." Evan snickers.

Cassie playfully slaps his arm. "Xander, you can't go wrong with any of the choices here. Go with your heart."

Mum says, "Xander, consider what Constance would want as you look around. You'll know what suits her when you see it. Evan and Cassie, follow me. I'll show you some interesting pieces on the other side of the vault. By the way, Cassie, what's your favorite stone?"

"It's rather overwhelming to see so many beautiful pieces in one place, but I do love emeralds," Cassie says.

"Then you must see Evan's great-grandmother's emerald jewels. The ring and tiara are spectacular. You may try them on," Mum says as they walk to the far side of the vault.

The problem is I don't know what Constance wants. She's never mentioned a favorite color. If it were Ariana, I'd pick the ring with the large yellow diamond in the center surrounded by white diamonds because when I first met her, she stood out like the moon surrounded by sparkling stars. She lit up that night. Too bad that was all a hoax.

Shaking myself from those thoughts, I wander from case to case. Stopping in front of one with a ring, tiara, bracelet, and necklace with white diamonds, I call out, "Mum, could you tell me about this set?"

They join me at the display case. Mum looks rather perplexed, but after a brief hesitation, she says, "This set belonged to your great-aunt. The platinum ring is set with a two-carat white diamond for the center stone and a half-carat trillion cut diamond on each side. The tiara is also set with white diamonds. It's one of the lighter-weight ones, which means it's comfortable to wear, but not as grand as many of the others."

"Am I allowed to select this ring?" I ask.

"You are," Mum says with a frown.

"Xander, that's a nice ring but given all the choices here, are you sure you don't want to pick something more unique? Did you see the yellow diamonds?" Evan asks.

"I can't give her a yellow diamond. It would remind me of someone else."

"Oh. Then definitely no yellow diamonds." Evan holds up his hands, palms out.

"We're done. Mum, may I take the ring with me? I plan to propose soon."

"You may. And Xander, when you propose, make it special for Lady Constance. A proposal should be a memorable moment," Mum says.

"I'll give it my best."

Texting Edmund, I leave the vault with the ring in the pocket of my trousers.

> Me: Did you arrange for Constance to be at the palace tonight? I need to add to the plans. Call me.

CHAPTER FORTY-FIVE

XANDER

Originally, I'd planned to meet Constance in the study to go over my proposed terms, and if she agreed, present the ring. But taking Mum's words to heart, the meeting has been moved to one of the palace's rooftop terraces, where Edmund told the staff to set up something romantic.

They did. Candles and white rose petals line the path from the door to sofas surrounding a firepit on the outdoor terrace. Twinkling lights are strung overhead. Champagne is chilling in a wine stand. Servers stand at the ready. Mum would be pleased.

Right on schedule, Lady Constance appears. Her shoulder-length auburn hair creates a striking contrast with her sleeveless, ankle-length white dress that skims her body. She could be a model for any top magazine. She even poses, seemingly waiting to be photographed before joining me.

Taking her hand, I raise it to my lips. "Constance, you look lovely tonight. I'm glad you're here."

"It is my pleasure."

With a nod to the servers, they pour champagne and present a silver tray of chocolate truffles and fresh strawberries.

"Please have a seat. We need to discuss a few things with you."

"Of course."

Dismissing the servers, we have some privacy now. "I want to talk about this matchmaking process. It has been rather short, and we've had limited time to get to know each other. Do you have any questions for me or concerns about life in Catalinius?"

"That's so considerate. Catalinius is a beautiful island. Anyone would want to live here. I can't imagine what would concern me but thank you for asking."

"You've grown up as a royal, so you know it can be difficult. Having watched Queen Josephine, life as a queen can be an even bigger challenge at times. Are you certain you would want to put yourself in that position?"

"Are you asking me to?" she asks coyly.

The setting for this proposal is intended to be romantic, so Constance will have a proper story to share. But I need to explain the terms of my offer before this goes any further.

"Constance, we haven't known each other long enough for either of us to promise, or expect, more than a union of two royals. If we were to marry, we'd be fulfilling our duties as we were raised to do. What I *can* offer you is the title of princess and soon the title of queen. You'd have almost anything you could ever want or need at your disposal. However, I have one important condition." Pausing, I look down.

"What is it?" she asks.

"We'll lead rather separate lives other than to produce an heir for Catalinius. Could you be happy with that?"

She nods. "As you said, we royals are raised to put duty first, so I'm prepared to do exactly that. So, yes, I'd be quite content with the arrangement you outlined as long as you're discreet and don't embarrass me publicly."

"Of course. I would expect the same of you."

"Understood."

I pull out my great-aunt's ring. Staring into her deep brown eyes, I say, "Constance, you're a charming and beautiful woman. I'm fortunate that fate has brought our paths together and given us the opportunity to join our royal families. Will you do me the honor of marrying me?"

She smiles. "I will."

Slipping the ring onto her finger, I pull her up into my arms. We kiss. It's rather chaste. How bizarre is it to have never kissed before proposing?

At my signal, the servers return to refill our glasses, and we enjoy the truffles and strawberries.

"Let's talk through some of the logistics. I'm sure you would prefer more time to plan, but our wedding will need to take place rather quickly," I say.

"I understand that we must marry before your father's birthday."

"Correct. The queen suggested we have the engagement ball this weekend with our wedding the following weekend. She's been planning with the assumption I'd marry before Father's deadline. Many of the arrangements are already in place."

Placing her hand on my arm, Constance says, "Please don't worry about me. I'm fine with that plan."

"Thank you. We'll need to meet with the palace PR team and the wedding planners early tomorrow. Will that work for you?"

"Yes. That's fine. It's going to be a whirlwind."

"It is."

We sip champagne and discuss plans for another half hour.

When conversation begins to slow, Constance says, "It's been quite an evening, and it's late. Would it be okay if I go back to The Shores now? I want to share the news with friends and rest up before tomorrow? I know it will be chaotic."

"Of course. I'll walk you to the car."

Two hours and a few drinks since the proposal, my arse is planted in a chair in the palace's library. Shaking the ice in my old-fashioned glass to draw out one last sip of scotch, it's not enough to improve my mood. I should be relieved that Constance agreed to marry me. She checks all the boxes. Father can retire and travel with Mum. All is well with the world. So why am I so completely depressed?

Grabbing the decanter from the side table, I pour another double. Oh hell, forget that, I might as well fill the glass. Taking a long sip, I'm hoping for some answers when my phone vibrates. It's Shelly responding to my text.

> Shelly: Your Highness, please reconsider. I can absolutely assure you that I have never revealed your identity to anyone, much less to my former employee. Maddie didn't know you are a prince. There must be a misunderstanding. We have had a highly successful working relationship with your charities. Please give me the opportunity to discuss this with you.

That's just great—a reminder of the woman I can't have. Why do I crave another night with Ariana even after she so thoroughly deceived me?

Or did she?

If Shelly is telling the truth, then it's possible she didn't know who I am. Did I jump to the wrong conclusion?

Now I'm engaged to Constance. Fuck.

CHAPTER FORTY-SIX

ARIANA

My request to go home to New York was denied. Instead, Edmund orchestrated my abrupt exit from the palace. And now he's sitting stiffly beside me as the black Mercedes speeds toward The Shores.

Forty-five minutes later, the driver drops us at a side entrance to Xander's beach house. "Follow me quietly if you prefer privacy."

He guides me through a service entrance, along an empty hallway, into a narrow staircase, and finally to my suite. Thanks to his kindness, we avoid Jessica and Constance, who are still here. I'm not ready to deal with the questions my tear-stained face would elicit.

At the door, Edmund gestures for me to enter. I sigh, relieved to have made it through the gauntlet from palace to privacy.

Unfortunately, that sense of relief is premature. A hulk of a man, dressed in a black suit, hands clasped behind his back, and feet spread shoulder-width apart, is waiting for us.

"Who are you and what are you doing in my room?" I ask, crossing my arms.

Edmund responds, "Ariana, this is Charles. He'll be *accompanying* you during the remainder of your stay in Catalinius."

Charles nods without speaking.

"Is my life in danger? Do I need a bodyguard?"

Edmund frowns and looks down.

Then it hits me. Steaming, I ask, "Are you serious? Xander doesn't trust me? He hired someone to guard me?" While packing and during the ride here, my emotions flip flopped between variations of anger and hurt, but right now, I'm completely pissed off.

Still refusing to look me in the eye, Edmund says, "Consider him your companion. If you need anything, he'll be stationed near your door."

"How fucking dare Xander treat me as a prisoner and have me guarded? Am I to be locked away in this suite until I'm cleared to fly home? You must be kidding me."

"You're not a prisoner. You can go anywhere you wish … with Charles. But I assume you'd prefer meals in your room for now given how upset you are," Edmund says, and Charles nods again.

I grit my teeth, staring at them. I'm living a nightmare. "I haven't done anything wrong other than stupidly fall for a prince. This is all Xander's fault," I whisper as my anger flips back to hurt, and ugly tears fall.

"Forgive me, but I must return to the palace now. And for what it's worth, I'm sorry." Edmund bows slightly and backs out of the room.

Glaring at Charles, my fists clench. "Please leave."

As the door clicks shut behind my effing guard, I throw myself face down on the bed, sobbing into the pillow.

My only sin was wanting to use my first name! I didn't hide anything. He never asked anything specific about my employment. I would've told him. Xander was the one doing business under an alias and misled *me*. It crushes me he's now convinced I'm some horrible person when he's the liar.

Eventually, the tears dry, and exhaustion sets in. Closing my eyes, sleep takes over.

Someone knocking at my door ends my blissful escape from reality. The room is pitch black. Hours must've passed. Releasing the pillow that I'm practically strangling, I climb out of bed. Rubbing my swollen, sore eyes while opening the door, I'm confronted with Charles, carrying a tray of food and a bottle of wine.

"Ms. Montgomery, you missed dinner, so the kitchen prepared something for you before they cleaned up for the evening." Charles places the tray on the coffee table.

"Thank you, but I'm not hungry. Do you know what time it is?"

"It's 9:30 p.m."

"The bottle of wine is calling me, but you're welcome to the food."

"I've already eaten, so I'll leave it in case you change your mind. Goodnight, Miss Montgomery." Charles closes the door on his way out.

The aroma of the food is making my stomach turn. Hoping fresh air will calm my queasiness, I retreat to the balcony with the bottle of wine, a glass, and a corkscrew. Falling into a chair at the small table and listening to the waves, I stare into the black nothingness.

With a full, and I mean *completely* full, glass of red wine, I reflect on the last twenty-four hours. I should regret sleeping with Xander, but I don't. When we first met, we had such an immediate ease with each other.

Initially, I thought it was just friendship. That's all I wanted, but then without trying, the chemistry grew from a simmer to a sizzle to full-on need. It's as if my subconscious knew that we weren't complete strangers and had already passed the initial flirting stage. He'd already softened my protective shell.

It's unimaginable that Xander accused me of lying and manipulating him. How could I have figured out he was Alex? My emotions are all over the place. I'm hurt, mad, disappointed, and mourning the loss of a love that was never mine. Shit, am I in love with him? How did that happen when we weren't even dating? How will I recover from Xander?

I'm such a fool to have thought one night would be enough. It wasn't even close to enough. But how can my body still want Xander when he doesn't trust me and said such awful things to me? He even has a guard at my door, treating me like some criminal planning to hurt him. That should be enough to make me never want to see him again.

Refilling my glass, I hear a muffled conversation. Someone must be on another one of the private balconies. It's a woman whispering. Did she say, "The prince proposed"?

I lean forward, straining to hear over the wind and crashing waves, but can't recognize the voice. It could be almost anyone.

Her voice is low and faint, but it sounded like she said, "There's no need to worry, Uncle Frank. The plan is working. Be patient. He won't be king."

After a long pause, she says something else that's indecipherable and then something about no backup plan.

Oh no! Someone is planning to kill Xander or his father.

I rush out of the suite, hoping to find the woman before it's too late. But Charles grabs my shoulders and stops me. Straining against his arms, I raise my voice, saying, "I heard someone talking on the phone on the adjoining balcony. They're threatening Xander or the king. We have to find out who it is and stop them."

"Miss Montgomery, you've had quite a bit to drink. Perhaps you fell asleep and had a bad dream."

"I've had a little wine. Okay, a lot. But I know what I heard. Hurry, before she's gone."

"Fine. Follow me."

The French doors at the end of the hall open onto a large balcony around the corner from mine. When we open the doors, the balcony's deserted. *Damn.*

"Miss Montgomery, no one is here. You must've had a bad dream."

Back in my room, I frantically find my phone and text Alex, who I now know is really Xander. Tapping my toe, I impatiently wait for the familiar "Delivered" confirmation. It never comes. Shit. The asshole blocked me.

I pace the floor. There must be a way to get word to him. He needs to know what was said on that balcony. Perhaps Edmund would take my call. That won't work. Charles won't back me up.

Then words I overheard register. Did the mystery woman say the prince proposed?

Gut punched again.

He couldn't even wait one day after our magical night together before proposing to someone else. Didn't it mean anything to him? Emptiness envelopes me. This is more devastating than what Brian or the others ever did. When those other assholes cheated on me, I wanted to make them hurt as much as they hurt me. This is different. My heart is burning with pain, knowing I'll never have his arms around me again. I love him so much it's crushing my soul. The way he made love to me last night, it's impossible to imagine he doesn't care about me too.

If only he would've listened to reason rather than jumped to ridiculous conclusions. Now he's engaged to someone else, and even our friendship is in a shambles.

If I don't do something to warn him, it won't matter. He'll be dead soon.

CHAPTER FORTY-SEVEN

ARIANA

I t's morning, and I'm hungover, out of tears, and desperately worried about Xander and his father.

Water, ibuprofen, and a shower later, I'm still trapped in my room, mentally pacing because my head is throbbing too much to actually pace. There must be a way to get word to someone who can protect Xander and the king.

I'm plotting my escape when there's a knock on the door. Hopefully, breakfast comes with a bottle of champagne that can be used to club Charles over the head, giving me time to run to freedom.

To my shock, it's Evan's girlfriend Cassie with breakfast for two. "What are you doing here?"

"Evan's concerned about his brother. Xander's moping but refuses to talk about it. We suspect something happened between the two of you, so Evan suggested I check on you to see if we can help. Please tell me what happened between you and Xander."

"There's no time, but I'm relieved to see you. Xander's in danger, but he blocked my calls. I overheard a woman on the phone last night out on the balcony. She threatened Xander and his father. That's why I need your help. We have to get word to him."

"Come with me. My driver will take us to the palace. Evan will know what to do. You can tell me about you and Xander on the way," Cassie says.

We blow past Charles. He follows, protesting. I explain everything on our way to the palace to find Evan.

When I finish the story, Cassie asks, "But you two got along extremely well, right?"

"We did. Now that I know Xander is Alex, it's not surprising we became fast friends. We worked together for a year, even though we never met in person. We even flirted a little over the phone."

"Evan and I could see the chemistry between you two. You became more than friends, didn't you?"

"Yes, a lot more."

"Then why is he settling for Constance?" Cassie asks.

"I wasn't looking for a relationship, and Xander wrongly believes I deceived him."

"This is a colossal misunderstanding. Are you still opposed to a relationship?"

"No. But he already proposed. It's too late."

"We'll see about that. But first, we need to keep him alive, which means we need to convince him to talk with you."

CHAPTER FORTY-EIGHT

XANDER

I tossed and turned all night. Half the time, nightmares took over, and I dreamed my wedding to Constance was like a funeral. The other half was spent staring at the ceiling trying to come to terms with Ariana's betrayal.

Then there's the text from Shelly. It has me second-guessing my conclusions about Ariana. What if she didn't know Alex Leonardo was really me? Was my reaction too extreme because of my college girlfriend's unforgivable betrayal?

It's just ... seeing the text on Ariana's phone, made me feel like such a fool for repeating the same mistake. The sense of being used again by another woman was too much, particularly when letting Ariana in was so unexpected. It was the first time since college my heart opened for someone. And damn it if I didn't fall in love—and then boom! Ariana turns out to be someone else entirely.

Eventually giving up on sleep, I shower and make coffee. While reviewing my briefing papers for today's appointments, Evan and Cassie arrive.

"Xander, you may be in danger. Can we talk?"

"Come in. What's this about?"

"Cassandra can explain."

"Let's go to the kitchen. I'll make more coffee."

Cassie's wringing her hands. What's with that? How would she become aware of an actual threat to me? It's probably nothing.

When everyone has coffee in hand, Cassie looks at me.

"Evan was worried about what happened between you and Ariana, so I went to see her. She was frantic. She's convinced someone is trying to kill you or your father. She tried to contact you, but you blocked her calls. You need to meet with her."

"If there was a real threat, she would have told Charles."

"She did. He brushed her off, but I believe her."

"What if she's a stellar actor, and this is a trick to see me."

"Why would she want to do that? Xander, Ariana is hurting. I don't think for a minute that it's an act," Cassie says.

"I don't know what to think."

"Meet with Ariana and let her tell you what she overheard. Do you have anything to lose? What if the threat is directed at Father? You can't ignore it simply because you're angry with her," Evan says.

"I'll think about it," I say.

As they're leaving, Evan lingers behind. "I don't care what you say. We saw the way you and Ariana interacted with each other. You were more than friends. At least talk with her. You need closure. If you don't, you'll regret it, which is not the way to go into a marriage."

Risking Father's life is not an option, so Edmund arranged for Ariana to meet with Carlson, the palace's chief investigator, to follow up on the threat to the monarchy. At my suggestion, the location is chosen to avoid the prying ears of the palace. Charles knows where to take her. Ariana hasn't been told where the meeting is taking place because security is of the upmost importance if there may truly be a threat.

I've wavered as to whether to attend the meeting. It's doubtful that she wants to see me after my harsh accusations. The problem is that

Evan's parting words haunt me. Will lack of closure eat away at me? Would seeing her again help me determine once and for all whether my accusations were justified?

Ultimately, my decision is to go, so an hour later, Carlson, Robert, and I arrive early and wait for Ariana downstairs.

Before long, footsteps click on the stone stairs. As they near, we overhear Ariana ask Charles, "Why are we at a winery?" He doesn't answer. The footsteps grow louder.

As she enters the barrel room, our eyes meet. She clasps her hands over her cheeks, coming to an abrupt halt.

"Hello, Ariana. Thank you for coming today. We're here because we need complete privacy," I explain as Charles and Robert each move to guard one of the staircases leading down to this room. "Please join us."

"Um. I didn't know you'd be here, Your Highness," she says as she moves closer and dips into a curtsy.

"Ariana Montgomery, this is Chief Inspector Carlson."

"Please tell us about the threat you reported. Take your time and don't leave out any details," he says.

Ariana explains the conversation she overheard, along with her frustration with Charles for delaying her attempt to catch the woman on the balcony.

"At the time you heard this one-sided conversation, what did you think the woman meant?" Carlson asks.

"When she said, 'He won't be king,' I assumed it was a threat to Prince Xander or King Louis."

"Couldn't she have meant that my father was going to retire because I'll be getting married and taking the throne?" I ask.

"She mentioned Prince Xander had proposed, but I couldn't tell whether that was part of the plan or whether she was reassuring the other person that it wouldn't impact what they were discussing. After the sabotage at the stables and on the yacht, I immediately interpreted the statement as a threat. I don't understand why no one is taking it seriously."

"Ms. Montgomery," Carlson says, "I assure you that the palace police take all threats to the monarchy seriously. That's why I'm following up with you today. We'll find out who was at The Shores last night."

Ariana lets out a deep breath. "That's a relief. I felt helpless when Charles didn't believe me."

"One last question. Who else have you told about what you overheard?" Carlson asks.

"I've only told Cassie, Evan, Charles, and the two of you."

"Please don't mention it to anyone else. While you likely misinterpreted the conversation, we cannot take any chances. Don't go anywhere without Charles close by to protect you. If it was an actual threat, you could also be in danger," Carlson says.

"My understanding is that Charles is not protecting me but rather protecting the monarchy *from* me. Apparently, Prince Xander has the misguided notion that I'm a threat. He's under the mistaken impression that I lied and orchestrated being here. But I did not know that His Royal Highness and I had met by phone prior to the reception in London. I had no clue Alex Leonardo was his alias." Ariana huffs as she hugs herself.

Turning to the inspector, I say, "Inspector Carlson, thank you for handling this matter personally. I know you need to follow up immediately, so please go ahead. I would like a word with Ariana in private now."

"Thank you, sir," Carlson says as he departs.

Ariana is sending me mixed signals. Her crossed arms and clenched jaw send one signal, but her sad eyes are trying to hold in tears, which conveys something else entirely. My first instinct is to hug her, but my judgment now is questionable at best.

Instead, I say, "Ariana, I apologize for my harshness yesterday. I should've given you an opportunity to defend yourself before I had you removed."

Her voice is tight, low, and barely controlled as she responds, "Your Highness, that's a lame apology at best. I shouldn't have had to *defend* myself. You shouldn't have assumed the worst after what we'd shared. You should have asked me what I knew or didn't know.

Instead, you jumped to the worst possible conclusion, which was dead wrong."

She closes her eyes tightly. I watch her inhale deeply and exhale slowly. She's trying to stop herself from lashing out further. I'm not sure how to respond.

When her eyes open, her neck moves as she swallows hard, and continues, "You didn't even have the courtesy to discuss the situation with me. Instead, you kicked me out of your room with only a sheet to cover my naked body and assigned a guard to shadow me like I was a threat to you and your country. And you engaged in that incredibly rude and humiliating treatment of me merely because I used my real first name for my novel instead of my nickname. Tell me, how does that supposed sin justify your abhorrent behavior toward me?"

Her lip trembles as the tears spill from her eyes.

Shite. I know now. Without a doubt, she's been telling the truth all along. "I'm an ass. It's a poor excuse. As we discussed before, my trust issues go back a long way."

"You know that I have trust issues too. And you've done nothing to restore my faith in men. Tell me, did you propose to Constance the same day you woke up in bed with me?"

"Yes," I whisper, staring at the ground. I can't look her in the eye, hearing how scummy that makes me sound. "In my defense, at that time I thought you'd lied to me. Now I know that wasn't true. At the time, I didn't."

"Will you be happy with Constance?"

"It doesn't matter. It's done now."

"You don't have to go through with it. Your father has no right to force you into a marriage."

"I have no choice at this point. It'll be for the best. That doesn't have to change what we have. Our night together will be a cherished memory. I'll be forever grateful to you, and I hope our friendship can survive my mistake. Will you forgive me?"

"You hurt me deeply. I care about you enough though to forgive you. And congratulations. I wish you and Constance the best." Her lips twitch upward in a half smile that doesn't quite meet her eyes.

"The winery was told I'm here for a private tasting. We have wine that's going to waste. Will you join me in a toast? Please."

She nods.

Handing her a tasting of the white wine in front of us, I say, "May our friendship survive my stupidity."

"I can drink to that, Your Highness," she says with a spark of mischievousness returning to her bloodshot eyes.

As we reach for glasses of the red wine, I say, "Your turn. Take your best shot," dreading what is coming.

She closes her eyes, leaving me to await the dagger coming my way. I can almost hear the seconds tick by. Finally, she raises her glass to me, saying, "May you rule Catalinius with enough strength to overcome adversity, enough conviction to do what's right, and enough compassion to help those in need."

We clink glasses and drink.

"You are remarkable. You repeatedly surprise me in such amazing and unexpected ways. Your toast was more generous and supportive than I deserve. Thank you. I'll try to live up to your lofty expectations of me."

"You better. Your people deserve that." She nods. "By the way, this red wine is exceptional. The white is nice too, but I much prefer the red."

"As do I." I sigh. It's ironic that she has the same tastes as me, but I'm marrying the woman who doesn't.

"Ariana, let me say it again. Please believe me. I truly am sorry for being upset yesterday. I was wrong. I now know that you didn't have a clue who I was, just as I didn't know who you were."

"Thank you."

"I have an idea. You can spend the rest of your sabbatical at the palace or at The Shores and finish your book. If you need longer, you could work as a PR adviser for me. We could plan my fundraisers together. We were a great team in the past, and I don't want to lose the friendship we've developed. What do you say?"

"Xander, I appreciate the offer, but I can't stay. Our friendship is important to me, despite the rocky part, but I doubt Constance will appreciate one of the other candidates remaining nearby. She doesn't know that I was never in the running to marry you. It's time for me to go home."

"The offer stands if you change your mind," I say, giving her a quick hug. Turning, I stride toward the staircase and bolt up the stone steps.

The waiting car shuttles me back to the palace where Mum and Constance are waiting to discuss wedding plans. Today is taking me on an emotional rollercoaster.

CHAPTER FORTY-NINE

ARIANA

Standing at the bottom of the palace's imposing stone steps, I wonder how to make it through the most awkward evening of my life—Xander and Constance's engagement party.

Why did the palace even invite me? It's beyond strange to have received an invitation from the king and queen themselves. I tried to decline it, but Edmund informed me that a guest of the royal family must accept such an invitation.

It's doubtful they would have physically forced me to attend, but my mom and Meredith would expect me to be polite and follow protocol. Too bad I didn't know until tonight that Jessica was going to feign illness to get out of coming. I could've done the same. Since she told Xander she wasn't interested in marrying him, she has kept to herself, so we haven't talked.

I let out a slow breath through my mouth and prepare to look happy. Lifting the skirt of my long periwinkle-blue dress, it's time to start my climb. With each deliberate step, I give myself a silent pep talk: *I've got this. No crying tonight. It's ending the way it should. I have awesome memories of one orgasm-filled night with Xander. Nothing else was promised. I have the info about matchmaking for my book. Mission accomplished. It's all good.*

Finally, reaching the top and cementing my smile, I'm ready to savor every moment of this once-in-a-lifetime palace gala. Yes, I've got this, or at least, I'll fake it until it's over.

Handing my invitation to a white-gloved tux-clad man, he reviews and returns it, gesturing for me to enter, saying, "Please follow the red carpet to the ballroom."

The instructions weren't necessary. No one will get lost given the long line of people ahead, leading the way. As the parade of guests slowly moves forward, my eyes scan everywhere, trying to memorize each detail of this spectacular palace from the statues to the oil paintings to the intricate woodwork on the walls and ceiling. I'm so lost in thought, the couple behind me has to gently nudge me to move forward.

At the ballroom entrance, the gentleman checks my invitation again. With practiced formality, he announces, "Miss Ariana Montgomery of the United States of America."

It's a living fairytale. Well, not exactly. The ending's wrong, but it's still magical.

Carefully, I maneuver down the three steps to where King Louis and Queen Josephine are greeting each guest.

I dip into what hopefully is a proper curtsy as Queen Josephine says, "Welcome, Miss Montgomery. My sons speak highly of you."

Her penetrating eyes fix on mine, searching for something.

"Your Majesty, it's a pleasure to meet you."

The queen says to the king, "This is Prince Xander's *good* friend from New York." The king politely welcomes me and moves on to the next guest.

Why did Xander mention me to his mother? It doesn't matter though.

I take a glass of wine from a passing waiter and survey the room. My body relaxes when Cassie's friendly face approaches.

"It's a relief to see someone I know," I say.

"Agreed. I wasn't sure you'd come, but I'm so glad you did."

"I was told I didn't have a choice."

"You're probably right. I'm still learning all the ins and outs of royal protocol." She laughs as Evan walks up and places his arm around her shoulders in an unexpected PDA that makes me warm all over. Cassie and Evan have found true love and aren't afraid to let the world know.

"Where are Xander and Constance?" I ask.

"They'll make their grand entrance in a few minutes," Evan says.

As we chat, my outer demeanor is calm enough, but I find myself drinking wine a little faster than advisable and sampling each appetizer that's offered.

So far, I've had spicy crab-filled wonton cups, gougères, a ham-and-asparagus puff pastry bite, and something topped with caviar. I can't help myself. It's stress eating. I'm internally frazzled waiting to see Xander and Constance together for the first time since they became engaged.

I'm snagging my second glass of wine when a trumpet sounds. All eyes turn to the far end of the ballroom where Xander and Constance are gracefully entering. Xander's perfectly fitting, snug black tuxedo is enough to make any woman's panties melt, but what it does to me is at another level. The heat wave that passes over me is unbearable. I was such an idiot not to have given us a real chance from the start.

With each step he takes, my emotions rise. I'll always regret that I wasn't open to the possibility of a relationship with Xander from the beginning. My stomach clenches. Why did I let the asshole Brian ruin something that could have been a once-in-a-lifetime love?

I need to hold it together until they pass. Buckle up. Stiff upper lip and all that rubbish ... I bite my lip and press my fingernails into my palm, hoping the pain will keep the tears from falling. You've got this; just another minute or two.

As they near us, Xander nods to Evan. Then Xander's eyes lock with mine, and his eyebrows shoot up. It hits me then. He didn't know I'd be here. How can that be? As they pass, Xander's head turns, keeping me in sight a few seconds longer. Constance whispers something to him, returning his focus to their procession toward his waiting parents.

The breath I've been holding escapes in a whoosh, causing Evan and Cassie to look at me.

"Please excuse me, I need to check my makeup," I say.

Hurrying out a side door, I go in search of a little privacy. I find myself on an outside terrace and spot a tall potted plant with dense foliage next to a pillar at the far end. Perfect.

Hiding behind the plant, I gaze into the night sky and again question why the king and queen invited me. I'd thought Xander wanted me here to show our friendship was intact. But clearly, he didn't expect me. His parents must've invited me by mistake. I'm plotting my exit to return to The Shores when footsteps click against the tile, growing louder as they approach. Before revealing myself to head back into the ballroom, I hear angry whispers.

A man says, "Are you trying to double-cross me? You must break up with him tonight."

"I'm not going to break up with him," a woman says.

Shit, that's Constance speaking! I lean closer to the plant and can barely see them through a small gap in the leaves.

"You know the plan. This wedding cannot, and will not, take place," he says.

"Uncle Frank, I'll soon be the queen of Catalinius. I'm not giving up that opportunity for your business deal. You have plenty of money already."

"Yes, you *are* giving it up. I've got too much riding on this. Xander cannot become king. He'll destroy my drilling business. I promise you that I'll not let that happen."

"I'll tell Xander what you've done." She huffs.

"That's priceless, sweetheart. You drugged the horse, released the butterflies, and sabotaged the boat. It wasn't me. I didn't tell you to kill anyone." He grabs her by the wrist. "So, you won't be telling Xander anything."

She struggles, attempting to free herself, growling, "Let me go. I didn't have a choice. You blackmailed me. You threatened to bleed my trust dry. Besides, no one will ever prove I did those things, but they'll believe that you did them. You're willing to do anything to protect your precious ocean drilling rights."

"Don't cross me, you spoiled rotten bitch. I promise you'll regret it."

"Watch me. I'm going to be queen. You can't touch me." She breaks free and disappears from my view from behind the plant.

The clicking of her high heels fades, and Frank mutters, "Oh, yes, I can. And then I'll take care of the prince."

A soft, involuntary gasp escapes before my hand covers my mouth. I have to find Xander and tell him what they said. Pressing myself against the railing, I try to hide better. Instead, I trip and accidentally drop my wine glass. It crashes to the ground with a thud as it shatters.

Frank whirls around the plant, grabs me, and twists my arm behind my back. I try to scream, but he shoves a wadded handkerchief into my mouth. He quickly forces me against the railing and positions a knife against my throat.

Heart pounding, I stomp my right heel, aiming for his foot but miss. He presses the cold tip of the blade harder against my neck, piercing my skin. I cringe, sensing blood trickling down my neck. My mind races. This can't be real.

"Either quit fighting me, or I'll end this now. Nod if you understand."

Having no choice, I nod. Tears well in my eyes, and my body sags. I thought losing Xander was my worst nightmare until now. Frank is going to kill us both.

"We're going to walk toward the door behind me, and you're going to open it. Now turn around and move."

He grabs my upper arm with one hand and shoves the tip of the knife against my lower back with the other. Slowly shuffling forward, we reach double doors, and he pushes me into an empty office.

Shoving me toward a door next to the desk, he says, "Open it."

I do. It's a small coat closet.

Think. Do something before he kills you and shoves you into this closet.

But there's no time. He slams me into the back wall. My head explodes. My shoulder goes numb. Blackness engulfs me as the lock clicks.

CHAPTER FIFTY

XANDER

E van, Cassie, and I are talking when a woman shouts, "Help me!"
It's Constance! She's rushing into the ballroom, holding her
side, and screaming as she falls to the floor.

My head swivels when Harper's familiar voice yells, "No! No! No!"

She's following closely behind and drops a bloody knife near
Constance.

Guards seize Harper as we rush to Constance. "Someone, get the
medics, now!" I order.

Her white dress is torn and stained. Ripping off my jacket, I press
it onto the wound in her side. "You're going to be ok. Don't worry.
They've got Harper."

She whispers, "No, it's not ..."

"What did you say?" I ask, but she turns ghostly white and sags
against the marble floor, lifeless.

The medics push me away and take over. As Robert helps me to
my feet, I rub my eyes. It's unbelievable that Harper would resort to
this. She has always been annoying, but we seriously underestimated
Harper's violent tendencies. Constance didn't deserve her wrath.
What if Constance dies? She can't.

Evan places a firm hand on my shoulder. "The medics need space to help Constance. You can't do anything else to help right now," he whispers.

We walk a few yards away, and Evan signals for Cassie to join us. "It'll be okay. They'll take care of her," she whispers, a strained look on her face.

I nod, sucking in a breath through gritted teeth. Plastering on my go-to neutral expression, I turn back to watch the medics as they work. My body's numb, and my mouth's so dry.

"Evan, I need something to drink."

"Robert, please bring a glass of water quickly. He's pale. Xander, are you okay? Let's find a chair where you can sit for a moment."

"No. I'm fine. My emotions are confusing me. I want Constance to be okay, but it's like I'm an outsider watching a scene play out before me. Shouldn't I be panicked? What's wrong with me?"

"There's no right or wrong way to react. You're in shock. Have a drink of water and catch your breath," Evan says.

The water helps.

Leaning toward Evan, I cover my mouth so no one will hear. "Where are our parents?"

"When the guards saw the knife, they hustled them out."

"Why didn't they remove us as well?"

"Robert was with you instantly, and the guards immediately detained Harper. We weren't in danger," Evan says.

Time moves in slow motion. Guests are clumped in small groups, murmuring softly, their eyes moving between me on the sidelines and Constance sprawled in the center of the floor. Tired of being on display, I shift to stand on the other side of Evan and Cassie.

What is taking the medics so long? They need to get Constance to the hospital. Turning to Robert, who is always nearby, I ask, "Do you have a car ready, so we can follow the ambulance?"

His response is interrupted with "Owwww!" Ariana is slipping down the marble stairs into the ballroom.

Running toward her, a path quickly clears to let me through. I kneel beside her and nestle her to me. Her dress is splattered with small red spots. "What happened? Did Harper hurt you too?"

She moans as she holds her shoulder. Blood is trickling from a cut on her neck and clumping in the waves of her long hair.

"It's all right. The guards have captured Harper. You're safe now."

She looks at me with narrowed eyes, whispering, "Harper didn't do this. You have to stop Frank and Constance. *They* killed Everly."

"What? Constance? That's doesn't make sense. She's been stabbed. And who is Frank?"

"Constance's uncle. He's here somewhere. You have to stop him. He has a knife. He's going to hurt you. Ohhhh. My head is throbbing …" She groans as her eyes flutter shut and her body goes limp.

No! Not again. I can't lose her. She's too important to me. "We need help here! Ariana's hurt. Hurry!" I yell.

"I've already radioed for assistance and told the guards not to let anyone leave the palace. They are locking the front gates now." Robert says.

More medics arrive and gently remove Ariana from my arms. I don't want to let go, but for the second time tonight, Evan's hand is on my shoulder. I nod.

Turning to Robert, I say, "We need to hurry and find Frank, whoever he is. He's probably outside trying to leave now."

"Cassie, please stay with Ariana. I'm going with Xander," Evan says.

Robert and I take off running, with Evan on our heels. We skid to a stop at the top of the palace steps, looking for anyone trying to leave.

Evan points toward the main gates, saying, "That's Franco's car. Robert, don't let that Jaguar leave the palace."

"Don't worry. The gates are locked. I already radioed for the guards to lock the gates. He won't get past them, sir."

The purple jaguar careens toward the palace gates at the far end of the drive. He's not braking.

Boom! The jaguar smashes into the locked iron gates at full speed.

We're frozen in place, staring.

CHAPTER FIFTY-ONE

ARIANA

A warm white light glows through my eyelids, causing me to squeeze them tighter. That hurts worse than the light. And what's that strong, floral scent? Oh, it's roses, my favorite. There must be dozens and dozens of roses.

Oh no! Did I die? Is this my funeral? Is that why there's a bright white light? I'm so confused, and my head is going to explode.

Do you feel pain when you're dead? Who knows? This could be a nightmare. Surely, I'll wake up in a minute. Trying to move my arms, they feel like lead weights. I'm stuck in place. Last time this happened, Xander was entangled with me. I wish that explained my current situation, but I know better.

There's a muffled voice. "Ariana, please wake up."

It sounds like Xander. It can't be. He wouldn't be here. And if I'm dead, he wouldn't be trying to wake me up. He'd know it wouldn't work.

"I heard her moan," a woman says.

She sounds like Cassie.

A warm hand strokes mine, "Ariana, wake up for me."

I shiver from the touch.

"She moved her finger, that's a good sign, right?" the Xander-sounding guy says.

"A good sign of what?" I murmur through parched lips.

"Thank fuck. You're finally awake," he says, kissing the back of my hand.

"Does that mean I'm not dead? Where am I?" I barely crack my eyelids apart. The light's dizzying. Gradually, my eyes open a little wider, adjusting to the brightness.

"You're in the hospital. We've been so worried about you, but you're going to be fine now," Cassie says.

Xander's beside me, his warm hand in mine. Evan's at the foot of my bed, and Cassie's on the other side.

"Thanks for being here," I cough out in a dry voice.

"Where else would we be?" Xander asks.

"We'll let the nurse know you're awake," Evan says as he and Cassie leave the room.

I squeeze Xander's fingers, saying, "I have so many questions."

"We'll have plenty of time to talk later. You need to rest now." He tenderly pushes a curl off my face.

"I can't rest unless I know your safe."

"I feel the same way about you. I'll be right here. I promise. We're both safe now."

Closing my eyes, I drift off, gripping Xander's hand.

CHAPTER FIFTY-TWO

ARIANA

W hen I awoke in the hospital this morning, I was still dizzy. Fortunately, I'm steadier, and the throbbing in my head is only a dull ache now. That convinced the doctor to let me move from the hospital to the palace.

That means I'm recuperating in Xander's guestroom again. He insisted. He also promised that we would discuss what happened at his engagement gala when he returns with food.

I didn't want to wait, but my growling stomach settled that disagreement.

My mind keeps replaying the evening of the engagement party until Xander returns with not only food, but also with Evan and Cassie.

"I hope you don't mind that I invited these two. I thought we should all share what we know while we eat."

"Thanks. I need to sort through all of this for peace of mind."

"If you're up to it, tell us what happened to you at the gala? How were you hurt?" Xander asks.

"After you and Constance walked by, I needed a little fresh air. I walked onto the terrace. I was standing against the railing hidden by a pillar and tall plant when I overheard a man named Frank threaten Constance if she didn't break up with you."

"Why did he want her to break up with me?" Xander asks.

"I'm not sure, but Frank also said he wouldn't let you become king because you'd terminate his offshore drilling rights."

"Before you passed out, you told me to stop Frank, so we locked down the palace. A man named Franco was trying to leave in a purple Jaguar."

"Remember I found a man named Franco associated with the offshore drilling company JagFire? You know, the one with the purple jaguar logo? Is it the same guy?" I ask.

"That appears to be the case."

"I knew a purple jaguar sounded familiar. It didn't click until we were standing on the palace steps, and I saw the car speeding away," Evan says.

"Why did Constance refer to him as Frank instead of Franco?" I ask.

"Her parents died when she was a young girl. He was put in charge of her trust and treated her like a niece. She had trouble saying Franco, so he became Frank to her. That's one reason we didn't find him when Chief Inspector Carlson searched for anyone with a relative named Frank. He's not her real uncle. Also, his real name is Franco, not Frank," Xander says.

"The pieces are falling into place," I say.

"But we don't know what role, if any, Constance played in his plot," Cassie says.

"I can answer that."

They look at me in surprise.

"From what I overheard, he blackmailed her into sabotaging the horse ride and the boat to scare away the other women you were considering for marriage. If she didn't help Frank, he was planning to destroy her trust fund, which he managed. It all makes sense now. They wanted to make sure you chose Constance and were left with no 'backup plan' when she broke up with you at the gala," I say.

"What an outlandish plan! That certainly fills in some major gaps. But what went wrong? Why was she stabbed?" Xander asks.

"Constance was going to double-cross Frank. She'd decided not to break up with you because she changed her mind. She finally realized that she wouldn't need money from Frank after becoming queen. She thought he wouldn't be able to hurt her at that point," I explain.

"I see. When she wouldn't break up with me, he decided to kill her because that would also eliminate my last option for marriage," Xander says.

"That must have been Frank's thinking. When Constance walked away, I heard him say that she was wrong. He *could* hurt her, and then he'd take care of you."

"That still doesn't explain how or why you were hurt, if they didn't know you overheard them." Evan says.

"I was so shocked that I dropped my wine glass. He heard me and put a knife to my throat. Then he marched me into a nearby office and threw me into a closet. That's when I hurt my shoulder, hit my head again, and passed out. When I came to, I knew I had to get word to you before he came back. But the closet was locked from the outside."

"That small storage closet is shared by two offices, each with its own door. Having locks on the outside prevents someone from the other office walking in unexpectedly. How did you get out?" Evan asks.

"It wasn't easy. I couldn't call for help because cell phones weren't allowed at the party. Then I tried to remember all the ways I've seen in movies to break down a door or pick a lock. My right shoulder was already sore from Frank slamming me into the closet wall, so I tried ramming my left shoulder into the door. It wouldn't give. I thought about removing the hinge bolts, but I didn't have any tools. Then I decided the only remaining option was to pick the lock, but I didn't have a credit card or hair pin with me."

"Too bad hair pins aren't common anymore," Cassie says.

"I thought all women carry hair pins. Mum uses them to hold her tiaras in place," Evan says.

"You're kidding, right? You do know that most of us have never worn a tiara before, don't you?" My laugh turns into a grimace. "Ouch! With this head injury, laughing hurts."

"We'll be careful not to say anything else amusing until you're recovered. Tell us how you got out of the closet," Xander says.

"I finally remembered some jackets were hanging in the closet, so I looked for a metal coat hanger. Luck was finally on my side. I found one, untwisted it, and felt for a hole in the doorknob. After some twisting and pushing, the lock clicked open."

"Brilliant! I'm impressed that you were able to do that, particularly given you had a head injury and were bleeding. Is that when you came back to the party?" Xander asks.

"Yes. I snuck out of the closet and stumbled to the ballroom. I was incredibly dizzy, causing me to slip on the stairs. The last thing I remember is you holding me."

"Thank goodness you overheard that conversation and escaped the closet in time to tell us that Constance and Frank were the killers," Xander says.

"Did he kill Constance?" I ask.

"No, she'll recover eventually and then be tried for her crimes. After what you've shared, I'm sure they'll be adding charges against her," Evan explains.

"Xander, I vaguely remember you telling me I was safe because Harper was in custody? What did she have to do with any of this?"

"Harper was repeatedly in the wrong place at the wrong time. Frank left Constance to die after he stabbed her outside the toilet. Constance pulled out the knife, threw it on the ground, and put pressure on the wound as she staggered back to the party for help. Harper walked by, picked up the knife, and followed Constance. When they entered the ballroom, we all thought Harper had stabbed Constance because she was holding a bloody knife. That's when the guards detained her," Xander explains.

"Does that mean Harper wasn't involved in any of the crimes?" I ask.

Cassie explains, "She wasn't. Harper had inside information from a friend in the palace about Xander's schedule. She thought if she was always around, Xander would eventually decide she was a better choice than you, Constance, or Jessica."

"Which wasn't going to happen. It also wasn't very smart of her to pick up a bloody knife. Thanks to you, we now know how Constance was involved," Xander says.

"It's still unclear how Constance managed to sabotage the horse-back ride. I assume she fed Cocoa muffins stuffed with pills, but how could she be sure that Cocoa would be anxious enough to run off with Lady Everly?" Cassie asks.

"That reminds me of something I forgot to mention. Frank reminded Constance that she was the one who released the butter-flies, not him," I say.

"That's it! That explains the butterfly wings in the water bottle. Remember, when I baked cookies with the pastry chef, one of the staff was complaining about finding butterfly wings in one of the water bottles from the stables. It didn't make sense at the time, but Constance must have dried out the water bottle and filled it with butterflies. When the drugs had had time to take effect, she released the butterflies to spook Cocoa," Cassie says.

"How did she get butterflies into a water bottle? That couldn't have been easy," Xander says.

"If you remember, she was the last one to come out of the stables for the ride. She must have done it then," I say.

"Where did she get the butterflies and how did she transport them to the stables?" Evan asks.

"Xander, can I borrow your phone?" I ask.

"No screen time remember. What do you need?"

"Google 'how to transport butterflies.'"

"Sure, why not?" He types. And suddenly, he says, "That's incredible."

"What is it? What does it say?" I ask.

"In a cool dark place, fold the butterfly's wings behind its back and place it in a thin parchment envelope. This will keep it calm until you are ready to release it," Xander reads.

"Bingo! Mr. Hamoncourt's stamp envelopes were actually butterfly envelopes. Another mystery solved," I say.

"I must admit I never suspected Constance. After all, she fell off the boat and was hurt when the gate broke open," Evan says.

"But that makes sense now. It diverted suspicion from her, and she was able to make sure Ariana went over with her. Since she was expecting the fall, she could avoid being hurt badly, and she could flail around and make sure Ariana was at least kicked a couple of times. We can't prove it, but I suspect Constance caused Ariana to hit her head on the hull," Xander says.

"She must have hoped you'd be too scared or hurt to continue. She also effectively took Jessica out at the same time. At that point, I thought Jessica was a prime suspect for two reasons. First, Jessica was the only one who hadn't been targeted, and second, Jessica is knowledgeable about both horses and sailboats. Of course, Jessica also decided she wanted no part of royal life. Constance probably thought that was a bonus," Xander says.

"This has been overwhelming. Forgive me, but I'm exhausted." I yawn.

"There's nothing to forgive. Get some rest," Cassie says.

"Inspector Carlson wanted to be here, but I pulled the prince card, promising to call him after we talked. He's going to be thrilled with these new details. I'm going to call him now, but I'll be back soon," Xander says.

"I hope so." I smile.

CHAPTER FIFTY-THREE

XANDER

Ariana has spent the last few days recuperating in my guestroom.

The first day, I apologized for being such an arsehole. It wasn't nearly enough to make up for the horrendous way I treated her or the terrible things I said. It was merely the first step and at least we have reestablished friendly communication.

I haven't shared with her my hope we can be more. With her injuries, I don't want to stress or pressure her. It could ruin any chance we may have. I can wait until she's well.

In the meantime, my desire for her continues to grow. If only I could take her in my arms and devour every inch of her body. Instead, I've jerked off in the shower so many times you'd think I'm a horny teenager.

We have talked about almost everything, teased each other, and spent long enjoyable days together.

She told me she's an only child. She's extremely close to her parents. They tend to hover and be overprotective. She gained much needed independence when she moved to New York. That's why she doesn't want them to find out she lost her job until she gets a new one. She fears they'll go back into ultra-protective mode.

I shared details about me and my family. She now knows my sister is a world-class tennis player. And she's sworn to secrecy for now about the meaning of the diamond key around Cassie's neck because Evan has a surprise in store for her. Ariana thought it was romantic.

Ariana's admitted that she's frustrated that her writing is going more slowly than she wishes, and she's apprehensive about where her career is headed next. The inheritance from her Nana won't last much longer.

We've bandied about ideas for promoting my Clean Oceans charity. I'm hoping she'll consider working with me again but haven't brought it up yet.

We've even played poker and watched the sunsets. I've never felt this connected to a woman before, and we're not even sharing a bed. Our friendship has strengthened, my admiration of her has soared, and my determination to win back her love has solidified.

But we've avoided the topic of my marriage dilemma. Fortunately, she hasn't asked about my plan, and I haven't wanted to bring it up until she has recovered.

While her shoulders are still a little sore, the cut on her neck is healing seamlessly. And, as of this morning, her headaches have finally subsided, so the doctor gave her an all-clear signal to resume most normal activities, except he thought she should wait a little longer before flying home. I'd have preferred he outright forbid it, but he didn't.

Now my problem is how to convince her to marry me before she books a ticket home. Evan and Cassie have been helping me with a plan, but I'm not sure it'll work.

Evan has convinced me that my best option is a grand gesture. It worked for him when he screwed up with Cassie, so I'm going to give it my best shot. And today's the day it plays out, but I need to make a couple of phone calls and meet Mum first.

After a day of planning, everything is finally in place. Hearing footsteps, I look up as Ariana emerges from the guestroom. She takes my breath away in the strapless, body-skimming silver cocktail dress with shimmering burgundy crystals scattered over the skirt.

"You're enchanting. That dress looks magnificent on you." My eyes remain glued to her.

"You're quite dashing in your tux. Skipping the bowtie and leaving a couple of buttons open is a good look for you. You're exuding the aura of a prince who wants to have fun. And thank you for this beautiful dress. It wasn't necessary."

I pull her into a gentle embrace, careful not to hurt her shoulders. "We're celebrating your recovery, the end of the murder investigation, and my good fortune in narrowly escaping marriage to a murderer. If that doesn't justify a special evening, nothing does. Would you join me for a little stroll? I've had dinner set up on one of the patios."

"Absolutely. I'm so tired of being cooped up indoors I'd do anything to spend an evening outdoors."

"Then let's go."

I guide her to the railing on the outdoor terrace and point to the garden that's lit with soft green lights.

Ariana says, "I've never seen so many rose bushes in bloom in one place. And they're so fragrant." She breathes deeply. "Roses are my favorite flower. I could stand here for hours."

"That's why your hospital room was filled with roses. I hoped your favorite scent would help you wake up."

"How did you know?"

I wink. "I'm a prince. I have my ways. Let's walk to the end of the terrace. Our dinner awaits."

Arriving at the large, round patio, a small band begins to play. Ariana gasps and quickly presses her palms over her mouth, staring at the oversized table for two. "You've recreated a mini version of the fundraiser I planned for you in London. The table, the flowers, the music. And I just realized that even my dress is a shorter version of what I described to you in our text messages."

"I wanted to take us back to the beginning. You deserved to be at the fundraiser and see how spectacular your hard work turned out. I'd looked forward to that night because I would finally meet the woman who amused me during our phone calls and texts. Tonight, I wanted to recreate that evening, but the way it should have been—with you and me together."

"This is the nicest gesture anyone has ever done for me. Thank you, thank you, thank you!" She throws her arms around me, kissing my cheek.

"Can you guess the menu?" I ask, pulling out the chair for her.

She grins, placing her index finger on the corner of her mouth, a twinkle in her eye as she gazes into the starlit sky. "Let's see. I'm betting it is filet mignon and lobster with truffle butter. Am I right?"

"Yes. It's the same meal you planned for the dinner in London."

"Mmm, my mouth is watering already."

We eat and chat while I try to quell my anxiety. Fortunately, as a prince, I have extensive experience suppressing my emotions, so hopefully, she doesn't suspect what's running through my head.

"Ariana, I have some good news to share. The king has decided to terminate the contract with JagFire and not renew the drilling rights for the other companies when their contracts expire."

Placing her hand on my arm, she says, "That's fantastic news. You must be so relieved."

"I am. It will have an enormously positive impact on the environment. He's also lifted his ban on discussing the pros and cons of drilling, so other countries will be better informed based on our experiences. He's leaving open the possibility of granting future drilling rights but only if the results of an environmental impact study are considered and sufficient safeguards are put in place."

"Oh, Xander, you must be ecstatic. What made King Louis change his mind?"

"After learning what motivated Franco and Constance, he opened his eyes. When he took a closer look at all his advisors, he finally realized what I'd been saying was correct. Many of them were looking out for their own bank accounts rather than the best interests of Catalinius. He's made some drastic changes in his advisors now."

"Thank goodness."

As dessert is served, I say, "There's another positive development."

"What is it?" she asks.

"The king has withdrawn his requirement that I marry before his birthday. He's decided to remain on the throne until death. That means when I propose and marry someone, it will be my choice, not his."

"Are you serious? He freed you from your obligation?"

"He did."

"Is your mother upset that they won't be able to retire and travel?"

"Not as much as I would have thought. She's the romantic of the two. She's now convinced that true love is in my future."

"Your mother sounds wonderful."

I give the band our prearranged signal to change to softer, slower music.

"She is, but that's enough about my parents. Let's enjoy this beautiful evening. Would you dance with me?"

Ariana nods and I guide her to the small dance floor in front of the band. Pulling her close, a bolt of electricity zaps me. I shouldn't have ignored all the sparks, tingles, and twinges that started in London. I've wasted weeks looking for the right person when she was in front of me all along. What a fool I've been. Hopefully, it's not too late to correct my mistakes.

"Thank you for sharing this evening with me. There's no one else I'd rather be with tonight," I whisper in her ear.

Ariana lays her head against my chest. I run my fingers through the long strands of her hair and gently kiss the edge of her ear, nibbling my way down to her earlobe. She softly moans. My tender kisses pepper her neck, and she shivers, tilting her head up to give me better access.

Raising my head, I stare into her eyes, letting my fingers trace her luscious ruby-red lips. The tip of her tongue slips out and caresses my thumb, sending blood rushing to my cock.

She's going to be the death of me. To hell with dancing. "Come with me. I have a surprise for you."

"I've already seen your *surprise*. We agreed that was a one-time thing," she says, wriggling her eyebrows.

Laughing at her adorable gestures I say, "This is something different. I promise. Please, let me show you."

Grabbing her hand, we hurry down the terrace, and I throw open a set of French doors.

"This room looks so comfy. What did you want to show me?" she asks.

"Everything here. There's an oversized chair and ottoman, a desk overlooking the garden, a bed loaded with puffy pillows, and a refrigerator with snacks and beverages, complete with an en suite bath. Is this what you meant when you described your ideal writing room?" I ask, pointing to each item in turn.

Mouth open, Ariana turns in a slow full circle taking in the details. "I'm shocked that you remembered. Why did you create this room? Are you planning to write a book?"

"No, silly. It's a writing room for you." I take her hands and interlace our fingers.

"But I'm leaving."

"I hope to change your mind about that."

I drop to one knee, keeping a firm grip on her hands.

"Ariana, you intrigued me when I knew you as Maddie. You enchanted me when we met at the reception. And despite your lack of interest, I couldn't help wanting to keep you close. I tried to convince myself we were going to be the best of friends, and I was right. But we quickly became much more than that even though we both refused to admit it. Then I ruined everything by letting trust issues overshadow my true feelings. I'll always regret that lost time. When you ended up in the hospital unconscious, I was terrified that I'd lose you forever. I couldn't bear the thought of life without you. I vowed to make you mine forever if you'd have me. I love you unconditionally. So, I kneel before you of my own free will with no obligation to propose to anyone. Ariana, will you marry me?" I pull the yellow-diamond ring from my trousers' pocket. It caught my eye on the first visit to the jewel vault. I knew then it belonged on Ariana's finger, but I let my past guide me in the wrong direction.

"Are you sure?" Ariana asks.

"Absolutely."

Time comes to a screeching halt as she stares into my eyes, searching my soul.

How can she not believe we're meant for each other?

She exhales a long breath, and tears slowly stream down her face. "Xander, please get up. I need to share some things with you."

Bloody hell. This is not how she's supposed to react. I rise slowly, staring down at her hand in mine.

"Xander, I loved flirting with you by text and phone when you were Alex. I was massively disappointed when Shelly fired me. And that was partly because it meant I wasn't going to meet you in person. The night of the matchmaking reception, I was drawn to you. In a sense, we were already friends and didn't know it. I rationalized accepting the invitation to join you in Catalinius because I needed to do research for my novel. Secretly, or subconsciously, I also looked forward to time with the intriguing prince I'd just met. Then we worked together investigating Everly's murder, and you kept taking care of me when I was hurt. Despite trying valiantly to avoid it, I fell for you. Then we shared the most sensuous night of my life, only for me to wake up and be devastated by your lack of trust in me. You accused me of lying and manipulating you. Nothing could've been further from the truth. You didn't even give me a chance to explain. You immediately assumed the worst. That hurt me deeply," she says.

"The night we spent together, I fell asleep planning to wake up convince you to reconsider relationships, and marry me. That next morning, I told you we needed to talk, but Shelly's text message interrupted us. Then I assumed the worst and lost it. Ariana, I can never apologize enough for what I did and how I treated you that day. I mucked it up. I was wrong. I never should have let my past get in the way of the best thing that ever happened to me: you. You're the most honest, loyal, dedicated, and beautiful person I know. You put your life on the line to warn and protect me. You are perfect. With every passing minute, I fall for you more. The thought of life without you is unbearable. I'll do whatever it takes to make it up to you every day for the rest of our lives. Please tell me that you can find it in your heart to forgive me. We're meant to be together. I love you and always will."

"You treated me badly. On the other hand, you grovel well, and anyone who recreates the night I missed in London and creates my dream writing room must have redeeming qualities. I happen to love you too, but I'm not sure that's enough."

"Why not?"

"I have three conditions before I could even consider your proposal."

"What are they?" I ask skeptically.

"You never let your trust issues invade our relationship again, you're completely faithful to me, and you promise me endless nights of mind-blowing sex." She grins.

"Done! Is that a long-winded yes?"

"Yes." She laughs.

I slip the sparkling, four-carat yellow diamond ring on her finger and pull her into my arms. Pressing my lips firmly against hers, I nibble her bottom lip, extracting a moan of pleasure.

Suddenly, I lean back, asking, "You were going to say yes the whole time, weren't you? You were enjoying making me sweat."

"Maybe a little," she says, holding her thumb and index finger close together, grinning.

"You naughty girl."

"I guess you'll have to punish me." She giggles.

Pulling her against me, I swat her tight little ass. "Thank fuck you wanted a bed in your writing room," I growl.

CHAPTER FIFTY-FOUR

XANDER

Ariana wraps her legs around me, and I carry her to the bed, softly kissing and nibbling the supple skin below her ear. The fear of losing Ariana, the relief of winning her back, and her naughty taunt that I should punish her has me wound tighter than a spring.

"Do you have any clue what you do to me?" I murmur. "I'm going to explode before we get started if I'm not careful."

Placing her on the bed, I snap the thin shoulder straps of her dress, and the slinky fabric falls, exposing her bare breasts. She's breathtaking. I'm the luckiest man on the planet that she lets me see her—all of her.

"The dress is better strapless. I'd have proposed over appetizers if I'd known you weren't wearing a bra."

Leaning over and taking one nipple into my mouth, I caress it with my tongue as my hands roam down her hips. "Are you bare under here too?" I ask, patting her.

"You're going to have to find out for yourself."

My teeth graze her nipple, winning me another moan. Trying to slow myself down, I move to her other side to give it equal attention.

With her back against the bed, she props up on her elbows and closes her eyes. "Please Xander, I need more."

Her begging is sexy as hell.

"You can and you will. Remember, you're being punished. You were very naughty." I smile, reaching for the hem of her dress. As I nudge it up to her waist, she lifts her hips to help. She's wearing a tiny burgundy lace triangle. It's sexier than if she were bare. I gently rub my thumb over the outside of the lace. "Fuuuck, you're wet for me."

"Please, touch me now." She arches against my hand. Slipping my finger under the lace, I explore almost everywhere, purposefully avoiding the one spot that will set her off too soon. She writhes trying to reposition my finger. Instead, I pull my hand away and press my lips against hers. My tongue explores and tangles with hers as I rub my hardness against her moist triangle. She gasps for breath.

"Xander, stop teasing me. Please," she begs.

"Anything you want." Giving in to our mutual desire, I retrieve a condom from my back pocket. As I start unbuttoning my trousers, Ariana reaches for the front of my shirt, ripping it open and sending studs flying.

"I want your skin against me now," she says, rubbing her warm palms across my pecs and down to my waist. We jointly push my trousers and boxer briefs out of the way, and she wraps her hand around me, giving me a gentle stroke.

She bends down and kisses my hard tip. "This is exclusively mine now."

"I'm only yours." I push her back against the bed, ripping off her knickers and tossing them away, while nudging her legs apart with my knee. I ease into her wetness, giving her time to accommodate me —while concentrating on how to make this last.

She pulls me closer, wrapping her legs around me, and I start to move, slowly at first. She urges me to move faster and harder. I readily comply, moaning from my own pleasure.

She tightens and spasms around me. I slow my thrusts and reach down to rub her, drawing out her orgasm. My elbows on either side of her shoulders, I move in and out, faster, and faster, sensing the wave coming strong. Another thrust and I crash over the edge, exploding as never before.

Fuuuck.

Collapsing on top of Ariana, I kiss her softly, and then roll off to avoid crushing her, but I keep her close. Our breathing slowly returns to normal.

"I want this moment to last. Will you hold me all night?" She snuggles closer.

"Don't worry. I'm not letting you go."

She cuddles against my shoulder, and I rest my chin against the top of her head. I'm exhausted from the emotional ride of the last few hours, not to mention the last few weeks. But I can't help smiling. She's mine now. Forever.

"Wake up. Wake up," a soft voice says.

Why is someone shaking me? "What's wrong?"

"It's morning. We fell asleep," Ariana says.

"What is it, love? I don't want to move. I've had the best dream. You agreed to marry me and then we had fantastic sex. Let me finish my dream. You just dropped an éclair down your shirt, and I'm about to lick the chocolate and cream off you," I murmur, pulling her closer and trying to go back to sleep.

"Xander, it wasn't a dream, well except for the éclair part, which we should try sometime, but not now. Wake up. It's morning. We're in my writing room, and someone's knocking."

I bolt upright, rubbing my eyes.

"Sir, are you in there? Your guests have arrived," Edmund says through the door.

"Yes, Edmund. We're here, but we need a minute."

"Very well, sir. Does this mean plans progressed in the direction you'd hoped?" Edmund asks.

"We're engaged if that's what you're asking. Can you distract the guests for a little while?"

"Of course, sir. And if I may say so, congratulations."

"What guests are you expecting?" Ariana asks.

"I was supposed to tell you last night, but we were distracted. Your parents and Meredith are here," I say.

"What?"

"I thought you would want them here regardless of your answer last night. I hope you don't mind."

Throwing her arms around me, she says, "That was incredibly thoughtful. How did you convince them to come? My parents don't even know you. I didn't tell them I was leaving London for a side trip to Catalinius. Did they know you were going to propose? They don't approve of taking risks. They must be worried sick that I ran off to an island without telling them."

"Slow down. It's all okay. Meredith helped explain everything to your parents. They aren't upset. And we have a little alone time while we wait for breakfast. Care to crawl under the covers so I can say a proper good morning to my fiancée?" I grin.

"How could I refuse that offer?" she says, pulling the covers over us.

EPILOGUE

ARIANA

I'm floating on air after spending the last week with Xander. Each night we've made love, and each day we've planned our wedding.

Queen Josephine is all smiles. Evan and Cassie had told her that Xander was marrying the wrong woman, so she decided to play cupid and invite the *right* woman to the fateful engagement party.

They all hoped seeing me again would open Xander's eyes to what he was missing. It didn't work exactly as they had planned, but the outcome was even better. The murderers were caught, and Xander and I are getting married today.

Meredith is quite proud of herself too. When we had lunch, she thought I was the perfect match for Xander and used my novel writing as the way to throw us together. She couldn't be sure that we would be open to finding a real match, but she hoped that creating the opportunity would be enough. Her intuition and ability to read people must be why billionaires pay so much for her matchmaking services. She knows what she's doing.

Soon after I left for Catalinius, Meredith also told my mom that she had set me up for a match. So, my parents weren't completely shocked when Xander called asking for their permission to propose. Fortunately, they're supporting my choice to jump into this marriage, and the planning has gone more smoothly than I could have ever hoped.

Our wedding colors are white, red, and chocolate. I know. Chocolate isn't a real color, but everyone is humoring me on this one. After all, it is *my* wedding.

Cassie has become the sister I never had, so it wasn't hard to talk her into working with the chef on the menu for the wedding. With only a week for planning, I needed all the help I could get. She and the chef have blended my American tastes with Xander's desire for traditional Catalinius fare.

As a result, we're having *four* wedding cakes—a German chocolate cake with coconut pecan frosting for me, a croquembouche to honor Xander's French heritage, a millefoglie to honor his Italian heritage, and an English fruitcake because we met in person for the first time in London.

When the guests arrive at the reception, they'll receive champagne in a glass rimmed with chocolate flecks, along with a frozen raspberry with a chocolate hazelnut filling floating in the bubbles. Dinner will consist of local fish and beef tenderloin served with California wines and wines from the royal vineyard.

I can't wait, but first, the wedding.

I'm holding an elaborate bouquet of red roses, white orchids, and chocolate-covered strawberries. The florist came up with the idea when I insisted chocolate was one of my colors. The result is spectacular. Cassie and Jessica are my bridesmaids. I would've asked Bri to also be a bridesmaid, but Xander wanted Evan and Bri as his groomspeople. They were the perfect choice.

My dress is one of fairytales. It's white satin with pearls to honor the queen, and my veil is the one Mom wore when she married Dad. The yellow-diamond tiara matches my engagement ring. It's glamorous and extremely heavy. I never knew tiaras weigh so much. Hopefully, my practice walking with it will help. It would be embarrassing if the tiara falls off when Dad walks me down the aisle of the palace chapel.

The opening notes of the wedding march signal it's time. Dad pats my hand, smiles, and nods. Holding back tears of joy, we take the next step toward my new life.

It's time to claim Xander as my husband.

EPILOGUE

XANDER

As we wait in an anteroom for the emcee to announce our arrival at the reception, I take Ariana into my arms and meld my mouth to hers.

"You're mine now, and I'm never letting you go. I love you more than I knew was possible. Now let's get through with this reception so I can show you just how much." I groan into her ear.

"Don't be silly. We're not hurrying through our only wedding reception. We're going to enjoy every minute of it. Then you can spend the rest of our lives showing me exactly how much you love me," she says.

"If you insist."

She wipes lipstick off my face as the emcee announces, "May I present His Royal Highness Prince Xander and Her Royal Highness Princess Ariana."

I guide my wife through the open door. We're met with thunderous applause.

"Did you hear that éclairs are on the menu? I had some sent to our apartment. We have unfinished business with chocolate and cream." She winks with a glint of mischief in her eye.

Finally! I found my match.

ACKNOWLEDGMENTS

I am extremely grateful to everyone who has supported my efforts to bring the characters and events of *Royally Deceived* to life. Thank you to my husband for his unending willingness to listen to ideas for plot twists and to proofread drafts. Thank you to my friends and family, especially Renée and Audrey for sharing their knowledge of horses, and Debbie for her support and encouragement. Special thanks to Suzi V. for her outstanding work and support. And thank you to my entire team for helping make this book possible.

ABOUT THE AUTHOR

When not consumed by her job as an attorney, J.D. Carothers loves to cook for her family and friends, read murder mysteries and romance novels, eat chocolate, and sip wine watching the sunset in Southern California.

Late at night or early on weekend mornings, she tries to find a quiet place to write her next novel and trade the stress of real life for a fantasy world where murder and romance are on the menu, along with the food she loves.

She just wishes there were more hours in each day!

For more information, visit
jdcarothers.com

Milton Keynes UK
Ingram Content Group UK Ltd.
UKHW040143030823
426240UK00013B/183/J

9 781957 997056